ROMANTIC TIMES PRAISES THERESA SCOTT'S HISTORICAL ROMANCES:

"*Yesterday's Dawn* is an entertaining read and an enticing beginning to the *Hunters of the Ice Age* series."

"Plenty of adventure and nonstop action.... Readers who thrive on Indian romance should particularly enjoy *Apache Conquest.*"

"*Forbidden Passion* is a light, charming tale. Theresa Scott has penned a pleasant read for all those who love exciting stories of the days of old."

"More than an Indian romance, more than a Viking tale, *Bride of Desire* is a unique combination of both."

"Theresa Scott's historical romances are tender, exciting, enjoyable, and satisfying!"

HUNTERS OF THE ICE AGE

PASSION AT THE DAWN OF TIME

"I do not hold you responsible for what your uncle did."

Summer looked up at him. "It was wrong, Talon! It was very wrong!"

His dark eyes went cold as he watched her. "It is done with."

"Yes, it is. And you are banished."

Silence fell between them. Summer fidgeted with the little sack at her neck. "I—I must go now. I have to hunt...."

"Wait. I owe you some meat. The shaman said I do. And I must do what the shaman said."

"You want to? Give meat for me?" She flushed. Surely he could not tell she had fantasized that he would give meat as bride-service for her.

Summer considered this. It would not be like bride-service, at all. He would only be fulfilling the shaman's requirements. "Very well. I will let you."

His smile twisted her heart. "Go home, Summer. I will bring the meat tonight."

HUNTERS OF THE ICE AGE

DARK RENEGADE

THERESA SCOTT

LOVE SPELL   ◆   NEW YORK CITY

LOVE SPELL®

June 1994

Published by

Dorchester Publishing Co., Inc.
276 Fifth Avenue
New York, NY 10001

For Debbie Macomber, dear friend and mentor,
with love and gratitude.

With special thanks to:
Daniel S. Meatte, archaeologist;
Karen Bean, gardener extraordinaire;
and Robert E. Kavanaugh Sr., naturalist.

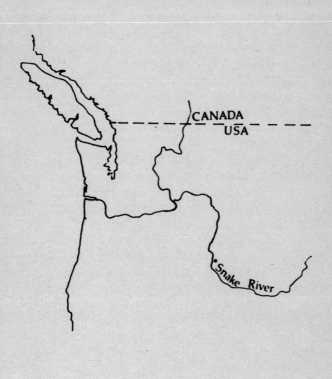

*the area where the story takes place 11,000 years ago.

Prologue

11,024 years ago
Site of what is present-day Snake River Plain,
Idaho

Beads of sweat trickled down the woman's brown forehead, dripped onto her naked chest and mingled in her tangled black hair. Her dark eyes screwed shut as she strained to expel the babe inside her.

Though it was not the Sun People's custom to let a woman give birth alone, far away from camp, Fleet had little choice. She had set out alone to pick the plants and herbs that the Sun shaman told her would aid the birth of her babe, not due for another full journey of the moon. But the birth pangs had come early, and

Fleet had been stricken far from her people's camp with no one to help her. She had been forced to quickly search out a place in which to give birth.

She'd had the good fortune to discover a sheltered, quiet glade surrounding a deep, leaf-green pond. A thin white waterfall rushed noisily over black rocks and splashed into the pool. Green willows and cottonwoods swayed in the warm breeze and insects hummed among the flowers.

Fleet had dropped her digging stick and basket of roots and herbs onto the soft green grass that grew thickly underfoot. She had plucked soft moss off the tree branches in preparation for the birth as other, stronger pangs assailed her.

Then many birth pains had come. The babe would soon be born.

Another strong pang shook her. She clenched her teeth and moaned. The pain receded. Fleet panted and looked around at the swaying green willows and flickering cottonwoods. The sun's rays warmed her and dried the sweat from her forehead; the tiny yellow violets that bloomed in the grass pleased her eyes and soothed her with their fragrance.

Fleet brushed aside her long black hair and sorely wished that someone was with her to help her give birth—her mother, her sister or even Shrond, her beloved husband. Though her mother had told her everything she knew about giving birth—and after birthing three sons and two daughters she knew much—her mother had, unfortunately, neglected to tell Fleet about the pain.

Another pain came then and she thought she would be ripped asunder from the heavy weight straining to leave her. She pushed, groaning. Every muscle in her body pushed.

She fell back exhausted, and waited. Another pain, another push. And then the babe slid out of her, out into the green world of the glade.

Fleet lay panting, chest heaving, black eyes huge with soaring delight as she looked upon this, her firstborn child.

Whispering a prayer of thanks to the Great Spirit, she sat up and crooned to the tiny boy. Using a sharp obsidian blade, she cut the umbilical cord that bound him to her. His cries echoed through the wood and she murmured soothing words to hush him. She smiled at him. He looked so like Shrond.

Once the placenta was expelled, Fleet lay back and placed her son on her stomach. Excitement at his birth kept her awake a good while, long enough for him to suck at her full breasts and then fall asleep. She curled up on her side, snuggled her son protectively in her arms, and then she, too, fell into a deep sleep.

While Fleet slept, slanted green eyes peered at her. A Fox woman with hair of a pale reddish color huddled behind a leafy bush; she had been out berry picking and had come upon the dark-haired woman straining to give birth. At first the Fox woman had thought to reveal herself to the laboring woman, perhaps to aid and comfort her, for she knew of a plant whose leaves could ease the birth pangs and hasten the babe's arrival. But something made her hesitate, and then it was too late. The babe was born, and the dark-haired woman no longer needed her help.

When the green-eyed Fox woman heard the baby's lusty cries, bitterness invaded her heart. It should be *she* who was giving birth, *she* who would be the mother.

She had buried five babes already; each one had died in her womb. True, when she was young and carrying her first baby, her lover had refused to marry her. She had taken a poison-plant then. But the other babies—no! She had done nothing to cause their deaths!

Tears pooled in her eyes. The Fox woman gripped the handle of her berry basket tighter. The old feelings of hopelessness and despair and grief washed over her. Born dead! To nourish a baby inside her for many moons, to labor through each birth, hoping, praying that *this* time the child would live, and then to have those hopes cruelly dashed! She gritted her teeth and shook her head. No! She could never endure such torture again!

Her husband knew it, too; he knew that she did not want to have another child. She had refused his advances, and he had started to talk about taking a second wife. Perhaps he would even set her aside.

The Fox woman's face clouded. What could she do? To labor through another stillbirth, to bury another baby would surely kill her.

But, came the tiny thought now, *the babe before you is alive. That babe is strong and healthy, too.*

The Fox woman regarded the sleeping mother and child through narrowed eyes. *If only I could be that woman,* she thought. Then, swift as an antelope, came another thought. *I could take that baby. While she sleeps. She is young, she will have other babies. But I, I will never bear a child as long as I live.* A sense of panic overwhelmed her suddenly. *The only chance I will ever have for a babe of my own is that tiny one lying at her breast!*

Glancing around the quiet glen, she hid her berry basket under the leaves of the bush, then took a step from behind the bush—then another, and another. Soon she was bending over the sleeping woman. She crouched down beside her and stared at the baby, unable to take her eyes off him. His little nose, his black, fluffy hair, his tiny thumb in his mouth, his long, perfect body entranced her.

A yearning such as she had never known washed over her and she reached out her arms to him. But she did not quite dare to touch him.

Great Spirit, forgive me for what I am about to do. Let me have this baby, just this one baby! Let me have him to stop the terrible ache in my heart, to bring peace to the tent of my husband and me. Grant me this one favor, and I will never ask you for anything again. Ever!

The silence of the glade was her only answer.

Hesitating, the Fox woman drew her arms back. Musingly, she plucked up a tiny yellow violet and held it to her nose.

Should she take the child or not? Her eyes turned again to the baby. He stirred in his sleep just then and his mouth made little sucking movements.

A deep longing swept through her. The violet fluttered to the ground. With the stealth of a stalking jaguar, the woman carefully pried the child from his mother's arms. Then she rose and clapped a hand over the baby's mouth to prevent his outcry. She fled as though pursued by the very spirits of the glade.

The Fox woman ran blindly through the brush. Branches slapped at her. Heedless, she clutched the child to her breast and kept running. Finally her shaking legs would not carry her a further step. Forced to halt, she froze like a hunted doe, intent only on listening for noises of pursuit.

But the only sounds that echoed in her straining ears were her own hoarse panting and the baby's muffled wails at her barren chest.

Back in the glade, Fleet, the Sun mother, slept on. She stirred once, and whimpered softly in her sleep as though from a bad dream. Then she grew quiet once more.

When she awoke, the glade was still and silent. Her arms were empty. She bolted upright, dazed, searching. Her son—where . . . ?

A single, tiny, wilted yellow violet lay on the ground beside her. She picked it up and pressed it to her breast.

Then she bowed her head and wept.

Chapter One

11,000 years ago
Site of present-day Snake River Plain, Idaho

Summer was staring at him. Again. She hugged her antelope fur cloak close about her thin shoulders and glanced away. But, unbidden, her eyes crept back to him.

He wore a thickly furred bison robe belted at the hip. Two black obsidian daggers, their blades honed sharp, rode in his belt of twisted leather. A wooden atlatl on a leather strap draped his shoulder and a quiver crowded with darts hung down his back.

The cold spring breeze ruffled the bison fur at his neck and Summer envied that soft caress to his skin. Because snow still lay on the rocky ground in ragged patches, he wore knee-high leather moccasins stuffed with straw. His legs were as sturdy as pine tree trunks. When she stared at his arms encased in the robe, she imagined those strong arms holding her.

Summer turned away swiftly, lest her wayward thoughts show upon her face. A flush rose to her pale cheeks and she brushed at a wisp of her straw-colored hair to distract herself.

Whatever was she doing, thinking such lustful thoughts about this man, Talon, who was promised in marriage to her own cousin? How could she be so depraved? Yet she felt helpless. Every time she saw him, her heart leapt in her chest. It had done so ever since he had come to reside with her people the previous year.

But Talon had not seen her and Summer's heart slowed its rapid pounding. It seemed he never noticed her. And why should he? She was but the orphaned young cousin of the fair, stunning Blizzard, the woman who was to be his bride.

Summer had been taken in to the tent of her mother's brother, Uncle Antler and his wife, Auntie Birdsong, when her mother and father had been killed in a hunting accident with a mammoth. She had lived with her uncle and aunt and their only daughter, Blizzard, eight winters now, but she still felt as though they had only granted her a favor, that she was not truly a part of their family. Not that they were cruel to her. No, not at all. It was just that she knew she was not as dear to them as was the lovely Blizzard.

Summer chastised herself for such ungrateful thoughts. It was natural they would love their daughter more, give her the finest clothes, the best pieces of meat. They gave Blizzard only one or two more pieces of meat when it was scarce, and she went just as hungry as Summer when there was no meat at all in the dead of winter. And Auntie and Uncle made sure that both young women had warm robes to wear in the winter, though Summer wore those that Blizzard no longer wanted.

The brown antelope cloak Summer now clutched about her shoulders had been Blizzard's but a short time before. Summer tried to ignore the cold that crept through the thin fur.

Her yellow agate eyes were still caught in the spell of Talon as she sat down and leaned against the rock wall next to the family's winter cave. Lifting her face to the sun, she forced her thoughts away from the man she could never have. Summer closed her eyes as she felt the life-giving rays warm her skin and gave silent thanks to the Great Spirit that her people, the Caribou, had survived another harsh winter.

Were she to open her eyes, Summer knew that she would see not only Blizzard's betrothed, but also the young green plants that had pushed their way to the earth's brown surface. Soon the plant leaves would be long and bushy, ready to be plucked and eaten. Spring was her favorite time of year.

She heard the crunch of footsteps on the gravel nearby. Someone was approaching the rock shelter and she hoped it was Talon. Still she kept her eyes closed, breath held, afraid to open them and find it was he—even more afraid to find it was not.

"Have you seen Blizzard?"

Slowly Summer opened her eyes. She looked up, past the leather belt, past the furred chest, past the strong chin with the cleft, past the firm mouth, the straight nose, the nostrils slightly flared, up, up into the slightly tilted black eyes.

Talon was the only one of her people who had such black, black eyes. Summer felt herself falling into their dark depths and for a moment she could not speak. Her palms were sweating, her tongue swelled in size in her dry mouth and still she could say nothing. She feared he could hear her heart thunder like a great storm inside her chest.

"Have you seen Blizzard?" he asked again, his dark eyes puzzled as he watched her. His long black hair fluttered in the wind.

"I—I—" Summer swallowed. She reached for a lock of her hair and wound it round her finger. She took a shaky breath. "At the river. She—she went to the river."

"Ah. My thanks."

There was a glistening in those dark eyes, and for a moment Summer wondered if he knew how she felt about him. She quickly squelched the thought. He could not know. No one must ever know.

She rose to her feet, intent on fleeing him. Suddenly there was a thunk! at her feet. "Oh, no! My sack!"

She stared at the small leather pouch that had fallen to the gravelly ledge. She desperately wanted to pick up the pouch and hide it. She ordered her body to obey, ordered her hands to reach for it, but they would not move, so mortified was she. Humiliation washed over her.

Summer watched in horror as Talon bent and picked up the sack. Her terrified eyes followed his hand as he raised it and opened his palm at eye-level to display the sack. He waited.

She lifted stricken eyes to his. Had he any idea what he had just done? No, she could see that he did not.

With a cry, Summer snatched the sack. As she did so, her fingers brushed his palm. His touch jolted her. She snatched her hand back as though she had caressed a live coal—as did he.

Summer whirled and ran into the cave with wildly beating heart, tucking the pouch back inside her tunic. Her hands trembled like cottonwood leaves. Oh, how could she have been so clumsy as to drop her precious treasure-sack?

25

She hastily pulled the sack out again and gazed at it in the dim light of the cave, then pressed it to her face and inhaled the leather scent. What was she going to do? Talon had touched her sack and the precious things she carried inside it. This should never have happened! That sack and its contents were not meant to be seen by other eyes, especially *male* eyes.

How would he like it if she had touched his atlatl? Or his darts? Or his spears? He would never be able to hunt with them again! No, no, such things were just not done!

She moaned. What would Auntie say? Oh, what should she do? And why Talon, of all men? Why did it have to be Talon who had touched something so private and personal? She moaned again.

Talon was loath to turn and leave. He stared at the cave where Summer had disappeared. Slowly he rubbed the place on his palm where she had touched him.

Her hesitancy had reached out to him. He wondered if she knew how vulnerable she looked in her ragged fur, her hair the color of dried grass, her eyes the color of a pale yellow willow leaf in autumn. Strange eyes, eyes of a color he had never seen before on another human being.

She would grow into a beauty, Talon thought, and the thought caused a sadness, an odd stirring in the depths of him. He would not be entitled to notice her beauty after he wed her cousin. He was an honorable man and once wedded would not admire another woman.

Talon frowned. Strange, the way Summer quivered like a yearling deer whenever he so much as glanced at her. Though she looked young, he had noticed that she wore the woman's neckcloth. Only girls who had had their first menses were entitled to a coming-of-age ceremony and a neckcloth.

And she had looked so frightened when he had returned the leather sack to her. He wondered if he had somehow offended her. Too late, he wished he knew more of the Caribou People's customs. He had joined them only a year before and was still learning how different they were from his own people, the Fox.

The girl was a quiet forest flower, he decided as he walked away from the cave. She was quite unlike lush, dramatic Blizzard, the woman he was to marry. Talon heaved a deep sigh. He had hunted meat for Blizzard's father for a year, and the time of bride-service was up. All his hard work was now to be rewarded by the marriage.

So Blizzard was at the river. He must find her before he went hunting again. The guests would be arriving over the next five days and he must be sure to have enough meat to feed them all.

As he neared the river, Talon spied the dark brown flash of a bison robe and a swirl of long brown hair. He knew it to be Blizzard. With a smile and a jaunty step he hurried toward her, all thoughts of the girl with the pale hair and yellow eyes vanishing from his mind.

Chapter Two

At last the guests had begun to arrive. Bison Eaters and Camel People, adults, children and dogs were everywhere. Summer watched her uncle run first to one group of people, then to another, bowing, talking, carrying packs, waving his arms, shooing children. It was indeed an honor for him to have so many people attend Blizzard's wedding feast, Summer knew, hoping her gladness for her uncle would force the sadness from her breast.

She leaned against the sun-warmed rock shelter wall as she poked an awl through a circle of deerskin. Now and then she glanced down at the visitors. From up on the ledge she could observe the festivities she had no desire to participate in.

29

Her eyes strayed to Talon as he greeted a group of guests with a gift of antelope meat. Her heart was in a turmoil whenever she looked at him. She was confused about Talon, about the way he had touched her personal possessions, and about how sad she felt as each day, each moment, brought him closer to marriage with Blizzard.

Summer's lips tightened as she fought back tears. During the past year while Talon had performed bride-service for Blizzard, it had seemed as if the marriage day was far off. But Summer had known that the Fox man was eventually to wed her cousin, and sometimes she had even prayed for the day to hurry so that she would no longer feel the strange yearnings that came over her whenever she looked at Talon.

But after what had happened yesterday with her treasure sack, she felt as if she had just discovered him. Summer had touched him, and everything had changed. Just as she was awakening to him, he was being taken from her. She would never get to know him once he married Blizzard, no matter what dances her heart did whenever he was near. Blizzard would keep him enthralled and certainly would not allow him to take a second or third wife.

"Oh, why, oh why," moaned Summer, "did I have to drop my treasure-sack? And why did it have to be Talon who retrieved it?"

She bit her lip as she recalled Auntie Birdsong's reaction when Summer had gained the courage to tell her what had happened. Auntie flailed her arms and screamed at Summer. Then she had stomped off to get the shaman.

She returned with him in tow and the two of them proceeded to argue over what to do now that Summer's treasure sack had been defiled. The shaman wanted a whole new woman's ceremony done but Auntie Birdsong refused, saying that she was not about to sew another neckcloth and feed the whole encampment, not after this wedding! One woman's ceremony for Summer would have to do!

Both turned ferocious scowls on Summer. Summer tried not to shrink away from their glares.

Then the shaman announced that at the time of her monthly courses, Summer must bury the sack and its contents. Only thus could she avoid the harm that would surely come to her for allowing a man to touch her woman's things. When Summer pointed out that she had not *allowed* Talon to touch them, the frowning shaman ordered her to be silent.

He continued his instructions. Once the sack was buried, she must dip herself in the cold river water every morning and every evening for three days. After her ablutions, she would be considered purified and free from Talon's touch. Also—and Summer cringed inside when she heard this—since it was the Fox man who had done this thing, he must present her with a gift of meat.

Summer did not know what to say. At first, she thought she never wanted to see Talon again, especially after such humiliating circumstances, but after she pondered for awhile, she decided it would be good to have him give meat to her. She could pretend he was performing bride-service for her, not for Blizzard.

"What are you doing, girl?" Auntie Birdsong's voice woke her from her reverie.

Summer flushed as though her aunt could read her thoughts.

"Your uncle calls you. Get down there and help him!"

Uncle Antler was gesturing to Summer to join him. She set aside the awl and deerskin and got to her feet, hastening down to where he stood talking with a group of guests.

"Girl, come!" Her uncle imperiously called. "Guide these fine Saber-Tooth People and their leader, Spotted Cat, to the grassy plain by the river to set up their tents." He bowed politely to the guests.

Summer stared. Spotted Cat, the Saber-Tooth headman, was a big, stern looking man. Flanking him on either side were two young men, each taller, slimmer replicas of the same sternness.

Accompanying them were six women bowed down with heavily laden baskets and packs, and enough men for each finger on both of Summer's hands. Some of the men were armed with spears. They all wore their long brown hair in a style unfamiliar to Summer: a thick braid hung to the left of the men's faces, to the right of the women's.

Caribou women wore their hair long and unbound when they were young. As they became older matrons, they twisted it into a neat coil at the back of their necks. Caribou men wore their hair long and straight, also, and sometimes tied something in it, like a strip of tree bark, a pine branch or a feather. Talon wore a red fox tail in his long black hair.

Summer noticed that the Saber-Tooth People's style of dress was different, too. Black spots were painted all over their leather clothes. Summer shifted her eyes, trying not to stare. She did not wish to be considered rude, but she thought they did look odd. Caribou women carefully decorated their tunics and dresses with designs in red, yellow, purple and black. They drew flowers and birds and stars and animals on their clothes, not black spots.

The Saber-Tooth People were staring back at her and Summer turned away, flushing. From their weary, impatient manner, she guessed that they had travelled a great distance to attend Blizzard's wedding.

Summer nodded to her uncle and trotted off in the direction of the grassy plain, looking back once or twice to be certain the Saber-Tooths followed. She led them to the level place, ideal for setting up tents, and Summer thought these

Saber-Tooth People must be very important if her uncle was giving them the best spot to camp.

Now, in the early spring, the grass on the plain was sparse. Here and there tiny green threads could be seen, but it would not be until later in the spring time, or even into the summer, the driest time, that grass would cover the reddish-brown dirt. But the camping spot was close to both the river and the pine woods so the Saber-Tooth People would have access to water and could gather wood for their fires. A very good place to camp, Summer thought in satisfaction as they reached the area.

As she turned to go, she was suddenly stopped by a brown arm shooting out and a brown hand clamping around her upper arm. Summer looked up in fright at one of the tall, slim, stern Saber-Tooth sons.

"What is your name, girl?" he asked. She did not like the way he stared down at her or the tone of his voice as he spoke to her, as though she were one of the camp dogs.

She tried to snatch her arm away.

"Your name, girl!"

"Spider," she said, the name just popping into her head.

"Come to my tent later this night, Spider. We will weave some interesting webs." He chuckled and let her go. His brother laughed, too. Summer flushed in anger at the men. Who did they think they were, speaking to her like that?

Then Spotted Cat, their father, walked over. The sons swiftly assumed solemn expressions.

"You. Girl. Come here."

Summer approached him warily.

"Tell me about the bride. Is she beautiful?"

Summer thought for a moment. "Yes, she is like a young antelope. She has long brown hair, green eyes and a graceful shape. She can run swiftly."

"And the groom, what of him?"

"Why are you asking me these questions?"

"I have heard that the groom is an orphan. That he has no people."

To have no people was an insult. It meant that a man had no one who would defend him or help him. "Not so," Summer answered. "The groom is no orphan. His mother lives, and he has people, the Fox People."

"Fox? Never heard of them."

"His people are five in number. They joined our Caribou People but a year ago, when their son Talon, the groom, took up bride-service for Blizzard."

"Five people?" Spotted Cat laughed.

Summer took a step backward.

"Blizzard? Is that the bride's name?"

Summer nodded.

"Pleasant enough name. So, girl, the groom has five people and the bride is beautiful." The headman took hold of a curl of Summer's hair. "How beautiful?" He yanked on the fine strands. "As beautiful as you?"

Summer winced in pain.

The Saber-Tooth and his sons laughed.

"Spider does not wish to catch you in her web," observed the younger son. "She means to catch me."

"Spider, hmmm?" said the headman. "Well, little Spider, you go and tell your headman that I will visit him this evening at his home. Tell him to have Blizzard in attendance. I want to see if she is truly beautiful." He laughed. "Perhaps she is ugly, hmmmm?"

Summer glared at him, but the Saber-Tooth only looked amused. "My sons will be with me. And, if we like what we see, we will have something most interesting to tell your headman." He released his grip on her hair. "I will bring my sons and afterwards, little Spider, we will bring you back here and—" His voice dropped to a whisper. He laughed coarsely.

Summer fled, not waiting to hear another word. She ran all the way back to the rock shelter and heaved herself through the doorway. She wanted to hide in its welcoming darkness, so awful did she feel after her encounter with the Saber-Tooths.

Later, she gave the message to her uncle, leaving out the part about the Saber-Tooths liking what they saw. Uncle Antler merely nodded. Summer shivered and picked up the deerskin circlet. She did not wish to be at home when the Saber-Tooths came to call.

Chapter Three

"Enter, enter!" Uncle Antler waved the Saber-Tooth headman and his two sons into the Caribou family's cave. Summer glanced up from where she was weaving a sage basket, and her heart sank. She had hoped to be visiting at the home of her friend, Blue Camas, when the Saber-Tooths arrived, but she had not finished her household tasks swiftly enough. Now she was trapped.

Blizzard had been forewarned by her father that the Saber-Tooths wanted to visit the bride, and so she sat demurely sewing by the flickering fire.

Summer had to admit her cousin looked even lovelier than usual. Blizzard's delicately chiseled face was seductively veiled by her long, tawny hair. Her slim, graceful arms were seen to best advantage when Blizzard carefully lifted the skin she was sewing and held it up as though to better see her fine design by firelight.

Earlier, Blizzard had demanded that Summer draw the design. But it seemed to the onlookers that she was showing off her own handiwork. Indeed, Blizzard was usually reluctant to turn her hand to any kind of artwork, preferring to get her mother, or Summer, to do the designs on her clothing. Summer watched the effect of her cousin's performance on the guests.

The eldest son gawked at Blizzard, Summer noticed. He seemed unable to pull his dull green eyes away from her cousin's lovely form.

Guiltily, Summer thought now that she should have warned Blizzard about the Saber-Tooths, but she had been so upset she had not thought of anyone but herself. She hoped her cousin would soon limit herself to sewing, and stop preening this evening.

The Saber-Tooths sat down and Uncle Antler offered them some dried pinyon nuts. The nuts were one of the few appetizing treats left after the winter.

When the nuts were devoured, Auntie Birdsong brought out a dish of roasted grasshoppers. The Saber-Tooths smiled and nodded. Uncle beamed expansively. Few guests could resist a taste of crunchy grasshoppers.

The men observed formalities for a time, talking about hunting prospects, where the best obsidian could be found to make fine knife blades, and what kind of plants were best for making duck nets. Finally, Spotted Cat said, "You have a truly lovely daughter, Antler. The man she marries will be most fortunate to have such beauty grace his home."

Uncle beamed proudly and glanced at Blizzard, who gave a tiny smile back. The Saber-Tooth's oldest son stared, obviously entranced.

Summer was barely able to concentrate on her weaving. *Be careful, my cousin,* she thought. *Be very, very careful!*

"Yes, we are pleased with the match, my wife and I," Uncle Antler said. "We know the young man well. He has hunted for us for over a year, doing bride-service, and he has never failed to bring home meat."

The Saber-Tooths considered this. It was an exceptional hunter that brought home meat every time he went out to hunt. "But your young man has few kinfolk, I understand," Spotted Cat said. "I confess I myself know nothing of the Fox People."

"It is most unfortunate, but you are right. He has few people to call upon."

Birdsong put another platter of roasted grasshoppers before her guests and there was a scrabbling sound as the Saber-Tooths greedily helped themselves.

"It was a difficult winter, was it not?" pursued Spotted Cat. "We Saber-Tooths lost three people. Two were hunters."

"A difficult winter," agreed Uncle Antler. "We lost a hunter as well."

Summer kept twisting the sage bark for her basket, wondering what the Saber-Tooths wanted. Perhaps they were merely indulging in a polite visit, but Summer felt uneasy. She shifted a little and stretched her back. Weaving was relaxing work, but one did need to stretch now and then.

"Ah, Spider, is that you?"

She froze.

It was Spotted Cat's second son. "I did not see you. Come on over here where we may see you, Spider," he coaxed.

"We met Spider earlier, when she guided us to our camping spot," explained the Saber-Tooth headman in a jocular fashion.

Summer got up and walked over to them. She wished she had never thought of the name "Spider."

"Is Spider a slave in your home?" asked Spotted Cat.

"*Summer* is our niece, but more like a younger daughter."

"Summer, you say? Your daughter? Why, I thought, from the state of her clothes—"

Mortified, Summer clutched her patched dress closer to her thin waist.

"That is, I . . ." The Saber-Tooth headman was genuinely baffled. "I thought from the way she was dressed that she was a slave."

"We Caribou do not have slaves." Uncle Antler looked affronted. There was an embarrassed silence. "We took my sister's daughter to live with us when she was but seven winters old," he said through stiff lips. "She has lived with us for another eight winters, and we have always treated her as a beloved daughter."

Summer wanted to run out of the cave.

"Orphan, hmmmm? Blizzard and Summer do not look much alike, do they?"

"They are but cousins," said Birdsong politely. She brought out another platter of roasted grasshoppers and shook the platter to draw attention to the food. Summer guessed that her aunt had just used the last of the winter supply of treats in her desperation to distract the Saber-Tooths.

The guests gobbled down the grasshoppers, then rose to their feet. "We must leave now," said Spotted Cat. "You are a most fortunate man, Antler, to have not one, but two beautiful—uh—daughters to grace your home. I thank you for your hospitality this evening."

After the Saber-Tooths had departed, Summer let out a little sigh of relief. Blizzard was glaring at her. "All they talked about was Summer!"

"Why did they call you Spider?" asked her aunt.

"What was so important that the Saber-Tooths were going to tell me?" asked her uncle. "They never told me anything important!"

Theresa Scott

Summer refused to answer the sharp questions that flew at her like cave bats. She whirled and ran to the back of the cave, where she crawled under her warm sleeping robe. Not even a single blonde hair was visible in the firelight.

She slept until morning when the family was awakened by someone calling, "Come out, come out! Gifts. Gifts for the Caribou headman!"

Blizzard and her parents threw off their covers and ran outside, heedless of the cold.

Summer recognized Spotted Cat's voice shouting, "Beautiful gifts! Costly gifts!"

Her stomach roiled. What were the wily Saber-Tooths up to now?

Chapter Four

Summer slipped out of the bed furs and dragged out her leather dress. Though she slept naked, she had stuffed the garment under the robes so that her body-heat kept the garment warm through the night.

From outside the cave came excited cries and loud talking. Summer was just pulling her dress over her head when Blizzard came back into the cave.

"Brrrr, it is cold!" Blizzard, wrapped in a robe, hastily searched for her clothes. When she had finished dressing, she demanded, "Where are my new moccasins? The Saber-Tooths are here and I must look my best."

The moccasins were decorated with purple and red threads sewn neatly in the design of a caribou head, and topped with yellow antlers. Summer had watched Auntie Birdsong labor over them through the winter. Her aunt had promised to make Summer a similar pair one day.

"Ohhh!" Blizzard cried suddenly. She leaned over the fire, snatched something from the glowing embers and pounded it against the dirt floor. "My moccasin!"

As Summer placed her woman's neckcloth over her head and adjusted it so that the fringe hung properly, she peered through the gloom and saw that one of Blizzard's newly made moccasins now sported a charred circle at the toe. Evidently, upon retiring for the night, Blizzard had flung the moccasins carelessly and one of them had landed too close to the fire.

"Now what will I wear?" Blizzard moaned. "Mother will be furious!" She tossed the damaged footwear at Summer. "You know how I hate to sew. Mend this for me!"

Summer glanced at the moccasin and saw that it could be easily patched. Then she looked up. "What are you doing?"

Blizzard was stuffing her feet into Summer's moccasins. "These used to be mine," Blizzard said. "I will wear them now. I just hope the Saber-Tooths do not notice how badly worn they are." And with that, she ran out of the cave.

Exasperated, Summer was tempted to throw the new moccasin into the embers to complete the job the fire had begun. Blizzard had no right to take what had been given to Summer! But of course Blizzard's wishes would come first. It had always been thus and Summer supposed it would always be so.

Wrapping her thin cloak around her shoulders, she sighed to herself and walked to the opening of the rock shelter to see what gifts the Saber-Tooths were shouting about. The cold of the floor seeped into her bare feet.

"Good morning, Spider—I mean, Summer," greeted the younger of the Saber-Tooth sons.

Around the Saber-Tooth headman and his sons clustered his men and their women. The Saber-Tooths were all dressed in their fine spotted garments, and all had their hair neatly braided. They looked bright and eager on this early morning. Summer saw a few of the men grinning and for the first time she noticed that the Saber-Tooth males all had their canine teeth sharpened to points in imitation of the long pointed canines of saber-tooth tigers.

The headman was talking to Uncle Antler, and with every word he spoke, his breath puffed in front of his face. Uncle's grey hair stood out around his head in a tangled mass, instead of in its usual neat style, and he clutched a large yellow camel skin around his middle to preserve his modesty. His bare legs shivered.

"I know it will be a fine marriage," Summer heard Spotted Cat saying. She looked over at Blizzard, who seemed unusually attentive to the conversation. Puzzled, Summer then flashed a glance at Auntie Birdsong, who was tugging on Uncle's arm as though urging him to return to the cave.

"But this cannot be," her uncle protested. "You know that, Spotted Cat."

"My son is a good hunter. He brings in much meat," the Saber-Tooth headman announced. One of the sons carried a pile of furs. Summer could see the layers: brown, white, black, dark brown. The top fur, just under his chin, was the soft, rippling brown of beaver. *Those furs could be sewn into warm dresses and cloaks*, she thought as she drew her own cloak a little closer around her shoulders, shivering in the cool morning air.

"He will make a fine husband for your daughter," Spotted Cat said in a stern voice. He drew himself up to his full height and glared down at Uncle.

Summer gasped as she suddenly realized that the Saber-Tooths were making a marriage offer for Blizzard! She shot a quick glance at Blizzard whose full lips parted in a tiny smile as she stared at the young man holding the furs.

"My son wants your daughter," Spotted Cat said.

"That is all very well," answered Uncle Antler. "But as I told you, she is already promised." He waved his hand at the tents dotting the land near the river. "We invited all these guests to the wedding between her and the Fox man."

Summer's stomach clenched and she glanced about, looking for Talon. Surely he deserved to know that the Saber-Tooths were bartering for his bride! His bride. . . . Summer was filled with confusion. Although in the secret place of her heart, she did not want Talon to marry Blizzard, she could foresee great trouble if these Saber-Tooths gained what Talon had already worked so hard to attain. Anxiously, she peered about for his tall form, but he was nowhere to be seen.

Spotted Cat waved a hand. "They came for a wedding, we will give them a wedding. They can be the guests at my son's wedding instead!"

"I can provide much meat, many furs, and many sons," said the elder Saber-Tooth son. He sounded very confident, and Summer thought from the way Blizzard was staring at him, as though he were a fat, roasted grasshopper, that perhaps he had good reason for his confidence.

"We cannot do this," Uncle Antler protested. "The Fox man has fulfilled his task of a year's hunting for my daughter. He expects to marry her."

"Where is he?" asked the Saber-Tooth headman. "He cannot be very concerned about her if he is not here this morning."

The Saber-Tooths murmured amongst themselves and several heads craned in different directions, pointedly looking about for the absent bridegroom. Summer shifted uneasily.

A small crowd of the other guests, Bison Eaters and Camels, had joined the Saber-Tooths. Word had already spread through the encampment that the Saber-Tooths were making a marriage offer for Blizzard.

"Where are his kin?" Spotted Cat demanded. "Who does he call upon to help him in his marriage negotiations?"

"He has no need to call upon anyone," answered Uncle Antler. "He is a part of our band. His people joined us last winter. He is one of us."

The Saber-Tooth leader snorted his contempt. "So he does not have any hunters to call upon. Then as your son-in-law, he will have no one to aid *you* when you need it. We Saber-Tooths number fifteen men. When you want to hunt mammoths, we will come and drive them into the river so your spears can bring them down."

Antler was silent, considering.

"When you need help with a bison run, we will bring our spears and atlatls and kill many bison with you, our friends, our new *kinsmen*."

Uncle Antler shifted restlessly from foot to foot. Summer could tell that he was tempted by the offer. She clutched her cloak more tightly about her as her heart pounded. Yes, she had wished Talon were free so that she could marry him, but oh, she did not want it to happen this way. She didn't want him to be humiliated!

Where was he? she wondered, gazing about with flashing yellow eyes.

"My eldest son, Rides Their Backs, has the power and medicine of the Saber-Tooths. He is a very strong man," Spotted Cat boasted. Summer noted that the eldest son was named for the style of hunting used by saber-tooth tigers. The predatory animal leaped onto its prey's back and tore into the victim's neck with its sharp fangs. She shivered.

Blizzard was coyly smiling at Rides Their Backs. He smiled back, his pointed yellow canines gleaming.

"What goes on here?"

Talon suddenly pushed through the crowd, shoving people aside as he strode up to the Saber-Tooth headman and Uncle Antler.

"Did you sleep late?" Spotted Cat sneered. "I have known some hunters who sleep until midmorning. Poor hunters they are, too."

Talon glared at him. "I have just returned from hunting," he said evenly. "Antelope." He jerked a thumb carelessly.

Summer saw a skinned antelope carcass of goodly size lying on the ground. Talon must have dropped it before marching up to the conferring headmen.

The Saber-Tooth frowned. "Small," he noted. Then he turned back to Uncle Antler. "Antler, you must know that my son, Rides Their Backs, will make a far better husband for Blizzard. He wants her. He will have her."

Talon glared at the Saber-Tooth. "I have already spoken for Blizzard. She is to be *my* wife. I have performed a year of bride-service for her. Your son has done nothing!"

Rides Their Backs handed the bundle of furs to his younger brother and sauntered up to Talon. The two men stood chest to chest, eye to eye. "I am providing these furs. They are the best, the most magnificent in my land. They are of great value, more valuable than a year's hunting by such as you!"

Talon recoiled as though struck. His face flushed. "I made a bargain with the Caribou people. The woman is mine!"

Rides Their Backs pushed Talon in the shoulder.

Talon pushed the Saber-Tooth back. Rides Their Backs stood his ground and did not budge. Then he lashed out at Talon. The Fox man ducked, barely avoiding the huge fist aimed at his head. He came up and pushed at the Saber-Tooth again, this time hitting the man's square chin and forcing Rides Their Backs' head at an unnatural angle. With a cry, the younger Saber-Tooth brother dropped the furs he had been holding and leaped into the fray.

He threw his arms around Talon from behind and his weight pulled the Fox man down on his back. Then both brothers threw themselves atop him and began hitting at whatever part of Talon that moved.

"Do something!" Summer cried in alarm.

Blizzard's face looked pale as she bit her lower lip and glanced at her mother. Birdsong frowned and continued to watch the combatants. Finally, she nudged her husband. "We cannot afford to lose a good man. They might kill him."

Antler turned to Spotted Cat. "Get your sons off the Fox man. They will kill him."

The Saber-Tooth grinned. "Let them."

"No," said Antler. "We need hunters. We have none to waste in a foolish fight."

Spotted Cat merely shrugged, watching the fight with proud interest. "So, is your daughter going to marry my son?"

Summer clapped both hands to her mouth and tried to stifle a scream. The sound of blows landing on Talon's body filled her heart with fear.

"Yes!" Antler said at last. "My daughter will marry your son."

The Saber-Tooth headman met Antler's eyes. "Very good," he said. He turned back to the fighting just as Rides Their Backs got in a particularly hard blow. "You can stop fighting now," Spotted Cat told his sons.

They ignored him.

"*Stop!*" said the headman, a little louder this time.

Summer could stand it no longer. "*Please stop!*" she screamed, but the men kept delivering body blows.

51

Summer picked up two long sticks from the ground and ran into the cave, returning a moment later with hot coals held tightly between the sticks. She raced up to the fighters and flung the burning embers on them.

"*Yow!*" cried the younger Saber-Tooth.

"*Aargh!*" cried the elder.

"Cease, foolish child!" ordered the Saber-Tooth headman, turning furiously upon Summer.

She cared nothing for what he had to say. She, too, was furious!

The Saber-Tooth brothers rolled off Talon and he groaned. As Rides Their Backs stood and shook hot coals off himself, the younger Saber-Tooth glared at Summer. "That was a nasty trick, little Spider," he muttered.

Talon lay there, unmoving. Summer hurried to his side. Fortunately none of the embers had landed on him. With relief, Summer saw that his thick hunting robe had protected him from the worst of the beating, though he did sport a bruise on one cheek. He rolled to his knees and then slowly got up.

The two Saber-Tooths looked ready to launch themselves at him once more.

"*No!*" cried Summer.

Talon staggered, then regained his balance. "I am ready to fight," he announced, between gasps. "But let us make this—" he took a deep breath "—a fair fight. One at a time!" Legs braced, he waited for Rides Their Backs' next attack.

Immediately, Summer ran back to the fire and scooped up more burning coals with the sticks. The eldest Saber-Tooth brother glanced from her to Talon. "Not me," he said. "Those coals hurt!"

Talon glanced around at the crowd, glaring at the men. No one had come to his aid—no one except Blizzard's little cousin, and she did not count. He wondered if no one had fought for him because he and the Fox People had joined the Caribou but a year ago. Evidently he had not yet established strong enough ties with the Caribou men to make them want to fight on his side. Having no male relatives or friends to call upon was proving a hindrance.

"I am giving my daughter to the Saber-Tooths," Uncle Antler announced.

"No!" cried Talon. "I worked for Blizzard. She is mine!"

"No," said Rides Their Backs. "She is mine!"

Blizzard looked on, a pleased smile curving her lips when she met Rides Their Backs' green eyes. Summer turned away, feeling sick. She did not want to be party to this. It was wrong.

She heard some jostling behind her and spun around to find that Talon had launched himself at Rides Their Backs and delivered a smashing blow to the Saber-Tooth's face. Rides Their Backs staggered and shook his head. He spat and his spittle came out red. A trickle of blood ran from one corner of his mouth.

With growls and snarls, his younger brother and Spotted Cat jumped on Talon, who was quickly brought to earth. The headman stood, legs astraddle, over Talon.

"I demand that you get rid of this man," he snarled at Antler. "He does not accept what has happened. He will be a danger to my sons. Banish him!"

Antler hesitated. "Do it," Birdsong muttered in his ear. "If you do not, we will have a fight with the Saber-Tooths on our hands. And there are too many of them."

Summer's eyes widened as she heard her aunt's whispered words.

"You are banished," Antler pronounced in a loud voice. "Fox man, you must leave the Caribou People."

Talon slowly sat up, rubbing one of his hands that had been injured in the fight. He got to his feet and dusted himself off. To be banished was the worst possible punishment for a man or woman of any people. It meant leaving one's own kind, leaving safety, leaving companionship, and going out into the land to survive alone.

"Uncle," implored Summer, gripping her uncle's hand, "do not do this thing. Our people need him." *I need him,* she wanted to say, but did not dare. "He is a good hunter," she added, hoping reason would sway her uncle.

But Antler would not be swayed, not with

the Saber-Tooth headman watching him with deadly, narrowed eyes.

"No. He is banished," Antler said heavily. He glanced at his pleading niece and shook his head.

The Saber-Tooth headman laughed at Antler's attempt to placate the girl. "In a year or two"—he shrugged—"he will die. A broken leg, a fall, a fight with wolves, a creeping lion while he sleeps, exhausted, unable to keep watch any longer. . . . Who is to say what can happen to a man alone?"

At those words, Summer's heart sank in despair. Talon would surely die! *No! No!* she cried silently, listening to the murmurings of the crowd as the banished man pushed his way through them.

"Get your things," Antler called to Talon's back. "Take your weapons, some food, and leave us. Do not come back!"

Talon turned then and his dark eyes flashed in defiance. "I am banished," he said in a deep voice. "But I will return!" His contemptuous gaze passed over the Caribou. Then his eyes came to rest on Blizzard. "Come with me," he said softly.

Blizzard lowered her eyes from that burning gaze. She shook her head, her shiny brown hair swaying, then took a quick peek at Rides Their Backs and gave him a slight smile.

Talon stared at her, then glared at the rest of the watching people. "Is there anyone who dares come with me?" he demanded.

Summer took a step forward and was about to lift her hand to catch his attention when Auntie Birdsong's heavy hand clamped onto her shoulder, pulling her back.

"I will go with him," Summer murmured.

"You will not!" snapped Auntie Birdsong. "Your place is with us, not with some dangerous renegade who has been driven out of our tribe!"

"I will go!" Summer insisted.

"I have seen how you look at him, girl!" hissed Auntie Birdsong. "You've always wanted him—your own cousin's betrothed!"

Summer's face flushed red.

"It is shameful, that is what it is! Shameful!" Auntie Birdsong snarled.

Summer hung her head, cheeks burning.

"It is not right to look at your cousin's betrothed that way!"

While Summer continued to stare miserably at the ground, her aunt crowed triumphantly, "And anyway, he does not want you!"

Dismayed, Summer lifted her head. It was true. Talon had turned away and she could only watch his broad back as he forced his way through the crowd. Had he not seen her? Did he not want her?

Behind him, Talon heard the Saber-Tooths' loud snickering. "He has no people. He is poor!"

"Poor hunter, too, from what I have heard!"

"He cannot fight at all."

"Never seen a worse fighter!"

"What a coward!"

"Those Caribou are wise to choose Rides Their Backs!"

"Yes, that Saber-Tooth is a great man!"

Humiliated, Talon gritted his teeth and quickened his pace, oblivious to the cluckings of the Caribou women.

"He is so handsome!"

"Blizzard is as foolish as a prairie hen to choose the Saber-Tooth."

"What a shame the Fox man cannot fight! He needs some of the men to help him, poor dear."

"There were two of them against one. That is not fair!"

"Fair or not, he just could not beat them! Too bad."

"I would like to comfort him . . ."

"Oh, you. Be quiet!"

At last the crowd was behind him. Talon strode to his tent and gathered his meager possessions.

That done, he tried to ignore the voices of the Saber-Tooths as he pushed his way through the crowd again to say farewell to his mother.

"My second son, Tuft, wants to marry your niece," the Saber-Tooth headman was saying loudly.

They are taking all the women, thought Talon. *Well, let them! It is nothing to me! Ah, but it* was. It was a wrenching, painful thing to be driven ignominiously away from the very people he had expected to marry into.

He glanced over one shoulder. Fickle Blizzard was even now casting flirtatious glances at the very man who had stolen her! Humiliation and rage twisted Talon's gut.

"Too soon," he heard the Caribou headman answer. "Wait until her eighteenth year. You can have Summer then. For now my wife needs her help digging roots and picking berries."

Talon's own predicament burst back upon him. To be banished! He was being sent to his death and he knew it. So did every one of the people he was leaving behind.

He reached his mother who was standing beside another elderly woman. When his mother looked up at him, her green eyes were sad. She reached out her arms and embraced him, patting his back gently. "My son," she said sadly. "I love you."

"I know, Mother," he said. "You would never turn against me."

"No, my son, I would not. I will come with you."

Talon pulled back and looked at her. Her red hair had long ago turned gray. Her face was wrinkled, her body stooped. He shook his head. "It would cause you much hardship and grief, mother. I cannot take you. It is better if you stay. You will be safe with the Caribou. You have friends who will help you . . ."

The other woman put an arm around her, and Talon thought he saw relief in his mother's eyes as she nodded sadly.

"I must go." He did not like it that his leave-taking was watched by sharp Saber-Tooth eyes.

"I will always love you, my son."

He hugged her. "And I, you."

Talon released his mother and left quickly, the crowd parting before him. Saber-Tooths put their noses in the air and turned away from him as though they smelled tainted meat.

Summer could not take her eyes off Talon as he strode away. She had seen him stop at his tent, and tears blurred her vision when he said farewell to his mother. The old woman now stood with head bowed, crying, while Talon walked away from her in the direction of the hills.

A sharp piercing in Summer's throat as though from a bone needle kept her sobs from welling up. She willed her tears away, striving to keep his proud, retreating figure in view until he disappeared.

Her heart felt empty. She let out a breath. He was gone. Talon was gone. She would never see him again. Never touch him. . . .

Auntie Birdsong's shaming words came back to her, and guilt again washed over her. Talon was free of Blizzard now. But he would not want a shameful woman like Summer, one who had lusted after her own cousin's betrothed. No man would.

A nasal voice at her side penetrated her blinding pain. "So, little Spider." It was the younger Saber-Tooth son, Tuft. "What think you? We are to be married in three years. My father says so." Tuft smiled, his pointed canines gleaming.

Summer's stomach lurched sickeningly. With a little cry, she whirled and fled to the safety of her cave.

Chapter Five

Talon awoke on a bed of dried pine needles. Chickadees twittered in the pine tree above his head. His muscles ached from the fight with the Saber-Tooth brothers. He consoled himself with the hope that their bodies hurt as much as his did.

But there was no consoling himself when he thought of Blizzard and her new husband. The woman he had done bride-service for had turned out to be fickle and unworthy of his efforts, and her father was no better.

But it was for the Saber-Tooths that he reserved his deepest disgust and anger. Rage filled him when he thought of the bullying headman and his two vicious sons. Bitterly, he hoped that Blizzard would have a miserable life with Rides Their Backs.

Talon had been treated badly and it galled him. His betrothed had been stolen from him; he had been publicly humiliated by the Saber-Tooths; his year of bride-service—the hunting, the fishing, all the meat he had provided to the ungrateful Caribous—had been disparaged and declared worthless.

But to be banished was the biggest blow of all. The Caribous had banished him merely because the Saber-Tooths demanded it. Those Saber-Tooths were not satisfied with stealing his woman. They wanted to ensure his death as well!

He left his pine-needle bed and wandered through the land for most of the day. He stopped on a little hillock that looked out over a lake. A cold wind blew in his face.

Bitter thoughts in a bitter wind, Talon thought. Over and over in his mind he replayed the terrible injustice done to him, wanting to right it, wanting to change the ending. But he never could. It was done. He had lost.

Finally, Talon could stand it no longer. He braced himself there on the solitary hilltop. Legs apart, weapons on the ground, he lifted his head and opened his mouth and howled out his anger and his pain. Rage poured out of him. He howled at the river, at the trees, at the hills and at the Great Spirit. From the very depths of his being arose the tortured sound. It was a cry for justice, a demand for revenge, a cry so strong he thought the very hills must reel at his pain. The sound soared up from his very soul and erupted from his throat. And it felt good.

After a long time, when Talon was finally weary of howling, when he could only force a croak from his throat, he sank to his haunches on the hill and stared out over the desolate, lonely terrain.

He felt drained, empty. He would be alone for the remainder of his life. But then he clenched his teeth. He would survive, Talon vowed to himself and to the Great Spirit. He would survive. The betraying Caribous and the cowardly Saber-Tooths would not win because he, Talon, would not die. He would live. And he would live to wreak vengeance on those who had hurt him.

The cold wind suddenly felt refreshing. A hard resolve formed in him, and he could feel his heart turn to a cold, hard piece of rock. He would survive, he vowed again. And when he was strong again, he would pursue the Caribou and the Saber-Tooths. They would feel the desperation, the pain that he felt now. They would taste his revenge!

As Talon picked up his weapons, he felt himself to be a new man, a colder man. He had lost his woman and his people. So be it. But he still possessed the life-force and he had his hunting skills. With the Great Spirit's help he would not be conquered.

His decision made, he raised his voice once more and howled at the heavens.

And then he heard an answering howl. First one voice, then another voice joined in, then another until there was a chorus of eerie, high-pitched sounds.

Talon knew what it was. A wolf pack had answered his cry.

The hairs on the back of his neck stood up. He turned in the direction of the howls and stared out across the barren land, searching for a glimpse of the only living beings who had responded to his lonely cry.

But Talon knew he must not forget, in his loneliness, that those same wolves could hunt him down and tear him apart.

He took a step down the hill, in a direction away from the voices of the wolves. He went forward, alone, to meet whatever fate the Great Spirit had prepared for him.

Chapter Six

"Farewell. Farewell, my dear, dear friend." Summer's eyes were clenched shut as she hugged Blue Camas. *Do not go,* she wanted to say but, alas, she knew that the older girl had no choice.

The Saber-Tooths waited in a tight little knot, surrounding their possessions. The wind fluttered their clothes.

Spotted Cat gripped Blue Camas' arm and tugged even as Summer still embraced her. "Time to go, wife," he said jovially.

Summer grimaced as she forced herself to take a step back. Her yellow eyes met Blue Camas' troubled brown ones and Summer saw the deep sadness there.

The second Saber-Tooth son, Tuft, watched

Summer and Blue Camas. "We will return," he announced in a surly voice and both women turned to regard him. When his father glanced at him, Tuft's lips parted in a snarl of a smile. "And when we return, I will claim you as my bride, Summer!"

But instead of meeting Summer's yellow gaze, Tuft was glaring at his father. Spotted Cat ignored him and tightened his grip on Blue Camas' arm. When she gave a little cry of pain, his hold slackened. "My regrets," the headman said. "I did not intend to hurt you."

Blue Camas rubbed her arm, glaring defiantly at him.

Spotted Cat grinned at her, complacent. "A man would be a fool to injure a new bride as beautiful as you."

Tuft bared his pointed teeth in a silent growl. Summer took another step back, wanting them only to be gone. She looked around. What was holding up their leaving? Where was Blizzard?

Uncle Antler stepped into the breach. "My daughter will return soon. She is merely saying good-bye to her mother in our home."

In truth, yells and angry shouts could be heard coming from the cave on the hillside.

"It is too late for your daughter to change her mind about the marriage," said Spotted Cat. "Rides Their Backs is her husband now. We have agreed. Remember the furs."

"I assure you she will be here any moment." Uncle Antler shot a nervous glance at the cave where more shouts could be heard.

"Load up," Spotted Cat said to Blue Camas.

Reluctantly, she lifted the baskets and furs that she was to carry on the journey back to Saber-Tooth territory. Her tan-colored leather dress was now painted with black spots in the Saber-Tooth fashion. Her hair, however, was not braided like theirs. In defiance, she kept it loose like the Caribou women's.

"When will I see you again?" Summer mouthed at her dearly beloved friend.

"I know not," Blue Camas answered just as silently.

Summer sighed. Perhaps she would be fortunate enough to see Blue Camas at her own wedding. Tuft and his father had announced that they would return to the Caribou People in her eighteenth year. Uncle Antler had looked unhappy about this, and Summer wondered if he was already regretting his decision to marry Blizzard off to Rides Their Backs.

"What is taking her so long?" demanded the Saber-Tooth headman, staring at the cave. "How long does it take for a woman to say goodbye to her mother?"

Uncle Antler cleared his throat. "Not long."

"Rides Their Backs," snarled Spotted Cat, "I am tired of waiting for your wife. Go and get her."

"I am certain," said Uncle Antler, "that Blizzard will be right down . . ."

"Quiet! I cannot abide idle talk—or idle talkers." Spotted Cat glared at Uncle Antler, who quickly subsided into silence.

Summer fiddled with the long fringe on her woman's neckcloth. She wished Tuft would stop staring at her like that. She glanced at her uncle. He was looking at the sky, at the ground, at the distant mountains, anywhere but at his soon-to-be-departing Saber-Tooth guests. Blue Camas lowered her heavy possessions to the ground and stared at the mountains, in the direction she would soon walk with the Saber-Tooths.

Rides Their Backs had reached the cave. After he entered, the shouting increased.

Summer concentrated on the long brown fringe of her neckcloth. Auntie Birdsong had sewn some Caribou designs in a circle on the frontpiece. Summer traced a tiny caribou calf with her finger.

More yells from the cave, but no one came out.

"Aargh," growled the Saber-Tooth headman. "I will go and see what takes them so long." He marched up the hill to the cave and disappeared inside. Still more yells issued forth.

"*I* was supposed to marry you," Tuft hissed at Blue Camas' back.

The young woman did not respond; Summer thought that perhaps she had not heard Tuft.

Tuft grabbed Blue Camas' arm and swung her around. His face was red with anger and his chest rose and fell with each quick breath.

"*I* was supposed to marry you. Instead you married my father!"

Blue Camas shrugged and stared at the far-off mountains. "It is not as though I had a choice."

"Look at me." Tuft choked on his words he was so furious. "Why did you choose my father instead of me?"

"I did not choose! I am not telling you anything new. You were there. You saw how it was. Your father told me, told you, told our Caribou headman, that he was going to marry me."

"He already has four wives!" Tuft growled. "What does he need with a fifth?"

Blue Camas shrugged again.

Summer started to edge away. She did not want to hear this conversation. Too late, Tuft saw her and swung upon her. "You!" he exclaimed. "It is all your fault!"

"Me?"

"Yes, you! If you were a woman, instead of a mere girl dressed up in a woman's neckcloth, I would not have had to ask for Blue Camas for a wife!"

Summer's fingers tightened on the fringe of the neckcloth. Her aunt and other women kinfolk had presented her with the woman's neckcloth when she had had her first menses. She deserved the cloth. It was her right to wear it. All Caribou women wore a neckcloth after their first menstruation. Tuft was mistaken to think that it meant she was eligible to marry.

For a moment she wanted to rip the deceptive cloth from her neck. Instead, she clenched her fingers. "My uncle says I must wait until I am able to marry."

"Your uncle is a camel plop! Now I have to wait. Alone." He glanced self-pityingly at Blue Camas, who stared stonily at the mountains.

Uncle Antler spoke up. "My niece, uh, daughter must stay with us. My wife is old. We have need of a girl to dig roots and pick berries for us. As for Blue Camas, why, we Caribou People would gladly have given her to you as your wife. But your father is headman. His request was the more, uh, powerful."

"You are afraid of him," accused Tuft.

Nobody said anything to that.

A loud yell caused them all to turn. Blizzard careened down the hill from the cave and stumbled into her father. The two fell to the ground. The Saber-Tooth headman and his son came running up, both puffing hard from their exertions. Rides Their Backs dumped Blizzard's possessions on the ground. A worried-looking Birdsong hovered behind them.

"This woman, Blizzard, is a problem," Spotted Cat snarled at Antler. "She says she does not want to come with us. But she is married to my son. She comes with us!"

"No!" cried Blizzard. "I do not want to go with you. You people are sloths. I do not like your son. He is a sloth, too!"

"My son is an excellent man!" roared the

70

Saber-Tooth headman. He glared at Rides Their Backs. "Take your wife with us. Drag her if you have to!" He turned his back on Blizzard and her grimacing husband. "Saber-Tooths!" he announced. "Load up."

Once again Blue Camas picked up her possessions. The other Saber-Tooth women loaded their baskets onto their backs and heads and proceeded to move slowly away from the Caribous.

Rides Their Backs pushed his new wife ahead of him. Blizzard dug her heels into the dirt, forcing her new husband to push her hard for every step taken.

That will not happen to me, thought Summer. *I will not be forced to marry a man of another's choosing. I will choose my own husband!* An image of Talon came to her mind. *A man like Talon!* Then she squashed the thought. Every time Summer thought about him, shame weighed her heart down like a heavy stone.

"We will be back," snarled Tuft, taking his place at the end of the Saber-Tooth line. He glared at Summer, then at her neckcloth, then at her uncle.

Uncle Antler shifted from foot to foot.

"I hope it is not too soon," whispered Summer.

"Three years," answered her uncle. "Come back to us in three years." He gazed after Blizzard, who was still taking slow steps, prodded forward this time by Rides Their Backs' spear.

71

Uncle Antler shook his head sadly. "If you return sooner than that," he called out to Tuft, "be sure to bring my daughter with you." He placed his hand over his heart. "An old man's heart longs for—"

"Hush," said Birdsong. "Those Saber-Tooths do not care how an old man feels about his daughter. They would just as soon cut out the old man's heart!"

Antler seemed to shrink into himself at his wife's words. Both of them looked suddenly old to Summer's eyes. They had aged much in the short time the Saber-Tooths had visited the Caribou camp.

Summer walked away, unable to bear the sadness of her best friend's departure or to watch her aunt and uncle any longer. As she walked, she again vowed to herself that she would never be forced to marry. Never! She would demand to marry the man of her choice, not be bullied into it like Blizzard and Blue Camas.

She reached a pine tree and glanced around, trying to calm her rapidly beating heart.

It was the time of her monthly courses and she decided to comply with part of the shaman's decree to bury her old leather sack and its contents.

Summer found a spot under the tree and dug a hole with her digging stick. Then she took out the treasure sack that hung on its frayed string around her neck. She opened it and studied her most precious possessions: a lock of hair from her deceased mother, a shriveled piece of Summer's own umbilical cord from the day of her birth, four dried blueberries, and a dried-up slice of tule root.

The berries were the first she had ever picked. They were to ensure that she would always find berries. The slice of tule root from the first root she had ever dug ensured that she would always find edible roots.

These were important to her. How did her Auntie and the shaman expect her to find berries and roots without these things? Summer tightened her lips.

She refused to be parted from her mother's hair, the only memento of her parent that she had. And saving the umbilical cord ensured she would have a long and happy life.

Glancing around, Summer noted she was alone. She lowered the sack into the hole. Then she stealthily pulled out the important objects, one by one and carefully placed them in a new leather pouch she had sewn and decorated.

The shaman's words came back to her: "The sack and everything in it must be buried. Only in that way can we be certain that no harm will come to Summer."

She peered around again, making sure no one could see her.

What possible harm could come to her? These were her things, important to her. Harm would come to her if she did *not* keep them.

Summer tucked the new sack and its precious contents inside her dress, then rose to her feet and used her digging stick to scrape dirt over the empty sack in the hole.

After one last glance around, Summer wandered back to the cave. She thought of the remainder of the shaman's instructions, the part about Talon bringing meat to her. But now that Talon was banished, he could not bring her any meat.

She wondered if he even knew of the shaman's decree. Probably not. She sighed. She would have liked to pretend he was performing bride-service. . . .

Alas, Talon would never perform bride-service for her, not if her uncle and the Saber-Tooths had their way. She did not like it that Tuft and Spotted Cat had negotiated with her uncle. She did not want to be forced into a marriage to Tuft.

Many things had changed since the Saber-Tooths' arrival, thought Summer. Blizzard was married, Blue Camas was married, and Talon had been driven away from the Caribou People.

Even Summer had changed. Her heart had been newly awakened to Talon mere days before he had been banished from her people. And now she was promised to another man, a violent stranger, a man she feared would make a poor husband. Yes, much had changed. And not for the better.

Chapter Seven

One year later

Talon sat on a black rocky outcrop overlooking a bleak, rocky land. He now knew it was possible to die of loneliness. That lack of his own kind could lead to this emptiness, this misery, was a sad revelation to him.

He had known when he had been banished from the Caribou People that he would face hardship and danger.

He had known that the short-faced bears, the lions, the saber-tooth tigers, the dire wolves, lay in wait for single hunters.

He had known that he risked accidents; he could break a leg and starve as had happened to Dart Thrower one summer.

But he had not guessed that the utter hollowness inside him would cause him such despair. One day loneliness would cause his death.

Talon had experienced to the full what loneliness could do to a man. It sapped his will to live, slowly, a day at a time, a heartbeat at a time, until when he saw a deer standing alone, he thought, not to kill it, but instead wondered if it, too, was lonely. The emptiness of his life was like a dirge that his heart kept chanting and he did not know how to stop or change it.

For many long moons, each moon totalling more days than the fingers and toes on both his hands and feet, Talon had not spoken to another human being. At first his anger at the Caribou People and the Saber-Tooth People and the rock hard feeling in his chest had kept him going. He had not needed anyone. He had hunted, killed game, eaten, made a shelter. He had survived and survived well.

Then, as the seasons passed, and he saw none of his own kind, there arose within Talon a feeling of bereavement. He knew himself to be the only thinking, speaking person in his world. And then the loneliness crept over him until it was dark and deep in its profundity.

It flowed through him like a cold glacier stream. It came and then went, but it always returned, intensified until sometimes, like now, he thought that he would die from this longing to be with another human being.

Talon sat eating the leg of a grouse he had snared and cooked. His grasp loosened on the birdbone. Of what use was it to eat, to stay alive, when there was no one to share meat with, no one to speak with? He picked the bone up and stared at it. *Eat,* he commanded himself. *Grow strong. You must go back to the Caribou People and revenge yourself.* He clung to his anger in the darkness of his loneliness as a wandering hunter clings to the North Star in the deepest night.

For solace, he began to remember people: his mother, who cried when he was banished but who was too old to come with him no matter how much she wanted to; his father, who had died when Talon was five summers old. Talon wished he'd had the chance to know his father. His bride-to-be, Blizzard, now the Saber-Tooth's wife; the Caribou headman, Antler, so afraid of the Saber-Tooths; Birdsong, who had cooked meals for him and seemed pleased that he was marrying her eldest daughter. . . . And the cousin, Summer. He remembered her pale yellow eyes, her light-colored hair. He wondered how she fared.

Something tugged at his memory then, something about the girl and the second Saber-Tooth son, but he could not capture it. He worried at it like a dire wolf does a caribou carcass, but the memory would not come and finally he let it go.

Talon thought about the Saber-Tooths now, carefully reviewing each one of them: Spotted

Cat, the overbearing father; his eldest son, so arrogant and confident when he took Blizzard away; the younger son, sly and overbearing like his brother and father.

It was then that Talon started to feel more than the dreaded loneliness. His heart pumped blood through his body at a faster pace, he felt that blood rush to his face, felt his fists clench and his teeth grit. It was solely his rage and humiliation that he could rely upon to sustain him.

He stood up and flung the birdbone away. He stalked over to get his weapons. Only thoughts of revenge kept him alive.

That his life should come to this single purpose—not listening to the bird as it called to its mate, not hearing the cricket as it sang its song—but that it should be hate, deep, dark hate and anger that drove him, this was a new thing to Talon. It was shaping him into a man he did not recognize. And if death by loneliness did not claim him, he shuddered at what kind of man he might become.

But still he would hunt. He would eat. He would build shelters. He would survive! He would live, for to live was far better than to die.

And he would revenge himself upon the Caribou People and the Saber-Tooth People. They would all pay dearly for what they had done to him!

Chapter Eight

Another year later
Summertime

Motionless, Talon crouched in a clump of pine trees and stared at a small cave under a rock ledge.

He had been watching the wolf pack and pups for several days. The pups' sire had a gray underbelly and dark brown markings streaking his back. He had a heavy face, with great jaws for snapping bones. His body was short and powerful. He was a dire wolf. Talon had seen many dire wolves and knew to keep out of their way.

The dam, however, was unlike any wolf he had seen before. She had longer legs, and a graceful gray body. Her face was much smaller, with intelligent yellow eyes, and she had small jaws.

Today was the first day that both parent wolves had left the pups and gone off hunting. On guard duty was a black two-year-old. He combined traits of both parents, having large jaws like his father and the yellow eyes of his mother. In another year, the black two-year-old would be a mature male, but now he still exhibited puppy playfulness.

The black wolf nosed his far younger siblings, three of them gray, one of them white. The pups clambered all over him in the warm sunshine. One of the grays tumbled off and staggered away from the low cave that was the wolf den and towards a swiftly flowing creek. A low growl from the black wolf halted the youngster. A short, sharp whine called the pup back to its elder brother.

The wolf family has chosen their home well, thought Talon. The cave was close to a stream in the midst of deer and antelope territory. He knew this because he hunted the same territory as the wolf family. Several times, Talon had come upon the small pack. Once, he allowed them to see him. Though he did not threaten them, the wolves preferred to melt back into the forest rather than challenge him.

He had not seen the small pack for a time until he discovered the cave. Now he knew their absence from his hunting territory was because the female had returned to the den to have her pups.

Talon sensed that the dire wolf and his mate tolerated his presence in their hunting area, but he did not know what they would do if they knew that he had found their cave and precious pups.

The white pup toddled over and bit the black wolf's tail. He gave a tiny yelp and jumped into the air, all four legs stiff. When he landed, the three grays swarmed over him again, tugging on his fur with their mouths. He pushed at them with his nose to keep their tiny sharp teeth from pinching him.

The pups' playful antics brought a smile, the first in several moons, to Talon's lips. Some of his loneliness eased as he watched the pups. Their little jaws opened and closed on great bunches of the black wolf's fur. He sat patiently through the torture.

Talon wondered what the black wolf would do if he were to approach and look at the pups. He knew that if the parents had been at the cave, they would have snarled and snapped at him and warned him away, but the black wolf was still young, and curious. Perhaps he would be friendly.

Loneliness propelled Talon forward and he stepped cautiously from behind the tree. The black wolf saw him and stood up hastily. The four cubs fell off him and tumbled to the ground. They climbed over each other, mock growling and ignoring Talon. The black wolf watched him warily, but did not growl. Encouraged, Talon took a step forward.

He started to speak to the wolf, and his voice felt hoarse from lack of use. "I have seen you before, elder brother wolf," Talon said, "while drinking water at the pond in the glade."

The sound of Talon's voice did not seem to alarm the black wolf, so Talon took another step. The wolf continued to gaze at him with yellow eyes, then sat down with his head cocked to one side as though considering Talon's words.

Taking slow steps, Talon continued to approach. Inwardly he wondered at the loneliness that would make him take such a risk. Yet the black wolf continued to watch him with those intelligent eyes. Finally Talon knew he must go no farther, no matter how lonely he was. This was still a wolf, and he could not forget how dangerous they were. "I admire your brothers and sisters," he said quietly. "They are very strong. They will make brave hunters like their mother and father and you."

He stood there for a time, watching the pups, and the black wolf allowed it. Realizing at last that the parents might return at any time to feed the pups, Talon backed away. "I will return another day for a visit, elder brother wolf. You need have no fear of me."

The black wolf watched him silently, and Talon slipped into the brush. It was with relief tinged with regret and sadness that he walked deeper into the forest, leaving behind the happy band of wolf pups and their watchful elder brother.

After that Talon found himself returning often to the den to watch the pups. Whenever the parent wolves left, he would step out quietly from behind the stand of pines and let the black one see him. When the wolf began to accept Talon's appearance as a natural part of his life, Talon was able to move closer and closer to the pups until one day he was able to pick up the plump white one. The animal's small, warm body squirmed in his hands until an anxious whine from the black wolf warned Talon to carefully set the pup down. But the next time he picked up a pup, a gray one this time, the black wolf watched in silence. "I will not hurt your younger brother," assured Talon. "I only want to play with him."

He held the pup up and looked into its alert brown eyes. This one possessed the same intelligent appearance of the parents and elder brother, it seemed. Talon rubbed the soft belly. "You have a fine family," he told the black wolf. "Someday they will be great hunters. I will have to work very hard to get deer for my—" He almost said "family," but he cut the word off. The loneliness that always receded when he watched or played with the pups came back in full strength. Slowly he bent and replaced the pup with its brothers and sisters.

He rose carefully so as not to alarm the wary elder brother. "You have a fine family," he repeated. He backed away from the den. He would return another day, when the sadness of his forced solitude was not upon him. The black wolf watched him leave, the wise yellow eyes following him.

Talon had no sooner stepped behind pine trees than the parents returned. The father padded up to his offspring and regurgitated the meat he had swallowed after his hunt. The female did the same. Talon watched as the pups eagerly ate the steaming meat. When the pups had finished eating, they sprawled out in the sun. Their mother licked them, bathing them, washing Talon's scent from their fuzzy fur.

As Talon watched the family, a longing grew in his heart. He could not live on hate and rage and loneliness. He wanted some goodness in his life. He was like the wolves. He wanted a family around him, children. He wanted someone to hunt for, care for, play with.

Talon turned and walked deeper into the forest, a lonely, solitary man.

Chapter Nine

Talon sat at his lonely fireside and stared into the flames. The black wolf suddenly appeared beside him. "Your mother is dying," said the wolf.

Talon rose in alarm. His mother was old, her red hair turned grey. "I must go to her."

"I will show you the way to the Fox woman," said the wolf and he trotted off. Talon followed the wolf swiftly across the land until he reached the tent of his mother. He entered the tent and sat down beside her. Her lips were caked with dry spittle, her forehead hot. He stroked her forehead. She opened her eyes, moved her lips silently, and then she died.

Talon got up and went outside the tent where the wolf was waiting. Talon's heart was heavy

*with sorrow and he turned away lest the wolf
see his grief.*

*"That is but one of your mothers," said the
wolf. "The Great Spirit gave you two." Then he
trotted off into the brush.*

Talon took a step to follow him. . . .

He woke up and bolted upright, crying out.
The cry died on his lips when he realized that
he was awake. He was no longer dreaming.

His heart thumping, Talon peered around
for the black wolf.

Gone.

Talon lay back down on his bedrobe and
stared up at the dark branches of the lodgepole
pine above his head. Dawn would come soon.

When the morning sun started her journey
across the sky, Talon arose and picked up his
spear, his robe and his few other possessions.
Then he followed the river bank until he came
to Caribou territory. The next day, he climbed
a hill and sat atop it, surveying the land. At
last he spied a faint wisp of grey smoke drifting across the face of a black basalt rock cliff.
Talon walked down the hill and headed in the
direction of the smoke.

It was the Caribou People. He waited until
nightfall and then he waited some more until
the Caribou had retired to their tents for the
evening. When all was silent, he crept to his
mother's tent and entered.

She was alone, and she was moaning. Her

long reddish-grey hair was tangled and her face looked sunken. Now and then she thrashed on the rumpled bedding. *The black wolf was right*, thought Talon. *She is dying.*

Just then his mother opened her eyes. She blinked and stared at him. "Is—is that you, my son?"

He approached her bedside. "Yes, Mother."

Snare smiled and took his hand. Her fingers felt like fine bark that crumbled at a touch. Her skin was dry and hot.

"You are a good son," she murmured and patted his hand.

Talon could not meet her eyes. A good son did not leave his mother when he was banished. A good son did not become banished in the first place.

His mother tried to sit up. "Talon, you must leave. The Saber-Tooths will find you!"

He saw then that she still understood what went on around her. He squeezed her fingers gently. "I will leave soon, Mother. They will not catch me."

"The Caribou might tell them," she warned. Then she sank back on the furs, groaning.

In alarm, Talon blurted, "Where do you hurt, Mother?"

"Every part of me hurts," Snare gasped. "I am dying!"

He felt helpless and powerless, seeing her pain. He wanted to do something for her, but what could he do? He could not hunt for her, he could not even stay near her.

Snare closed her eyes and moaned again. Then she slept for a time. When she awoke, she murmured, "Is that you, Summer?"

"No, Mother. It is I, Talon."

"Ah, Talon. So it is. I thought perhaps it was Summer. She brings me my morning meal."

Talon was relieved that his mother was being cared for by Blizzard's cousin.

"Did I tell you how I found you, my son?"

"Yes, Mother, you told me. Rest now." He touched her forehead. Hot. Dry.

"I want to tell you again," she rasped. When he saw that she insisted, he nodded assent.

"I found you in the forest," Snare began. "I was hunting for my herbs and special medicine plants . . ." She waved a hand at the baskets lining one side of the tent. They were full of dried leaves and gnarled roots and dead stalks.

Talon's mother had always collected plants. When he was a little boy, he had gone with her up the hillsides, through the valleys and down by the river, wherever it was she needed to go to find a particular plant she sought.

"A great, fierce saber-tooth tiger came to the pond to drink. I saw you lying close by, under a big green fern. Swiftly I snatched you up before the tiger could see you and eat you. Then I ran away, holding you to my breast. And that is how you became my son." She smiled happily.

Talon smiled sadly. He had always wondered why his birth story was so different from other people's stories.

"A great, fierce saber-tooth tiger . . ." murmured his mother, drifting off to sleep, "with long black hair . . ."

Talon was alone with his thoughts. He got up and stirred the embers of the fire, then he went back and sat down beside his mother.

Suddenly he noticed that her breathing had quickened. Her breath whistled and she cried out, waking herself with the cry.

"Ah, Talon! You are still here. It is good. It is good . . ." She patted his hand, but her eyes were strange.

"Talon! I see them, the babies!" She seemed to be focusing on something he could not see. She tried to sit up, and Talon gently pushed her back down. "There, Mother," he soothed. "Rest."

"The babies! They are here! Four of them! Only they are no longer babies, Talon. Why, they are grown! Your sisters and brothers. My babies!"

He shook his head sadly. She was confused. Talon had no sisters and brothers. Snare had no other sons or daughters.

She sat up, her arms opened wide as if to gather the unseen children to herself.

Talon made her lie down again. "Easy, Mother," he murmured.

"Oh, Talon, I love them so! And—oh, here comes another! Oh! Oh!" This time when she sat up, Talon's strength was not enough to overcome hers.

"She is here too! My first baby! The one I was carrying when I ate the poison-plant." After a long silence, Snare whispered, "I did not tell you about that, Talon. I ate a plant one time so I would not have a baby. But she is here. She is here!"

Snare sank back on the covers and covered her face with her hands. "Tell her to go away, Talon! I am too sad. I am too sorry."

Gently Talon pried her hands from her face, his heart pounding. He did not understand what his mother was talking about.

"She is crying, Talon." Snare had tears in her eyes. "She is crying and saying she loves me. Oh, Talon, I made a terrible mistake! I love her too! Oh, why did I do it? I cannot remember now! She is coming to me. Her arms are open. She loves me! Oh, Talon, help me!"

Snare's arms were open and she was trying to rise out of the bed furs.

Talon did not know what to do. *Help her, Great Spirit*, he prayed. *Help my mother!*

"Talon! I have wronged your mother terribly. And you. Oh, why did I do such a cruel— Oh, no! But wait! I learned to love by being your mother. I can go now. I can go now. I can go to the Great Spirit. My babies—

come with me! Goodbye, goodbye Talon!"

And his mother died.

Talon wept.

Before it was light, he crept away from the tent and disappeared into the forest.

Chapter Ten

Early Fall

Talon was dragging back an antelope to the
small camp he had made when he first saw
the man.

He almost did not see him, for the light was
waning. But something, a movement perhaps,
alerted him suddenly that he was not alone.

The stranger lay on the ground, one leg disappearing into a deep hole. On the thick limb
of a tree above him crouched a snarling saber-
tooth tiger.

Talon glanced around warily. Sometimes
saber-tooth tigers hunted in pairs and he
had no wish to be attacked by the big cat's
mate.

The tiger heard Talon's approach and whirled to face him, teeth bared. Talon dropped the antelope to the ground and swung around to face the beast, raising his spear.

The cat bared its glistening yellow fangs. Talon looked into its snarling red mouth. Tufted ears lay flat against the large head. It was the biggest tiger Talon had ever seen.

He shook the spear menacingly, hoping to scare the cat, but the growling animal rose to a launching position.

Before Talon had time to brace himself, the tiger sprang. A loud *crack!* sounded as the branch broke from the powerful thrust of the animal's hindquarters. The tiger flew through the air at Talon, deadly claws extended, and hit Talon like a huge rock. As he fell, he shoved the spear up through the animal's shaggy fur, aiming for the heart. The cat's sharp claws ripped at him and the searing pain caused Talon to gasp. He tried to yank his spear out of that powerful chest, but it was caught fast. He was caught fast, too, in a bone-crunching hold.

Desperately, Talon felt at his waist for one of the obsidian knives he always wore. He found one and plunged its blade deep into the beast's stomach, then into its heart, again and again. The cat roared in agony, and its legs shook, clawing convulsively. Its huge mouth sought blindly to impale Talon on its dagger teeth. Talon kept ducking his head out of reach.

He feared the tiger would never die. But at Talon's last plunge of the knife, the cat gave a huge gasp and went limp. For a long time Talon did not move, only lay panting into the stinking fur. Blood soaked his back from the wounds.

"Better you die than I," he suddenly heard.

He had forgotten about the injured man. Slowly Talon withdrew the bloody knife blade. Next he tugged his spear from the tiger's heart and rolled out of the cat's death embrace. He staggered to his feet, prepared to fight anew.

The stranger's jaw dropped open. Clearly he had thought both Talon and the tiger were dead. The man's eyes turned angry when he saw Talon staring at him.

"Kill me, then. Kill me and be done!"

Talon approached the man cautiously, far more cautiously than he had approached the tiger. He saw now that the man's leg lay at a strange angle, probably broken.

The injured man watched Talon out of hate-filled, bleak eyes. He reached for his spear, but in his fall, it had landed out of reach. "Kill me and be done," he growled again.

Talon had to listen carefully to understand the stranger's words, for they sounded different than the way he, Talon, spoke.

The man was big, and his leather shirt was poorly sewn, as if clumsy large fingers had sewn the stitches. His tangled brown hair was cut in a manner that Talon had not seen before, hacked off just below his ears. Talon walked over and kicked the man's spear even farther away. He would take no chances with a man who looked this fierce.

"I will kill you if you do not kill me," snarled the man on the ground.

Talon shook his head. He was not anxious to kill the first human being he had seen in many moons, especially after killing the saber-tooth. He was bleeding and still trying to catch his breath.

He glanced the length of the man and saw that he was well stuck in the soft dirt of the hole. He was alone, with a broken leg, unarmed and mean. Talon shook his head again. This man had few prospects for survival.

"What happened?" he asked, wondering if he should just walk away. *He is perhaps worse than the Saber-Tooth People who took Blizzard,* Talon thought. But something within him did not want to let the man die; he sensed the other's desperation.

The man glanced down at his leg. "You can see for yourself," he snarled.

Talon frowned. This man was not grateful to be saved from the saber-tooth tiger. He was not relieved that someone had come along who might help him. What kind of a man was he?

Talon shrugged and picked up the man's spear. The man glared at him. "Go ahead. Take my spear. Leave me unarmed."

He seemed to think that Talon wished to hurt him. Why would Talon want to take the man's spear? He had his own spear, and atlatl and darts. "Where is your atlatl?" he asked the stranger.

"So you want that too? Is my spear not enough?"

Was the stranger giving away his things now that he was going to die? It was very confusing to speak with this man, Talon thought.

"I do not have an atlatl," the man said then, but his eyes glanced to the side. To Talon, it looked like he was hiding something. Talon walked in circles around the man, larger and larger circles, combing the ground—for what, he did not know. He gave a small cry when he found the atlatl some distance away. Next to it was a dead rabbit and a small sack. Talon knelt and opened the sack. It contained two firemaking rocks, some moss, a piece of black obsidian, and two blue feathers.

The stranger must have seen the saber-tooth, dropped the dead rabbit in hopes the animal would eat it, then dropped his atlatl and run. After that, he had stumbled into the hole and injured his leg, Talon surmised.

Carrying the atlatl and the hunter's sack, Talon walked back to the man. He squatted on his heels and stared at him. "Where are your people?" he asked.

The man spat in disgust. "I have no people," he growled.

This was very strange, Talon thought. Here was another man with no people, like himself. "Are you banished?"

The man glared at him, his jaw working. "No need to tell you."

From what little he had come to understand of this stranger, Talon judged that this answer meant that he had indeed been banished from his people. Men were only banished for desperate reasons like murder or kidnapping—or if a certain headman feared the Saber-Tooth People. "Who are your people?" Talon tried again.

The man just scowled, tightening his lips.

Talon rose and dropped the man's things beside him. What strange trick of the Great Spirit's was this that he should find such a man? He started to walk away.

"You!" the man called.

Talon turned.

"Will—will you help me?"

Talon frowned. "I thought you wished to die. You told me to kill you." He shook his head. "But I will not do that."

The man stared at him. "I thought you were going to kill me."

"No."

The man watched him warily. "Will you help me out of this hole? I will surely die here if you do not."

"Do you want to die?" Talon asked.

The man choked out his answer. "No."

Talon walked back until he stood next to the stranger. He looked down at the big fist grasping the spear. He looked into the light brown eyes staring up at him and saw pleading in them. He knew then that this man found it difficult to ask for help.

Talon knelt and began digging at the dirt surrounding the injured leg. He saw the man wince once or twice when he accidentally bumped the injured limb, but no sound crossed those tight lips. Finally the hole was wide enough to hoist the man's leg out of it without further damage to his other leg.

Talon gripped the man under the armpits and pulled until the leg came free. With a loud gasp, the man fainted.

Talon laid him carefully on the ground. It was dark now, and he glanced around, still watching for the dead saber-tooth's mate. Leaving the man where he was, Talon built a fire close by. When the flames were crackling and the rabbit cooking, he went back to the stranger. Using a strip of hide cut from the dead saber-tooth, Talon straightened and bound the injured leg to a long stick. He thought the man was fortunate to be unconscious.

When the rabbit was cooked, the man came to.

Talon handed him a fat rabbit haunch with hot juice dripping off it. The man devoured the meat. Then Talon gave him some fresh water from the bison bladder he always carried with him. When the man had eaten and drunk his fill, Talon asked him as he had before, "Who are your people?"

The man wiped his fist across his mouth, smearing rabbit grease. He considered for a time, then answered, "My people are the Bear People."

Talon chewed on the rabbit haunch he had selected for himself. "Where are they?" he asked.

The man jerked his thumb carelessly to where the sun rises.

"Why are you not with your people?" Talon asked.

The man reached for the spear and placed it across his lap. He stared at his broken leg, now bound and straight, then met Talon's eyes warily. "I killed a man. I, Blue Feather, killed the shaman of my people."

Talon did not like the sound of that. To kill a shaman was the worst thing a man could do. Shaman were respected and needed. They cured the sick, made ceremonies for hunting, chanted for babies to be born. They did many things to help their people. He moved a little farther away from the man.

Blue Feather smiled. "You do well to keep away from me," he said. He swung his spear around until the sharp tip pointed in Talon's direction. "Where are your people?" he asked.

Talon gently pushed the spear point away.

Blue Feather's smile widened.

Then Talon told him about the Saber-Tooths' offer for Blizzard, about the cowardly Caribou betrayal, and how he had come to be banished. He felt as though he had not said so many words to one person in his life. *That is what living alone for so many seasons does to a man*, he mused.

When he fell quiet, the man said, "So. You are on your own."

Talon glanced at him. "Have been for a long time."

Blue Feather laughed. "Yes, being banished for life makes for a long time. I know that!"

Talon stared into the orange flames. "I want to return and revenge myself upon those Caribou People and those Saber-Tooths."

Blue Feather also stared at the fire for some time. "If I survive, I will help you," he said at last.

Talon stared at him in surprise. He did not think Blue Feather made offers such as this often. Talon pushed a chunk of wood, the limb that the saber-tooth had crouched upon, further into the fire.

"My thanks," said Blue Feather. "That saber-tooth cat would have killed me." He laid his spear aside. "The shaman tried to kill me. He wanted my wife. He wanted my brother's wife, too. So he poisoned my brother, and he also poisoned my cousin. They both fell sick and died. When I started to get sick, I knew it was the shaman who had done it. I killed him and I recovered."

Talon listened in silence.

Blue Feather continued, "But I had to leave my people and my wife after that. I was banished and it was as though I was dead. After I left the Bear People, I sneaked back one night—oh, not to talk to her, not even to let her know I was there, but just to watch her." He threw a stick on the fire. "She had married somebody else."

Talon did not know what to say. It made him uncomfortable to be with a man who had killed another man, yet he knew such things happened. He might be forced to do it when he returned to the Caribou People.

And even though this man was a killer, he was still a human being. Talon did not want to go more moons without another person to talk to. Perhaps he and Blue Feather might be able to help each other with hunting.

"I know of a wolf cave," Talon said.

The man stared at him, surprised at the change of topic.

"When your leg is better, I will show it to you."

Blue Feather met his eyes. In that light brown gaze, lit only by the flames, Talon saw understanding dawn that he was suggesting a pact. A pact that the two of them live together, travel together, hunt together. Neither would have to be alone. Talon found himself letting out his breath when he saw Blue Feather slowly nodding. "That would be good," he answered. "I like wolves."

"Wolves are fierce when they have to fight off a predator," Talon said. "They take good care of their families; they hunt for them and protect them. They play with their pups. They hide deep in the forests and in the canyons. They run great distances after deer and antelope and never tire. They are good hunters."

"And sometimes," added Blue Feather, "they kill their own kind."

Talon acknowledged, "They do. We are like wolves."

Blue Feather nodded.

"We can learn from the wolves," Talon said. "We can learn to grow cunning, skilled at hunting, and ferocious to our enemies."

Blue Feather grunted in agreement.

"We are Wolves! We will call ourselves the Wolves," Talon exclaimed. "Not the Wolf People, for we have no women or children." Strange how the image of the pale-haired Summer flitted through his mind. "There are only two of us. But we will be the Wolves and we will be fierce!"

"Hunh," agreed Blue Feather.

Chapter Eleven

The warm weather almost made Summer forget that winter was soon to come. Though it was now autumn, it was still warm and dry. She eased the basket she was carrying to the ground. It was half-full of purple choke cherries. *A good day's work,* she thought, wiping one hand across her perspiring brow as she glanced at the laden basket. She liked picking choke cherries. They grew along the river and it was always pleasant to walk there.

Auntie Birdsong was picking with the other Caribou women. *I will just wade in the river,* thought Summer. *Perhaps there will be more choke cherries farther upstream.*

She told Auntie of her plan. Birdsong nodded absently as she talked with one of the other women, her fingers swiftly plucking the fruit as she spoke.

Summer wandered idly, the cool water soothing to her legs and feet. The river rushed swiftly here and mosquitoes were not the plague they were wherever the water stood still.

As she rounded the bend of the river, Summer spotted a thicket crowded with choke cherries. She gave a happy cry. It was bountifully laden with ripe fruit and she picked her way through the thicket, away from the river and deeper into the forest. To her surprise and delight, she came to a little glade, far away from the noise of the river. Green willows and silver and green cottonwoods quivered alongside the quiet banks of a small pool. At one end, a thin white waterfall cascaded over black, mossy rocks and rushed headlong into the pool. A pair of blue jays screeched high overhead.

Summer stood enchanted. *What a lovely place,* she thought. She stepped further into the glade. Soft moss cushioned her feet and she moved forward noiselessly. When she bent to dip her hand in the water of the pool, she gave a little exclamation of delight. The water was warm and clear.

Without another thought, Summer deposited her berry basket on the moss and swiftly shed her clothes. She waded into the pool and closing her eyes in bliss, sank up to her neck in the water.

She played in the water, paddling a little. It was not often she had such a fine opportunity to swim.

Talon was tired and hot. It had been a long day and though he had followed the river, no deer or antelope had crossed his path. He squinted at the sun. There was still some time before dark when he must return to the Wolves' camp. There was a glade he knew of not far away, with a pool. He could cool and refresh himself there.

Summer splashed happily in the water. She swam across the pond and then back again. Suddenly the screeching of the blue jays ceased abruptly and they flew off. Silence reigned. Summer froze. Only her eyes moved, searching for whatever had alarmed the birds.

Seeing nothing, she swam to the bank where her clothes lay. She was halfway out of the water, almost to the pool's edge, when she saw it.

A black wolf.

Summer's yellow eyes widened in fright and her heart pounded as she stared at the wolf. He was huge, and like no wolf she had ever seen before. His jaws were large, yet his body was graceful. He stared back at her and then, to her utter dismay, he prowled forward.

She stood motionless, frantically forming and discarding plans of what to do. The wolf stopped several man-lengths away. His eyes captured hers.

Yellow eyes stared into yellow eyes.

Suddenly Summer knew what the wolf wanted. He was telling her with those fierce yellow eyes, *You are my prey. It is time to die.*

She stared at him as that uncanny thought burned its way through her brain. And at that moment she knew that if she made one move for her clothes, moved a single finger or toe, he would leap upon her and tear her limb from limb.

She stared back at him and to his silent threat of death she answered aloud, "I want to live. I will fight you. I am strong!"

The wolf stared at her while Summer's heart slammed in her chest. Did he understand her reply? Did he believe her?

She could feel the blood thudding in her veins. Would this be the last time she felt it? A tiny breeze caressed her hot cheeks. Would she ever again feel the wind on her face, in her hair? A tiny fish darted against her leg and away. She took the touch for inspiration.

"I will not flee," she told the wolf. "You must leave me. Find someone else to kill, to eat."

Hearing her own words spoken aloud gave her courage. Still the wolf watched her. She dared not take her eyes from his.

"Go," she commanded. "Leave me."

Still he watched her and she felt herself growing weak. The fear was in her, coursing through her with every beat of her heart. *I must not give into it,* she thought. *This fear is deadly.*

Then, as she watched, the wolf lowered his head and walked away, melting into the bush, the greenery closing around him. He was gone.

Only the quiet of the forest told Summer that she had not imagined the encounter.

Slowly, her knees trembling, she staggered to the bank where her clothes lay, scanning the trees where he had disappeared. She was alone. She was safe!

Talon could not take his eyes off her. He watched her lithe body, the long graceful length of her brown back flaring out into full, rounded hips, and his body tensed.

She flicked her head, sending her long wet hair falling down her back. Talon swallowed. She bent over to pick up her dress. When she straightened, she glanced around and he saw her yellow eyes searching again for the black wolf.

Talon started to sweat. His hungry eyes followed her every move. As she stepped into her dress, he imagined her long legs holding him, wrapping around him. He shook his head, trying to dispel the vision.

She picked up her basket and walked away from the glade. The dense choke cherry thicket swallowed her up.

He watched her go. His whole body felt on fire. His heart drummed in his breast.

It was the girl from the Caribou camp! Summer. He recognized her. Blizzard's little cousin. But she was little no longer. She had grown into a woman, a lovely, brave woman.

And he wanted her.

Chapter Twelve

"It is easy to sneak up on you Wolves," Talon said as he strode into camp. He dropped two large rabbits and his spear next to the rock by the fire and held out his hands to warm them.

Blue Feather grunted. "We heard you. You thrash around in the brush like a mammoth with a broken leg."

Weasel, one of the new men, chuckled. So did his brother, Sloth, though silently.

Talon squatted by the fire. "We should move camp. There are no deer anymore."

"Again?" asked Weasel. "Winter's coming. What are we going to do for meat if we have to move all the time? We cannot move in the snows. We should be putting away dried roots and berries for the winter."

"Roots and berries indeed!" snorted Blue Feather. "We are not women!"

"When we were with my people, my brother and I helped harvest camas bulbs," Weasel retorted. "Did we not?" Sloth nodded.

"That is what I would expect of two brothers who were once members of the Camas Eater People," Blue Feather sneered. "*Men* do not dig roots."

"If they are hungry they do," said Weasel. Both brothers stared glumly at the orange flames.

"I do not mind digging roots," said Talon. "Though it would be better if we had a woman to do it for us." He was thinking of the young woman he had seen at the pool.

Blue Feather snorted. "Woman! What woman would join us? Who has even seen a woman in many moons? I have not. I forget what they look like." But by his angry eyes, Talon was sure he was remembering the wife who had remarried.

Weasel chuckled. "When I was with the Camas Eaters, before they drove us off . . ." He glanced at his brother, who kept staring at the fire. " . . . I had three wives."

"We are four men," said Blue Feather. "And we have no wives."

They were all silent.

"Women are not to be trusted," Blue Feather cautioned. "I know this. My former wife refused to follow me into banishment."

"As did mine," said Weasel. "Not one of the three would come with me."

"Hunh. Afraid of starving, no doubt."

"What about you, Talon?"

Talon shook his head. "Blizzard was most eager to go away with the Saber-Tooth," he said bitterly.

Weasel volunteered, "Sloth did not have a wife. She died the winter before."

Sloth nodded sadly.

"Four men and no women," said Blue Feather. "What a pitiful lot we are."

"Wolves have mates," observed Talon.

"Hunh. Every animal has a mate."

"Except us," said Weasel.

"Perhaps we should take mates."

The others looked at Talon as though he were suddenly deranged.

"Who would we go to for women?" demanded Blue Feather. "No people will allow us near them. The nearest woman to us, if we could find her, would be protected by other men. If we even show ourselves, the men will drive us away with stones."

Talon touched the warm cloak he wore. "We did well trading with the Mammoth Eaters. They were eager to trade these warm clothes for the bison meat and hides we provided."

"Hunh. But they would not let us speak to their women!" Blue Feather shook his head. "My people, the Bear, will attack us if they see us. Your people, the Caribou, will do the same. And the Camas Eaters do not ever want to see Weasel and Sloth again. They are too afraid of Sloth."

"My brother has harmed no one!" snorted Weasel.

Sloth looked up from the fire and glared at Blue Feather.

"I have told you why we were forced to leave the Camas Eaters," said Weasel. He placed a restraining hand on his brother's shoulder. "One of our hunters was killed down by the river. His body was found—half-eaten."

Sloth shuddered.

"My people accused Sloth. But Sloth cannot speak to defend himself. I told them he did not do that horrible thing, that a bear did it. But no one believed me.

"When the Camas Eaters forced my brother to leave, I left with him. My hair was the color of obsidian before my brother and I were banished. But grief has turned my hair white."

All four men were quiet for a time, each preoccupied with his own thoughts.

"I saw a woman," said Talon quietly. "Today."

The others swung their heads to stare at him. "You what?" demanded Blue Feather.

"Alone," said Talon. "She was alone."

"A woman," breathed Weasel.

"She would make a good mate for a Wolf," Talon mused aloud.

114

"*Any* woman would make a good mate for a Wolf," snorted Blue Feather. "We would put her to work digging roots, picking berries, sewing clothes—and doing other things.." He grinned. "Is she old?"

"No."

"Young?"

"Yes."

"Ugly?"

Talon shrugged.

"She *is* ugly. Hunh. I do not think I want to see this ugly woman of yours, Fox man."

"She has yellow eyes. Like a wolf."

The other three pondered this information. "Where did you see her?" asked Weasel.

Talon jerked his thumb over his shoulder in the direction of the glade. The men peered into the darkness as if they might discover her hiding behind an aspen tree. "I do not understand why she has no people," said Weasel.

"Oh, she has people."

"Who?" Blue Feather asked. He leaned forward, watching Talon intently. "Who is this ugly young woman with the yellow eyes, Fox man? Tell us."

Talon stared into the fire. "Nobody," he said. "Just the younger cousin of the woman I did bride-service for. Her name is Summer."

"Summer," murmured Blue Feather.

Talon grinned a wolfish grin. "I would like to steal that woman. That would be a fine revenge on the Caribou!"

Blue Feather and Weasel hooted like owls in delight. Sloth, with a huge grin on his face, gave a silent laugh of joy. Talon stared at the orange flames and thought of Summer.

Chapter Thirteen

Winter

It was cold, so cold in the winter cave. Summer shivered and thought she had never been so cold. The tiny fire in the cave flickered and burned low, casting long dark shadows on the black rock walls. Summer prayed the remaining wood would keep the fire aflame a little longer; she needed time to rest before she dragged herself forth to search for more wood. She intended to go soon, truly. She just needed to rest first.

Uncle Antler groaned and Summer watched as her aunt patted his hand. But when Birdsong reached over to rub his wounded leg, he pushed her hand away. The jaguar's vicious claws had torn through the muscle of his thigh right down to the bone.

"Summer, make a poultice," Auntie Birdsong demanded.

Summer hesitated. "There is only one yampa root left, Auntie. It is the last of our roots. Perhaps we should use it for food instead of a poultice."

"If we cannot heal the man who hunts for us, of what use are a few paltry roots? Make the poultice!"

Summer shuffled out of the cave. She scraped snow into a stone bowl and lugged it back inside. When the snow melted, she soaked their last piece of dried yampa root in it. Her lips quivered as she stared at the gray root. After Uncle Antler had been attacked by the jaguar, her family had been forced to rely upon the small store of roots they had gathered in the summer and fall. But those roots had been swiftly eaten.

The accident had happened when Uncle Antler went hunting in the snow. He killed a camel he found floundering in a deep snow bank. Unfortunately, a jaguar had also been stalking the camel. Deprived of its prey, the big cat attacked Uncle Antler and left him for dead. After the jaguar dragged the camel away, Uncle Antler managed to crawl back to the cave, leaving a bloody trail in the snow. He fainted at the entrance to the cave and Summer found him early the next morning. Only the warmth and protection of the two camp dogs lying beside him had kept him alive through the cold night.

Summer wished the jaguar had never appeared. He had sorely wounded her uncle and he had taken meat they badly needed. Camel would taste so good to her now! Any meat would taste good to her. She was terribly hungry and she could count each of her ribs with ease. Her stomach caved inwards from lack of food. Yes, the camel would have tasted very good.

She took a tiny nibble of yampa root. She held it in her mouth a long time, savoring the spongy texture, sucking the last taste from it. Then she bit off a bigger piece.

"Do not eat that. I told you your uncle needs it on his wound!"

Summer held out a piece of the root. "Try it, Auntie. It is good."

Her aunt snorted and turned her face away. "I will give mine to my husband. He needs it. You should do the same."

Summer did not want to give the root to Uncle Antler. She was so very, very hungry, she wanted to eat it all. But that was not the Caribou People's way, she knew. The Caribou People helped one another, especially in hungry times.

"Perhaps the parents of Blue Camas will return soon," Summer said, still savoring the bit of yampa root.

"Perhaps," Auntie Birdsong acknowledged. "It is better for families to hunt for their

119

own food in the winter. Blue Camas' parents know this. Every winter they hunt along the river for food. Sometimes they cut into the ice for fish."

Blue Camas' parents and her young sister and brother had tried to winter with Uncle Antler's family, but food was getting low. Just before the jaguar had attacked Uncle Antler, they had left the winter cave shelter and set out to search for their own food. They did not want to further burden Uncle Antler and Auntie Birdsong, so they had taken only a few roots and a little of the dried meat. Summer hoped that they would meet with some success, perhaps finding fish under the ice, or an occasional stray deer.

Blue Camas' father had promised to come back when they had meat, but Summer did not expect them to return very soon. She knew that Blue Camas' family would be fortunate to feed themselves now, never mind Antler and his family.

"They should have gone to their daughter's people," said Auntie Birdsong. "Blue Camas' husband, Spotted Cat, would have fed them. He is obliged to since he is their son-in-law."

"It is too far away," Summer answered. "They would never find the Saber-Tooths in the snow."

"*We* should have gone to the Saber-Tooths. Then *we* would not be starving." Auntie Birdsong said this several times a day.

"Uncle Antler was wounded after the first big snowfall," Summer reminded her. "It was too late to travel by then. And now the snow is too deep . . ." She sighed drowsily. She would wait just a little longer before she got up to get the wood for the fire. Summer fell quietly to sleep.

She was awakened by Auntie Birdsong slapping her arm. "Wake up, girl! Fetch some wood. The fire dies and you lie there sleeping like a lazy camp dog!"

Summer staggered outside; she felt dizzy. Swaying, she tried to get her bearings. She glanced at the thicket of snow-draped pine trees, the best place to find branches for the fire. But it looked so far away. Perhaps she should just sit down and rest first. . . .

"Get going, girl," her aunt called. "The fire is out!"

Summer shook her head to clear it. She must get wood for the fire. If she did not, they would all freeze to death. She wrapped her warm cloak over her head to protect her face from the cold and trudged toward the pines. She tried to keep her mind on her task, but it was difficult. How many days had it been since she had eaten— two? Three? She could not remember. She concentrated on putting one foot in front of the other, breaking a trail through the knee-deep snow.

Summer had to stop and rest several times. Each time she prodded herself up again, knowing that she must not fall asleep in the snow. She must get the wood. Uncle Antler and Auntie

Birdsong depended upon her.

At last she reached the clump of pine trees and stood there, panting. Then she started to scrape at the snow, searching for fallen twigs and branches. When she had an armful, she began the long trek back to the cave. The walk would not have been so difficult, if only she had not been so hungry.

Summer bent down and swiped up a handful of snow. She set the cold stuff to her lips and licked it. At least she would not die of thirst. . . .

Brow furrowed, Talon watched the woman's actions. He and Blue Feather had been hunting. Finding themselves close to the Caribou People's winter caves, Talon had been irresistibly drawn to see what his old enemies were up to.

"She is elderly," whispered Blue Feather, beside him. "See how she staggers under such a light load."

"There is only one elderly woman with the Caribou People," answered Talon. "It is Birdsong, Blizzard's mother." He squinted into the distance. "That does not look like her—too thin. Birdsong is hefty and plump."

"Some other family with an old woman may have joined them."

"Perhaps." Talon watched the woman make her way slowly to the cave. "She rests often," he observed.

"Not worth the meat it takes to feed her," Blue Feather scoffed. "They should just leave her out in the snow. One less mouth to feed."

Talon just grunted. The Caribou did not expose their old people to the snows, leaving them to die as Blue Feather's Bear People did.

"Let us go now," Blue Feather said. "I have seen enough. Let the Caribou People take care of the old one."

Talon nodded. He, too, had seen enough. If the Caribou People were able to feed such a weak, elderly woman, they were doing well this winter. Very well.

"Come," he said. "Let us take this deer back to our camp. Perhaps Weasel and Sloth have had a successful hunt, too."

Chapter Fourteen

Summer awoke to the sound of Auntie Birdsong singing as she swirled something in the stone pot over the little fire. Summer rubbed her eyes, wondering what there was about their situation to make Auntie sing. Then the smell of meat drifted to Summer's nose. She sat up, fully awake now.

"Come," sang her aunt. "Meat. Delicious meat!"

"Meat?" Summer heard her uncle scramble up from the robes where he lay. Most days he stayed there, and she thought he healed but slowly. All three of them spent most of their time in the cave, huddled under thick robes to keep warm.

"Come! There is meat to eat. Now you will get strong and healthy!"

"How—? Where—?" began Summer.

Her aunt smiled and shook her head. "Eat, eat. Enjoy."

Without needing further encouragement, Summer and her uncle fell to eating the nourishing stew. Summer could feel her strength return as the warm meat reached her stomach. Warmth quickly spread throughout her whole body.

"Careful," Auntie warned. "A little at a time. It will not do to overeat." She smiled benignly as Summer forced herself to set aside several of the bigger chunks and sip the hot broth instead.

"There is more," crooned her aunt. "No need to eat it all at once."

Never had meat tasted so good to Summer. Never. And there was more food. They would not starve, not today, not tomorrow. "Where did you get this meat?" she asked.

Auntie smiled and pointed to the robes. One of the dogs, the gaunt wolf-like one, lifted his head.

Awareness dawned slowly on Summer. "The other dog? Where—where is the little dog?"

Her aunt's lifted eyebrow told her. Summer swallowed.

"Those dogs saved my life!" Uncle Antler exclaimed. "When the jaguar attacked me and I dragged myself home, it was the dogs that

126

kept me warm. They saved me from freezing to death in my own doorway!"

"And they saved you again," Auntie Birdsong said. "Just now."

Summer felt sick. The dogs were an ordinary part of camp life; she was not particularly attached to them. But she saw them every day. She also knew her uncle relied on them for hunting, and for warning against approaching bears. It had never occurred to her to eat the dogs.

"Perhaps you would rather starve?" Birdsong's narrowed eyes dared them to answer.

Summer stayed silent. So did her uncle. All three of them stared at the gray wolf-dog on the robes. He stared back.

The next morning, the gaunt wolf-dog was missing.

"Ran away," Auntie Birdsong sighed. "He knew we were going to eat him, too."

Summer shrugged. She did not regret the loss. Eating one dog she had known was enough.

Three days later, they were out of food again and Uncle's leg still had not healed enough for him to go hunting. Summer wished now that the wolf-dog had stayed. Then she would not be feeling this pain in her guts, the listlessness, the dull fear. It was hunger. Again.

Talon watched the beaver dwelling, a pile of logs and sticks melded to the ice of the lake. He stood behind the tree and waited. Beavers were very tricky to hunt. They could hide in their stout homes for a long time. But he reasoned the beavers had to come out some time. Finally one of them waddled out. It was huge, enough to feed four men for several days. *If* he could kill it.

Slowly Talon raised his spear, drew his arm back, and let the weapon fly. The beaver gave a high-pitched squeal and fell over. It writhed helplessly, trying to dislodge the spear in its throat. Another spear swiftly followed the first. The beaver gave one last great shudder and died.

A second beaver, drawn by the squeals, came out to investigate. He lifted his big snout to the air and sniffed. Then he waddled over to the blood-drained carcass on the ice. Soon that beaver too was squealing and writhing in his own death throes.

Talon smiled grimly to himself. Getting enough meat to survive the winter was proving to be easy. Of course, it helped to have four strong, healthy hunters.

Suddenly he heard a howl—a dire wolf! The wolves were in his territory. They were hungry and they were looking for food.

Swiftly he butchered the two huge animals before the wolves arrived and before the meat froze. When he was done separating the tasty parts from the bones, he lumped the chunks of warm meat into the freshly skinned hides and bundled them up. Then he set out for camp with more food than he and his Wolves could eat in seven days.

Chapter Fifteen

Snow blew in Talon's face and swirled lightly around him. He kept his balance against the wind, plodding steadily along on his snowshoes. Snowshoes were a necessary part of a hunter's winter equipment. Talon had made his out of deer gut strung on a wood frame. They were narrow and pointed and he navigated on them with ease.

"What is so important that we have to leave our warm camp and walk through this snow?" complained Blue Feather.

"I want to walk," said Talon. "If you do not, then go back to our winter camp." Winter camp was a rock shelter they had taken away from a bear. The angry bear had fought for his home but he had been no match for four armed hunters.

Blue Feather shook his head. "No. It is too quiet at camp. I do not want to miss out on whatever it is you are up to."

Talon laughed. Life was good. He had companions. He had food. He was healthy and strong. The cold snow stung his cheeks and he knew himself to be fortunate. Yes, life was much better now than when he had been banished by the Caribou. His face clouded. *The Caribou.* Just the thought of them brought the dull, warming heat of anger to Talon's chest.

They walked for some time until Talon could see a dark cave on a rocky hillside.

"Hunh," Blue Feather grunted. "I see the winter caves of the Caribou People. You just cannot forget, can you?"

"You would not forget if it happened to you."

"No, I would not. That unfaithful woman I was married to . . ."

Talon let him talk on. By now he had memorized most of Blue Feather's speech about his former wife, as no doubt Blue Feather had memorized Talon's impassioned railings against the Caribou. Talk around the Wolves' campfire sometimes became very repetitive indeed.

The two stood watching the cave for some time. Today, blue smoke hung low outside the cave entrance. They were home. "Why not just go up to them?" Blue Feather stamped his feet to warm them. "What can they do? There are two of us, and we have our spears."

"I am banished. They can remind me of that."

"Hunh. Words. Nothing else." He sighed. "How many times have you been past these caves?"

Talon did not tell him that this was the fourth time he had sought out the Caribou People's winter caves. He had not seen anyone else since that first time he had seen the old woman gathering wood, but each time he knew they were there. Twice he had seen smoke from their fire and once he had seen a dog lingering at the entrance.

"You could bring a gift," Blue Feather suggested. "Something so they do not spear you or throw stones at you."

Talon considered. "Yes. Let us do that."

They soon snared two fat grouse. Night was not far away when they approached the Caribou caves. No dogs rushed forward to bark at them and warn them away.

Talon was ready to walk up to the cave entrance, but Blue Feather put out a hand to stop him. "It is too quiet," he whispered. "I am suspicious."

Talon surveyed the land. Snow covered the gravel outside the cave's ledge and no one could hide there without being seen. Any danger would come from inside.

"Let us go closer," he said.

Blue Feather said, "I will sneak up to the side of the cave. Then, if they attack you, I will throw my spear at them." He set off, his snowshoes leaving tracks in a wide half-circle. When he was in position so Talon could see him but the occupants could not, Talon started forward.

"Greetings," he called out. "I bring gifts."

There was a commotion in the cave. An old woman came to the entrance. "Who is it?" she called.

"Friends," said Talon, laughing to himself. "Enemies" would have been closer to the truth. He wondered where the hunters were, why he had not been greeted with frowns and spears and rocks.

"Come ahead," called the woman. She tottered back into the cave.

With a shrug, Talon walked up to the entrance. Blue Feather swung into step behind him. They unlaced their snowshoes and stamped their feet to get the blood moving. No one stopped them as they entered the darkness of the cave. A tiny fire lit the way, and Talon followed the beacon of light.

He arrived at the living space, one he knew well. Many times he had sat at this fireside, when he was doing bride-service—before the Caribou headman had given his woman to the Saber-Tooths. Talon clenched his teeth to bite back bitter accusations and his fists tightened on the feet of the grouse. He would have dashed the dead birds to the cave floor if he had not reminded himself of the stone that had taken the place of his heart. These were his enemies. He had come to seek out their weaknesses.

"I bid you greeting."

The deep male voice startled Summer out of her doze. She spent many days drowsing now—fetching wood and drowsing and drinking a little melted snow. She had even tried eating boiled black moss. It had tasted sweet and it kept her stomach from cramping in hunger, but she knew it would not keep her alive. She could die with a stomach full of black moss. Others had.

"I bring you a gift."

Summer blinked, pushed aside the robes and sat up. Who was it? What was he saying? She did not recognize the voice, perhaps she was too tired. . . . Was it Blue Camas' father?

Her aunt and uncle were murmuring. Auntie Birdsong sounded most appreciative. What had the man brought?

"I will fix them now." Auntie Birdsong's fingers faltered with the grouse feathers, slowly plucking them one by one.

Talon watched. He saw the thin arms of the old woman. He glanced at the old man who lay on the fur robes. Talon's eyes narrowed when he saw the jagged red scars on the old man's injured leg.

On the other side of the fire, a young woman sat on the bedrobes. Talon recognized the pale hair, the huge yellow eyes reflecting the flames. It was Summer, the woman he had seen in the glade. His pulse quickened. His eyes followed her hand as she brushed a strand of hair back from her face. She was thin, her cheekbones prominent. He frowned.

Then his eyes returned to the old couple. Antler was drooling as he watched his wife pluck the dead birds.

Talon smiled to himself. His enemies, the Caribou, were starving.

Chapter Sixteen

Summer chewed a piece of the sweet-tasting meat. She had always liked grouse, but never had it tasted as good as this. The thick, soft chunk rolled on her tongue, the savory juices tantalized. "Mmmm," she murmured. She bit off a bigger chunk and gulped it down.

"Eat slowly," cautioned the stranger with the deep voice.

She glanced up at him, but the cave was so dark and smoky that she could not see his face. The fire reflected in black, black eyes that narrowed at her. Summer ignored him and fell upon the juicy fowl once again.

Auntie Birdsong hummed to herself as she ate the meat, so happy was she. Uncle Antler gnawed deliberately on a grouse leg. When he finished with that one, he tossed it in the fire and pulled off another leg.

The second stranger watched in silence. In fact, both strangers spoke little; they seemed satisfied to watch Summer and her family eat. When the two grouse were completely devoured down to the bones, Summer contented herself with licking the delicious fat off her fingers. She failed to notice the dark eyes that followed every dart of her tongue.

Talon could not tear his eyes away from her. From what little he could see of Summer, she was much thinner than she had been on that autumn day long ago. He watched her darting tongue and images of what he would like her to do to him with that tongue came to his mind. He shook his head to dispel the lusty notion.

Neither Antler nor Birdsong had offered the two men any of the food. Talon did not expect it once he realized how hungry they were. How was it that the Caribou had come to this? They were an energetic people, and when he had worked bride-service for them, he had seen how they carefully dried roots and smoked meat and stored berries in preparation for the winter. "Where is all your food?" he asked now.

"Gone," Auntie Birdsong answered. "It has been a long, cold winter. We were nearing the end of our stored food even before my husband was injured. After a jaguar attacked him, we were forced to eat the rest of our food. He cannot hunt," she added unnecessarily, pointing at Uncle Antler's leg.

"Where are the rest of your people?" Talon asked.

Antler set aside the last bare grouse bone with a contented sigh. "Gone also," he said. "The families dispersed, each thinking they could better survive the winter if they hunted only for themselves."

A good strategy, thought Talon. *One that wolf families use also.*

"They will join up with us again in the spring," said Birdsong. "If they survive."

Summer stared at the stranger, trying to recall where she had seen him before. There was something about him . . .

Talon felt her eyes upon him. That none of them recognized him added to his delight at seeing his enemies brought so low. "We will leave now," he said, turning to the cave entrance.

"Wait!" cried Antler. "We want to thank you properly for the food. And it is night. You must not leave. The night animals are too dangerous. You are most welcome to stay!"

Talon would rather face an enraged short-faced bear or a pack of dire wolves than spend a single night under his enemy's roof. He shook his head and kept walking toward the entrance. Blue Feather followed him on silent feet.

Summer and her aunt and uncle watched them strap on their snowshoes and depart.

139

Her uncle shook his head. "I do not understand why they did not stay. It is cold out there. And dangerous. Here they are safe."

As Summer glanced at the puzzled looks on their faces, dread started a slow coil in her stomach. Suddenly she suspected why the stranger did not want to stay. She was not certain, but the way he walked, his deep voice, his large body—all of it was somehow familiar. The coiling dread told her the man who had just left their cave was Talon, the very man her uncle had banished in so humiliating a fashion so many seasons before.

"Pitiful, were they not?" Blue Feather's words drifted behind to Talon as Blue Feather broke trail through the crusty snow. It was fortunate that the moon was full and could light their way.

"Most people who are starving look pitiful to those with full bellies," answered Talon. "But it is good to see my enemies brought so low."

"Yes. Let them starve!"

Talon laughed at the thought. He did not need to lift a finger to get his revenge. Starvation would do it all! They would be dead by spring and he would laugh and do a dance outside the cave that would be their tomb. An image of the yellow-eyed woman flickered through his mind, but he quickly squashed it.

"Let them starve!" he murmured.

"Did you see how the old woman grabbed

those grouse from you?" Blue Feather chuckled.

"And the old man was drooling before he even bit into a grouse leg! I hope I never get that hungry."

Both men fell silent and sober at that thought.

"We will not get that hungry," said Blue Feather. "We are good hunters. So are the brothers. We will never suffer like that."

"The Caribou are suffering, are they not? It is painful to be hungry."

"Have you ever been hungry?" asked Blue Feather.

"Twice. Both times during harsh winters when I was a child."

"Yes, children suffer the most in those long winters."

"So do old people."

"Those two old people will not live long. There is scant flesh left on those bones." Blue Feather laughed.

"The young woman will not last long either," commented Talon. "Once the old ones are dead, she will soon follow." A spark of sadness flickered through him, but his anger quenched it.

"Yes. She will last the longest," said Blue Feather. "It will be cold and lonely for her when the old ones die."

Talon felt a twinge of guilt. "Why do they not call upon their precious son-in-law, the mighty Saber-Tooth? He is their kinsman now.

He should be feeding them!"

"He probably does not know they need help," answered Blue Feather. "That wound to the old man's leg looks recent—the last moon or so, I would say. Who would they send for help? The girl? She is thin and weak. She would soon be lost in the snow while looking for the Saber-Tooth camp."

"She must have been the one I saw the first time," mused Talon. "I thought she was old because she rested so many times."

"Probably half-starved by then." Blue Feather halted in mid-step. "Talon! That is not the ugly yellow-eyed woman that you saw in the glade, is it? The one you wanted to steal?"

Talon stopped and turned to face his companion. "It is."

Blue Feather snorted. "Not much to look at, is she? Who would want her? Not me!" He shook his head and kept walking.

Talon's thoughts remained on the girl. He no longer had any need to steal her to revenge himself upon the Caribou. Starvation was taking his revenge for him. He need not do a thing and his enemies would be dead by spring.

He was pleased. They *should* die for what they had done to him! He had worked hard for the bride-service meat he had provided. They had promised him the woman, Blizzard; he had deserved her!

The thought that she was faithless and that he was fortunate to be rid of her suddenly crept into his mind. Yes, Blizzard was aptly named. She was cold and uncaring of him and his labors.

But what of her young cousin, Summer of the yellow eyes? Was it right, was it *just* that she suffer for what Blizzard had done? For what her foolish uncle and aunt had done?

Talon tried to erase the memory of the young woman as he had seen her in the glade that day, but her words kept coming back to him, words she had spoken to the black wolf. *'I want to live. I will fight you. I am strong.'*

She can fight no one now, he thought. *And she is no longer strong. She will die soon.*

But try as he might, he could not forget her first words. They haunted him all the way back to the Wolves' camp. *'I want to live!'*

Chapter Seventeen

Summer crept to the entrance of the cave. Now and then the sun shone from behind the clouds upon the snow. She looked out across the land. Here and there clumps of green pine wore white snowy cloaks. Snow covered the flat grassland and the river was frozen and gray. A cold wind blew.

She spied Auntie Birdsong gathering wood in the pine thicket. Inside the cave, Uncle Antler was sitting up for the first time in many days. The two plump grouse that the visitors had given her family brought them all renewed strength. But they would all become weak again if she did not find them some food, thought Summer. Her lips tightened. She must put it off no longer.

"Uncle, give me your spear."

Her uncle looked up from where he was resting on the skins. "Foolish child! I cannot give you my spear. It is a man's weapon, meant for a man to use. If you try to use it, nothing will happen. You will find no animals and I will never be able to use that spear again!" He flapped his arms at her in his distress.

Summer fingered the little leather pouch that hung around her neck, remembering how upset her aunt and the shaman had been about a man touching her woman's things. Now her uncle was just as upset about a woman touching his man's things.

"Uncle, I *must* use your spear," she said. "Do you not understand? It is the only way I can get food for us. I need to hunt."

"Hunt? Hunt? Lack of food has driven you strange, girl! I will not listen to any more such talk. Hunt, indeed! *I* am the only hunter here!"

"Uncle, I want you to give me your spear before Auntie Birdsong gets back. Give it to me."

"No!" He grabbed the spear and held onto it. His knuckles were white. "This spear is to be touched by no woman! Do you understand?"

Summer turned away. She understood. All too well.

When he was asleep, still clutching the spear, she crept up to him and took it away, running out of the cave before her aunt returned. She must start hunting right away.

It looked easy the way the men did it. They waited patiently behind a tree or in a thicket until an animal came along and then they killed it with the spear. But watching it and doing it were two very different things, Summer soon discovered.

The long wait was tiresome and frustrating. Dressed warmly in furs, she hid for a long time behind a small snow-covered bush. She only moved her eyes as she stared about, looking for a grouse or a hare.

Once she saw a fox taking dainty steps on the snow crust, but he was out of her range. Even if she threw the spear, she probably would not hit the fox. She would have to wait until the animal came closer. He wandered off.

Summer thought about deer. Perhaps a fat deer would walk by. She wished she knew the proper rituals to summon deer. Hunters knew them. Women who stole spears did not.

She heard some scratching under the snow at her feet. Making as little noise as possible, she scraped away the top layer. She saw some of the sagebrush under the snow wiggle. Something was down there. But was it big enough to eat?

A red-tailed hawk swooped overhead, casting a black shadow on the snow. The scratching sound at her feet ceased. She glanced up, wondering if the hawk had heard the scratching.

Summer waited, but the sound did not come again. It would be dark soon. She was cold and stiff from sitting in one position for so long. She dreaded returning to the cave with nothing. How furious her uncle would be, and her aunt would rail at her.

Slowly, reluctantly, she rose, and heard more scratching in the snow, near the roots of the sagebrush. Without thinking, she dropped the spear and pounced, leather clad hands cupped, upon whatever was making the noise. A little squeak alerted her to her prey. She had caught a tiny meadow mouse!

Summer picked it up by its tail and looked at it. It swung there, its black eyes regarding her solemnly. It was very small, but it was food. She used the spear to kill it, then hurried through the snow back to the cave.

When her uncle saw her, he sat up. His face was grim. "Give me my spear, girl. Do not ever take it from me again!"

"Summer! What have you done?" screeched her aunt. "You must not take your uncle's spear! You know that!"

"I was trying to get meat," Summer said. "We need someone to hunt. Uncle cannot. You cannot. Therefore I must."

"But to take his weapon! He will no longer be able to hunt with it!" Her aunt's eyes were wild with fear.

"Give me that spear!" Uncle Antler howled.

Summer walked over and handed it to him.

"And you got nothing!" He looked triumphant, his gray-green eyes glowing. "I knew it! She cannot hunt! The spear will not kill for her. It will only kill for a man!"

"Why are you so glad that I bring home nothing?" demanded Summer. She ignored her aunt's affronted gasp. "We will all starve if I do not find meat!"

"That hunter will be back," said her uncle. "I know it. He will bring us meat. We will not starve."

"Yes, surely he will return with more meat." Auntie Birdsong sounded hopeful.

"So you think he will return?" demanded Summer. "Do you know who he is?"

"Some kind stranger . . ." began her aunt.

"A fine man," said her uncle. "A man who knows how to hunt!"

Summer laughed harshly. "Think you so? I will tell you who he is. I recognized him."

"Who?" Her aunt's voice was suddenly cautious. "I wanted to ask him his name, but I did not want to press him . . ."

"That 'kind stranger,' that 'fine hunter,'" sneered Summer, "is Talon, the man who performed bride-service for Blizzard. The man you banished from the Caribou People!"

The two old people fell silent. Auntie Birdsong looked sick. Her uncle looked pale.

"I—I found some moss," Auntie Birdsong said, turning away to prepare the evening meal. She busied herself with a stone bowl and poured hot water over the black moss. Summer felt her stomach churn just thinking of eating the wretched stuff.

"Here," she said at last, holding up the mouse.

Her aunt's mouth dropped open. "Antler! Look what she found."

He glanced up. "A mouse!" he snorted.

Summer cringed.

"A scrawny mouse! You defiled my spear to kill a scrawny, tiny, useless mouse!" He turned his head and stared at the cave wall.

But Auntie Birdsong reached for the mouse. "Give me that! I will cook it," she said to Summer. Summer glanced at her, expecting a harangue from that quarter too. "I have eaten mouse before. It is better than moss."

The soup that night was tasty and nourishing. And though Uncle refused to speak, he ate every drop that Auntie Birdsong gave him.

After he fell asleep that night, Auntie Birdsong picked up the spear that lay beside him. "Since it is already defiled," she said to Summer, "you might as well use it. That hunter—" She grimaced. "I do not think he will be back."

Summer took the spear and placed it carefully against the cave wall. She would leave early in the morning. She would find something else to kill. And it would be bigger than a mouse.

Chapter Eighteen

The black wolf was outside the cave. Summer saw him the next morning when she went out to practice throwing the spear. He sat a little distance away, tongue lolling. At the cave entrance, three big slabs of raw meat lay on the gravel.

Summer scanned the landscape, trying to determine if he was alone. Only a single set of wolf tracks led through the snow to the cave entrance.

When he saw her, the beast got to his feet, stared at her with those yellow eyes, then loped off into the snow. Summer picked up the meat and sniffed it. It was fresh.

She took it inside. Her aunt and uncle were still·asleep. She put more wood on the fire and cut the meat into long strips. These she wove onto sticks to cook over the flames. Soon the pungent smell made Summer's mouth water. The sputtering sizzle of fat dripping on the embers awoke her aunt and uncle.

They hastily dressed and approached the fire. "Where did you get the meat, Summer?" asked her uncle, eyeing the fresh slabs. He sniffed. "Smells like deer."

"It is." Summer wished she could say that she had been the one to kill the deer, but she could not.

"Yes, where did you get this meat?" Auntie Birdsong was eyeing her in puzzlement.

"From a wolf," Summer answered.

Both elders looked amazed.

"A wolf. I have never heard of a wolf bringing food to people." Her uncle sounded confused.

"A black wolf," continued Summer. "I have seen him before." But she did not tell them where and when she had seen the wolf.

Auntie Birdsong picked up a piece of the meat and sniffed it. "Smells good."

"How did he get here? How did he know we needed food? Did someone send him?" Uncle Antler looked completely baffled. "Never have I heard of such a thing!"

"Neither have I," Summer said. Indeed, she had been pondering the mystery ever since she had first stepped out of the cave.

"Do you think," her uncle said, "that it is from that hunter?"

Summer had been wondering the same thing. She noticed that her uncle did not use Talon's name.

Her aunt sniffed again. "It might be poisoned."

Summer had considered that too.

"Too bad we cannot feed it to a dog," said her uncle. "Then we would know."

All three took turns sniffing the meat. They all agreed that the meat smelled fresh, not poisoned.

"The grouse were tasty and good," said Summer. "He could have poisoned those, but he chose not to."

Her aunt and uncle nodded. "This meat is no doubt good," said her uncle at last. "He would not want to kill us."

"How do you know this, husband? Do you know what the Fox man thinks?" Auntie Birdsong said angrily. "He did not like it that we gave Blizzard to the Saber-Tooth. Now the Fox man has come to poison us!"

"Pah! If that were so, we would be dead now. We ate the grouse he gave us!"

"I am not going to eat this meat," declared Auntie Birdsong.

"I will," said Uncle Antler. "I am not afraid."

Summer handed him a chunk of the cooked meat.

He took it from the stick, looked at it, sniffed it again. He saw both women watching him so he put the meat in his mouth and chewed it.

"Tastes good," he said with his mouth full.

They watched him for awhile. When he did not fall down sick upon the cave floor, Summer and her aunt, too, nibbled at the cooked chunks. The meat tasted good.

Three days later Summer found more fresh slabs of meat, this time beaver meat, at the entrance to the cave. And again all she saw in the snow was the tracks of a single wolf, one set leading to the cave, one set leading away.

She studied the tracks, bent down and traced the cold imprint with her finger. Sudden fear twisted her vitals. Could Talon change himself into a wolf?

Chapter Nineteen

Summer picked up the spear and left the cave.

Most of the snow had melted, leaving white patches here and there on the gravel. She walked along the rough ground, pausing now and then to peer about for animals. Once she spotted a hare. Swiftly she threw the spear, but missed the hare. Shoulders slumped in defeat, Summer trudged on. Though the weather was cool, sweat dewed her forehead.

She traveled a worn deer trail for some distance, hoping to see another hare, or even a deer. Glancing about, she saw she had come a considerable distance from the cave. Indeed, the territory looked new to her eyes. She memorized a rock formation near a gnarled tree so she could find her way back along the same trail.

Suddenly a brown grouse whirred out of a bush ahead of her on the path. Summer drew back her arm and threw the spear with all her strength. The grouse flew out of the spear's path. Disappointed, Summer retrieved the spear and walked on.

She spotted an opening between two rocks in the ground. A burrow, she thought. Creeping noiselessly, she sneaked closer and then crouched down to wait, spear poised for a throw.

It was a long wait. Just when she thought the occupant of the burrow must be in the deep sleep of hibernation, she was rewarded with a scratching sound and a glimpse of brown. Barely breathing, she watched as a golden-mantled ground squirrel crawled out the door. He stretched and sat down to lick his fur.

Summer's eyes narrowed as she waited. Finally he got up and sniffed the air. Then he sat down again to wash his face this time, interrupting the cleansing to scratch vigorously with his hindfeet for fleas.

Summer waited. The little brown creature stopped scratching, got to his feet and took several steps in her direction. Motionless, Summer waited until the ground squirrel came within her spear's reach.

She launched the spear. It hit the animal in the head, stunning him. Summer ran up and killed the squirrel with the tip of the spear.

Elation soared through her. Her first big kill! She had done it—stalked and hunted and killed an animal! Auntie Birdsong would make a fine stew from this meat, she exulted. Her family would eat! And *she* had done it!

She picked up the carcass and examined the dead animal. It had a thick coat of golden fur and she could feel the fat under it. She touched the ears, saw the teeth closed in a death grimace. Blood seeped out of the mouth in the little dead face.

With trembling fingers, Summer stroked the head. The life spirit was gone from the animal, driven out by her hand. The eyes, so bright only a short time before, were now closed forever. Because of her, this winsome creature would never again stretch in the sun, or lick its fur. Remorsefully, she set the animal back on the ground. Finally, not knowing what else to do, she took out her knife and skinned and gutted the ground squirrel. Then she tied the skin to one side of her belt and the meat to the other.

Summer picked up her spear and walked on, past several boulders that lined the trail. As she walked, her spirits lifted. To kill an animal that would feed her family was a fine accomplishment, one she now felt confident she could repeat.

Because the days were short, Summer knew the sun would disappear soon. She headed back to the cave.

When Auntie Birdsong saw the ground squirrel she crowed happily and bustled about preparing the evening meal. Uncle Antler just snorted and stared at the cave wall. But again he ate every morsel of meat that Auntie Birdsong served.

Summer smiled to herself.

The next day Summer went hunting again, tying the skin of the ground squirrel to her belt to remind herself of her success.

This time she headed directly for the spot where she had killed the squirrel. She watched and waited for awhile but saw nothing. With a shrug, she wandered up the boulder-lined trail. No sooner had she rounded a large rock than a man's voice stopped her.

"What are you doing?"

Summer whirled and came face-to-face with him. Black eyes with a hard glint stared at her. Her hand went to her throat. "Talon?"

He stood but a short distance from her. How had he sneaked up on her without her hearing him? Atop his head he wore a snarling wolf's face, the gaping mouth showed deadly fangs. The wolf's skin draped down Talon's back in a gray cape. His long black hair flowed past his shoulders. The brown tunic he wore looked warm and well-made. His feet and legs were protected by thigh-high moccasins.

He looked taller than before, filled out. He did not look friendly. His dark eyes watched her as though she was a ground squirrel. His well-sculpted lips were firm and she thought she detected a muscle twitching in his jaw.

She glanced around, suddenly aware of how alone the two of them were. Sweat popped out on her forehead. Summer thought of the banishment and the cruelty of her people to him, and she took a step backward.

"Whose spear is that?" Talon's obsidian eyes held hers.

"Mine."

"Women do not use spears."

"I—I do."

He took a step forward. "You killed a ground squirrel."

Summer nodded and tensed for an insult about her hunting abilities.

"They are difficult to kill. A hunter must be patient."

Summer blushed, proud of her kill and pleased that Talon respected her effort. "Thank you," she replied. "And thank you for the deer meat for my family."

She saw that he was unaware of the trap she had set. It had been the black wolf who had brought deer meat to her family, not Talon. The only time Talon had appeared at the cave, he had brought two grouse.

He nodded acknowledgment. Her suspicions confirmed, Summer tightened her grip on the spear. Either Talon told the wolf to bring the meat, or he had the ability to change into a wolf. Neither choice reassured her. This man was dangerous. She took another step back.

"I—I must go," she said. "It will be dark soon. My people will be looking for me."

His eyes were still on her face. She flushed under his penetrating stare, and was relieved when he bent down to pick some dried sage-brush leaves off a weathered stem. "Rub this on your hands and arms," he commanded, holding the leaves out to her.

Though taken aback, she took the leaves, her cold hand brushing his warm one. She rubbed the scented sage leaves on her skin. The aroma filled her nostrils.

"Rub the skin at the back of your neck also." His eyes followed her actions and she saw him swallow.

"Your face, too." His black eyes followed the sage wherever she rubbed it. Summer flushed at the hunger she saw in his eyes.

Thoroughly soaked in sage scent, she demanded, "Now I want to go home."

"This is a good time of day to hunt," he said. He glanced toward the river; it was a goodly distance from where they stood. "You must be silent when you walk," he warned.

"You will take me hunting?" Summer asked eagerly.

He nodded.

"That is very good. I will kill more game for my family."

Talon gave a snort when she said that. Perhaps he did not like to be reminded of her family, Summer thought uneasily.

She was conscious of his every move as she walked beside him toward the river where trees grew along the banks. Talon's thick moccasins made no sound. Summer's whispered now and then. Once she stumbled on the rough terrain and he caught her before she fell. As he restored her to her feet, she wondered if he could hear her heart thumping like that of a bird caught in a snare.

They came to the river and Talon halted by a cottonwood tree. "We wait."

Summer waited too, peering about for animals. The scent of sage came to her. Talon must have rubbed scent on his own skin before she saw him. She sniffed the air, liking the smell. Now she would always think of him whenever she smelled sage.

She slanted a glance at him. How could she have forgotten how handsome he was? She stared at him hungrily, admiring his straight nose, high cheekbones, his cleft chin. She took another breath. And always, sage.

She saw Talon move his head slowly, careful not to attract attention. Had he spotted an animal? She leaned forward, craning her neck in the direction he looked.

No animals.

She glanced around, taking care to move her head slowly, too, so as not to startle any game. And his shoulders. Magnificent they were, in the leather tunic he wore. An atlatl on a leather strap hung on his broad back. Her eyes roved over him. His legs were long and powerful. She liked how the moccasins fit him.

Talon shifted imperceptibly, but she saw the move and glanced away, not wanting him to catch her staring.

"Where are the animals? What are we waiting for?" she whispered.

Talon barely moved his head in the direction of a stand of brush. Summer glanced to where he indicated. She studied the brush, trying to discover what he was looking at. Was it a rabbit? A grouse?

Dimly the outline of a small deer took shape to her straining eyes. She gasped. The deer, with velvet nubs atop his head, turned to look at them.

The buck must have heard her gasp, she realized with a sinking heart. The animal stared at them for several heartbeats, then flicked his tail and bounded away.

Talon drew his arm back and threw his spear. The spear hurtled forward. The buck wheeled to avoid the spear and took several high leaps away.

In the blink of an eye, Summer watched Talon reach for his atlatl and slam a long dart into the handle. He drew his right arm back and launched the dart, still holding onto the spear thrower. The whole weight of his body propelled the thrust. The dart sang through the air and entered the deer in its right side. Half the dart shaft was buried in the rib cage.

Summer gasped and stared in awe at Talon. Never had she seen a man react so swiftly. He had launched both spear and dart in the time it took her to pick up her spear!

The buck staggered into the brush and disappeared.

Summer began to run after it, but Talon lunged after her and gripped her arm. "Wait!"

Summer glanced from his strong brown hand up to his obsidian eyes where anger lit tiny flames. Dismayed, she tried to pull her arm free.

"We wait," he said in a low voice. "The buck is injured. We will wait until he dies, Caribou woman."

Talon dropped his hand as though she scorched him.

He retrieved his spear and they waited another long watch. Summer huddled in a tiny ball, feeling like a reprimanded child. After awhile she peeked at him. He was alert yet relaxed. She took a breath, secretly pleased with her handsome hunting companion.

At last Talon moved forward after the wounded deer, and Summer followed him.

They arrived at the stand of brush and Talon pushed carefully through. As they walked in the direction the deer had gone, he pointed to the trail of blood on the ground. Summer had to strain to see the brown drops, so blended

163

against the dark ground were they.

The two came upon the deer at a little distance from the stand. The dart shaft stuck out of the animal's side. The buck's head thrashed from side to side as he groaned in pain.

Summer saw to her astonishment that the power of Talon's throw had buried the dart deeper in the deer than a mere spear thrust would ever have done. She frowned at her spear. She wanted an atlatl and a dart, too.

She ran ahead of Talon to get to the buck. With a sharp tug on her dress, Talon again halted her. "Do not approach a wounded animal! It can be dangerous." He shook his head. "Caribou people know nothing."

As if to prove the truth of his words, the buck rose to his knees and lunged at Summer. She barely jumped out of the way in time.

Talon waved her back. Summer stood where she was as he pulled out a knife from his belt and cautiously approached the prone animal from behind. In a swift movement he kneeled on the animal's back and grabbed the animal's head from behind. With a single efficient stroke he slashed the buck's throat. The groans stopped, the head drooped; the animal was dead.

Summer gazed at the deer, thinking of all that meat feeding her aunt and her uncle and herself. Saliva dribbled into her mouth and she swallowed. Stepping closer, she saw the buck's eyes, round, brown and beautiful, staring lifelessly at her. Sadness shafted through her that the animal was dead, the same sadness she had felt after killing the ground squirrel.

Talon spoke. "We thank you, Great Spirit, for this animal. We thank you, honored animal, for giving your life that we may eat."

Summer was silent, but her heart lifted a little. It was fitting that he who had killed the animal had also thanked the Great Spirit for it. There was a rightness to Talon's prayer that moved Summer and she gave a relieved little sigh. The deer's spirit would understand now that they needed his meat to feed themselves and their families.

In swift imitation, she whispered a prayer of thanks to the Great Spirit for the ground squirrel, and remembered to thank the squirrel for the gift of its life. Suddenly she felt much better about her part in the kills.

Summer's eyes followed Talon's every move as he rolled the deer onto its back. She found herself staring at *his* back, the leather of his tunic straining across his broad shoulders. She could see the play of his powerful muscles as he used his black obsidian knife to make a long incision from the top of the animal's ribcage to the vent. With skillful strokes, he cut away the skin from the flesh until the hide was only attached at the backbone. He removed the intestines, the heart, the liver and the fatty kidneys from the gut.

Summer glanced at the tasty liver and kidneys and her mouth watered again. Talon picked up a heavy stick and, pounding it like a mallet on his skinning knife, he expertly dislocated the deer's hindquarters at the ball and socket joint. He sliced through the hamhock tendon. When that was done, he walked over and hung the haunch on the stout limb of a tree. He came back and did the same to the other hindquarter.

Summer tore her eyes away from him and glanced at the two hindquarters with long legs cooling in the slight breeze. Steam rose from the meat. She knew it was important to cool the meat as soon as possible after a kill because otherwise it would spoil.

Talon used his sharp obsidian blade to slice through the front shoulders. He hung them on a branch also. All that was left were rib cage, tenderloin and the backbone with ribs attached. These were light to carry as the deer was small.

He opened up the gut and drained off the juices, then tied off one end of the stomach and squeezed out the digested stomach contents. The stomach would make an excellent bladder for carrying water.

Full of nutrients, the digested grasses and mosses and buds in the buck's stomach were also delicious.

"Here."

Summer gasped when he thrust a handful of the delicacy at her. She took it and demurely nibbled at the steaming food. What she really wanted to do was gobble it down as she had always done as a child, but now she was no longer a child. She would not act like one, not in front of Talon.

She daintily wiped her mouth afterwards with her hand and smiled her thanks at Talon. He stared at her, but did not smile back. Summer was reminded suddenly that he had good reason to be angry at her people. And at her?

Silently, he ate his share of the stomach contents.

Summer ignored his simmering anger. Her own stomach was full and her spirits rose.

"We will leave the rest for the eagles and the foxes," Talon said.

But little was left, only the urine bladder and the lower intestines. Every other part of the deer was useful to Summer's people. Even the hooves had their uses: they could be melted down for glue or dried for rattles.

She was glad that Talon had not mentioned wolves and saber-tooth tigers. She glanced around. Strange how safe she felt with him. Every time Summer went hunting alone, she had constantly been aware of the dangers of lions, saber-tooths, wolves and bears. She had felt afraid. With this man, she felt safe. She fingered the treasure sack at her neck as she watched him, wondering if the safe feeling was an illusion. Perhaps she was in more danger from Talon than from any wolf or lion.

He cleaned his weapons of blood. "We will go to your cave now." He indicated she should carry the tenderloin, backbone and ribs, skull and hide. He hefted a single hindquarter over his shoulder.

When she remembered how deeply the atlatl dart had penetrated the buck after Talon had launched it, Summer was content to carry the load of meat. Talon needed to have both hands free to use his weapons in the event a big cat or bear or wolf attacked them.

She felt carefree as they walked along. She was safe with this man she lov—what? Summer forced down the rising thought. She merely felt grateful to him for helping her hunt. Yes, that was all.

"Do you hunt in this area often?" she asked.

"No."

"Where is the other man? The one who was with you the other time you came to our cave?"

"Hunting."

After awhile, Summer gave up trying to converse with Talon. His one-word answers told her he did not want to talk. Perhaps he regretted teaching a Caribou woman to hunt after her people had treated him so badly.

When they arrived at the entrance to the cave, Talon cracked open the deer skull, saying, "You may have the brains for tanning." He also gave her the buck's tongue, a great delicacy to the Caribou people.

"Thank you," Summer said shyly.

"It is an honorable thing to help your family," he told her. "Even if it means a woman must take up hunting."

She reddened with pleasure. "There is much about hunting I need to learn."

Summer thought of the swift, coordinated movements Talon used to launch a spear or a dart. He had practiced many years, but she was trying to learn it all in a very short time.

"You have taught me much this day," she added. "You taught me to cover myself with sage to disguise my scent, to creep silently up on the animals, and to wait patiently for game." She laughed ruefully. "You also taught me not to run after a wounded animal and to carefully walk up to a downed animal from behind, not to march up to it so it can lunge at me."

For just a moment she thought she saw a warm glint in Talon's black eyes, but he quickly hid it. His eyes became as hard as the obsidian blade he carried at his side. "Go."

Summer handed him the deer meat she had carried. She would not assume that he meant to give it all to her family, not after what they had done to him. "I thank you," she said, "for teaching me to hunt."

Talon pushed the venison back at her. "Take the meat."

Her eyes met his. "Will you join us for the evening meal?" Good manners dictated she ask him this. After all, he had provided the meat. But it was more than good manners that made her hold her breath. She *wanted* him to stay.

169

Talon shook his head.

"You are most welcome to stay and eat with us," she urged.

Again, he shook his head.

Summer stared into the dark depths of his eyes. "Thank you," she whispered. "You have returned kindness for cruelty." Then she turned and ran into the cave.

He glared after her into the darkness. "Not kindness, Caribou woman. It is cold, cold revenge." He laughed shortly and muttered, "I have my reasons. Kindness is not one of them."

With those words, he headed out across the gravel, away from the cave, away from the warm fire and the woman he wanted. Badly.

Chapter Twenty

"I tell you, I can hunt. My leg is better!"

Summer glanced at Uncle Antler. He did not look able to hunt to her. His leg was still swollen and he moved slowly. Yet she knew there was a stubbornness in him. "I will go, this one last time," she answered. She knew that stubbornness also helped make him a successful hunter. "Give your leg one more day to heal."

"I need a new spear. The power has gone out of my old one."

Summer picked up his old spear, now hers.

"There is enough power left in it to kill ground squirrels and rabbits," Auntie Birdsong reminded him as she sat weaving cattail rushes into a mat.

Uncle Antler snorted. "I hate ground squirrel. Too puny. Almost as bad as mouse meat."

Summer flushed.

"It kept you alive." Auntie Birdsong looked unperturbed as she wove the brown strands of grass.

"Bring home more deer meat," Uncle Antler said to Summer, knowing full well that it was the banished Fox man who had provided the deer meat she had brought. Her uncle and aunt asked no questions once they had learned who had provided that meat, and they had eaten every scrap of it.

Summer started toward the entrance of the cave.

"Where are you going, girl?" called her uncle.

"Hunting."

"Try the creek bottom. Plenty of animals live near the water. They like to hide in the willows there."

Summer called over her shoulder, "I will." That was where Talon had taken her when he had killed the deer. She wondered if she would see him there. She shivered and quickened her step.

"Remember to walk quietly. Deer have good hearing."

"Do you want a buck or a doe?" Summer pretended to go along with her uncle's outrageous demand for deer meat. He knew as well as she that she would be fortunate indeed to return with a rabbit.

"A doe. Remember to thank the Great Spirit for the animal."

"I will." Talon had done that, too.

"Remember to rub your skin. Use sagebrush or pine. Pine is good."

"Yes, Uncle." She walked faster but his words came after her.

"The spear point must be sharp. It must slice through and be very sharp. Did you sharpen it?"

"Yes, Uncle." Summer was out of the cave now.

"Women should not hunt," she heard him grumbling to Auntie Birdsong. "They do not know what they are doing."

Summer ran down the gravel slope, away from the sound of her uncle's voice. His words tore at her like an eagle's beak at a deer carcass, leaving her weak and bloodied. How could she hunt? How could she, a mere woman, even presume to hunt?

After awhile, she slowed to a trot, leaving her uncle and his belittling words far behind. She reached the brush that grew along the river bank and pushed aside branches as quietly as she could. She walked up to the water and stared into the cold depths. Dark shadows of fish flitted in the clear water. Perhaps she could spear a fish.

Summer picked a spot on the bank and waited, but the fish stayed out in the middle of the shallow stream. She moved slightly, wondering if there was a better place to stand. Then she caught a glimpse of movement on the water and tensed, spear poised.

She lowered the spear. It was merely her shadow moving. Summer walked along the bank, looking for somewhere else to spear from. As she walked, she watched her shadow move along the water with her.

Suddenly a fish darted ahead of the shadow shape. Summer halted. The fish could see her shadow! That was why she was not able to sneak up on them. Fish were smarter than she had thought.

She sidled over to stand beside a patch of brush that grew near the river. The brush broke up the outline of Summer's shadow on the water. Perhaps that would fool the fish.

She waited. A fish, a big one, came closer to the bank. Summer leaned forward and thrust the spear into the water. The fish swam away.

Summer frowned. She had aimed for the head, but she had missed. Something was wrong with her spear—it looked bent under the water. She pulled it out, but the shaft looked as straight as ever. Summer put it back in the water. Again it looked bent. She pulled it out.

As she pondered, another fish swam by. This time she aimed the spear toward the middle of his back and thrust. He got away too, but she thought she came closer to spearing him than she had with the first one.

She waited. No more fish came near her.

With a sigh, Summer decided to see what land animal she could find.

She walked through the brush along the bank as silently as possible, yet she still snapped the occasional twig underfoot. Once, after a particularly loud snap, she saw a deer leap away. Uncle's doe, she thought. Summer had not even seen it in the brush, but it had seen and heard her. Would she ever learn how to hunt? If only she knew the ritual to call the animals to her. She must remember to ask Uncle.

Feeling disheartened, Summer set her spear down and sat down herself, leaning against a rock. She pretended she was a stone, and after awhile little sounds started up around her. There was a rustle in a bush. Peering into the dead branches, she saw a brown grouse. Heart pounding, she snatched up her spear. The grouse rustled away, out of range. Summer lowered her spear and became a stone again.

She was a stone for a long while. Soon her stone eyes felt tired. They wanted to close. She yawned. Hunting meant waiting and waiting and waiting. . . . Her stone head fell lower on her stone chest and she finally succumbed to closing her stone eyes. She would rest for just a moment. . . .

"Hunting, Summer?" said a deep voice.

She jerked awake, shaking her head, glancing about for the speaker. "Talon!"

Another grouse took wing out of the brush. "Oh!" Dismayed, she watched it fly away.

Talon, arms crossed over his broad chest, strong legs braced apart, regarded her.

Summer felt his eyes on her hair, her face, her breasts. She rose. "Yes," she answered with dignity. "I am hunting. And you?"

"The same."

"You have killed no game yet?"

"Not yet."

"It is late in the day, Talon. I am surprised you have found nothing."

Should she tease him this way? After all, her family had greatly insulted him. Perhaps he did not like her or her family. But he did not look hostile. Interested, yes, but not hostile.

Talon gave a quirk of the lips. "I do not get game every time I hunt."

"My uncle told the Saber-Tooths you did." Summer clapped her hand over her mouth. She had not meant to bring up the past.

There was a hard glint in his eye. "Your uncle told the Saber-Tooths much. Too much."

She twisted the leather sack on a string about her neck. His black eyes followed her nervous movements. She dropped her hands.

"I see you have a new sack," Talon observed.

"It is none of your concern."

"Did I offend you that day when I returned it?"

She nodded. "The shaman said—" She stopped. It was unlikely he wanted to hear what the shaman had said.

"He said what?"

"That—that I must bury the sack and everything in it. That I must make a new one."

"Why?"

"He said that you had taken away my woman's power."

Talon considered this. "Summer, you are a strong woman, hunting alone. And courageous in learning to hunt to save your family. You have not lost your woman's power."

Summer smiled up at him. "I did not bury everything. I kept my most precious things . . ." Perhaps she should not be telling him this. Perhaps harm would come of it.

"Defying the shaman, Summer?"

She flushed and looked at the ground. "No. Yes."

"Who else would you defy? Your uncle, perhaps? Your aunt?"

He was laughing at her. She knew it. Summer lifted her chin and glared at him. "You are defying the shaman, too!"

"Me?"

"The shaman said you were to gift me with meat. You were the man who caused the loss of my power and you were supposed to compensate me for that."

"No one told me that."

"The Saber-Tooths came. Blizzard got married. I had no—no chance to tell you. My aunt— The shaman—" Aware she was mumbling, Summer stared at the ground. She could feel his dark eyes upon her but she would say no more about the circumstances under which he had been banished.

"I do not hold you responsible for what your uncle did."

She looked up at him. "It was wrong, Talon! It was very wrong!"

His dark eyes went cold as watched her. "It is done with."

"Yes, it is. And you are banished."

Silence fell between them. Summer fidgeted with the little sack at her neck. "I—I must go now. I have to hunt . . ."

"Wait. I owe you some meat. The shaman said I do, remember? And I must do what the shaman said."

She glanced at him. Obsidian eyes, Talon had. Cold and hard like the rock that made the sharpest, deadliest knives. She lowered her head. "You are not one of the Caribou People any longer. There is no need for you to do what the Caribou shaman said."

"Ah, but I want to."

"You want to? Give meat for me?" She flushed. Surely he could not tell she had fantasized that he give meat as bride-service for her.

"Yes."

Summer considered this. It would not be like bride-service, not at all. He would only be fulfilling the shaman's requirements. "Very well. I will let you."

His smile twisted her heart. "Go home, Summer. I will bring the meat tonight."

"But you have caught nothing. And it will soon be dark."

"All the more reason to return to your home. I will find something."

"Uncle Antler wanted a doe."

"Your uncle might not get quite what he wants."

"Of course not. A hunter cannot control what animal walks across his path, can he? My uncle should know that."

Talon's smile was a flash of white teeth against brown skin. "A good hunter can get exactly what he wants. Sometimes he just has to wait longer."

"I know about that!" She laughed. "It seems to me that I do nothing but wait when I hunt. Do you?"

For a moment, warmth lit the dark depths of his eyes. "I have learned patience. I find that if I but wait a little longer, the right game crosses my path."

"Every time?"

"Every time."

Summer had the uncomfortable feeling that he was speaking about something else. "I will go now." She picked up her spear. "Do not forget to bring the meat."

"Is it important to you, Summer?"

"Yes! I—" She stopped and shrugged. "It is up to you. If you want to bring the meat, that is fine with me." Just a tiny fantasy, that was all. The fantasy that Talon was bringing bride-service meat for *her* tonight. Just this one time. This one tiny fantasy was all she would allow herself.

He waved her away. "Tell your uncle to expect me."

He sounded like a lover promising to bring meat for his bride! Summer flushed and waved back. Then she fled, running as fast as she could. Never had her feet run so fast. Never had the air felt so good to her heaving lungs. Talon was bringing meat. For her!

Talon watched her lithe form darting among the rocks. He smiled to himself at her excitement. Keeping the Caribou family alive was an important part of his plan. Though the girl was brave to hunt, she could not get the meat her family needed to sustain life. But he could. He would keep her alive.

Then his eyes grew as cold and as hard as black rock. The Caribou People must be kept alive. Dead people could not feel his revenge. And *she* would be part of his revenge.

Chapter Twenty-One

Talon entered the cave and placed a large doe beside the fire. The animal had been gutted and skinned and the meat still steamed, so fresh was it. Talon was giving Uncle Antler every part of the deer.

Summer's eyes widened as she noted the size of the doe. She flashed a broad smile at Talon, but he ignored her.

"Thank you. My wife and I appreciate the meat."

Talon nodded once. "It is because the shaman requested it."

Antler and Birdsong glanced knowingly at each other. Auntie Birdsong had explained the shaman's demand to her husband earlier.

Summer gazed at the doe, pretending all the

while that Talon courted her. This was merely the first part of his bride-service. Of course there would be more meat, and then they would marry. Talon would be so smitten with her that he would be most reluctant to leave her and go hunting. And whenever he returned from the hunt, they would celebrate with many kisses. He would grow gaunt and thin from all the kissing they did until she finally pushed him out to hunt once more. Summer smiled to herself as she sat sewing by the warm fire.

"Will—will you join us for a meal?" Auntie Birdsong's voice sounded timorous. Summer glanced at Uncle who frowned at the fire.

"No."

Auntie sighed and followed Talon's gaze. He was staring at Summer. Her eyes narrowed. "We thank you for the meat. Your obligation to Summer is now fulfilled. We will speak no more about it."

Talon's lips tightened. "Just as you would rather not speak of my banishment."

Uncle Antler snorted. "You are still troublesome, boy."

Summer scowled at her uncle. Had he not noticed Talon's size and demeanor? Talon was no longer a stripling youth to be called names and driven away at a Saber-Tooth's whim. He was a fully grown man, far bigger and stronger than Uncle.

"I was not troublesome when I provided a year's bride-service for you. You were glad enough to take the meat then. You are glad to take it now."

Uncle Antler glared at Talon. Then he glared down at his own leg. Summer realized how much he hated being helpless.

"I will remind you that I have relatives I may call upon. Saber-Tooth relatives!"

"As you called upon them when you were starving?"

"I injured my leg after the snows. We could not find them. But it is none of your concern."

Auntie Birdsong looked ready to cry. "We had no choice! The Saber-Tooths forced us to banish you!"

Talon ignored her. "When are the rest of your Caribou People going to join up with you? There should be five more families."

Uncle shrugged. "In the spring." He glanced at Talon. "But do not come here then or I will be forced to hunt you down and kill you. That is what banishment is supposed to mean."

Talon laughed.

"When my leg is healed, you will not laugh!"

"No. I will not laugh then," said Talon. "But I warn you: I have men who will fight with me. You will not find us easy prey to hunt."

"Stay away from my family and my people and I will not have to hunt you."

Talon swung his head and speared Summer with his glare. Her cheeks reddened when she saw the fire in his eyes. "I may come and visit you in the spring."

Summer's heart thundered. She lowered her head as though to carefully take a stitch of her sewing, peeking at him through the waterfall of her long hair. She gave a tiny smile. How she would welcome a visit from him!

"No! Neither I nor my wife nor our people want you here. Stay away!"

Summer's smile disappeared.

Talon's appeared, a slash of white teeth against his darker skin. "I will go wherever I want in the spring."

Her uncle's voice shook with anger. "I warn you: stay away from us. I will be forced to fight you. I do not want to fight you, but I must appease my Saber-Tooth relatives. They do not want you here."

"They will not know."

"Yes, they will," piped up Auntie Birdsong. "They are coming for a spring visit. That is when Summer is to be married to Tuft, the second Saber-Tooth son."

Summer shivered. No matter how hard she tried to forget Tuft and his marriage demand, she never succeeded. She must convince Uncle and Auntie that they could *not* marry her off.

Talon whirled to face Summer. "Married? To the second Saber-Tooth son? Allow me to wish you great happiness. You must be very pleased."

Summer opened her mouth but before she

could speak, Talon added, "I will come to the wedding."

"No!" cried Uncle and Auntie in unison.

Auntie fanned herself in agitation. "You must not do that!"

"When are they marrying?"

"Late spring, perhaps even into the summer. We do not know exactly," said Auntie Birdsong, shooting Summer a sharp warning glance. It had been arranged that the marriage would take place in *early* spring.

"Late spring or early summer," Talon repeated. "That is most unfortunate."

"Oh?" said Uncle. "We thought it an auspicious time for a wedding."

"It is, I am sure," Talon answered. "It is just that I suddenly remembered that my men and I will be gone from here at that time. I will not be able to attend the wedding after all."

Auntie Birdsong sagged in relief. Uncle Antler shot Talon a cautious stare.

Summer's face crumpled in disappointment. Did he not even care that she was being married off? Did their time hunting together mean nothing? A wayward tear fell on the sewing she held in her lap and she brushed the wetness away with a finger before anyone could see it. She had been reading promises in his eyes, promises that did not exist.

Through the smoke of the chamber, Summer caught those dark eyes intent upon her. She recoiled from the stony rage she read there and groped for her sewing.

Her heart pounded as she pretended to sew. When she finally found the courage to look up again, Talon was gone.

Chapter Twenty-Two

Meat was left at the cave entrance eight more times. The snow was gone, and though Summer searched the ground avidly, she found no tracks of either man or wolf, leading up to the cave. Talon did not contact her family again and the gifts of meat stopped when Uncle Antler's leg healed enough for him to go hunting and bring home two rabbits.

The days became warmer and Summer left the cave often. While her uncle went about assembling the wood and obsidian he needed to make his new spear, he showed Summer a place where she could set a snare to catch grouse. Snaring, at least, he would allow.

A stick fence was built into the ground with an opening in it wide enough for a grouse to pass through. As the grouse squeezed through the opening to eat some seeds, a snare collar tightened on its neck. When Summer came to check the snare, the bird was well and truly caught. Her family enjoyed several tasty meals of grouse because of that snare.

Uncle Antler also showed her where the pits were located on the caribou migration path. These were deep holes dug into the ground and big enough to hold a large animal. Sharp pointed stakes poked upward from the bottom of the pit. Its opening was covered with boughs, moss and branches so that it resembled the ground around it. When the caribou herds migrated, looking for food, an unwary animal would step on the boughs and fall into the pit. Thus captured and wounded, it was a simple task to dispatch the bawling animal.

But pits were only useful when the herds migrated and sometimes years went by before a caribou herd passed this way again. The three pits Summer's uncle showed her were empty.

While Uncle Antler did not encourage Summer to hunt with his old spear, she noticed he no longer demanded that she return it. Over and over, she practiced throwing it until she was able to hit her target. Her family would not starve next winter, she vowed, because by then she would be a skillful hunter. Summer had one tiny futile wish: she wished that Talon would hunt with her again.

As the days started to warm, the other Caribou families, one by one, wandered back to the caves to join Antler's family group. First came the shaman's family. The shaman looked thinner, and his wife walked slowly, but they were healthy and they had survived.

Next came Blue Camas' parents, Screech Owl and Tule, with their two small children. Summer was relieved to see they had survived the winter. Then the remaining three families arrived and Uncle Antler's Caribou People were complete again. A feast was held outside to bid farewell to the harsh winter.

One evening, two nights after the feast, Summer sat with her aunt and Blue Camas' mother, Tule, at the open air fire down on the grassland. Screech Owl was off hunting with the other men.

"Blue Camas should be returning to us soon," Tule said as she sewed. Her two other children, a girl, Wren, and the boy, Raw, were asleep. "It is a long time since I have seen her. Wren and Raw will not remember their sister if much more time passes."

While Summer longed to see her dear friend, she did not long at all for those who would return with her: Spotted Cat, Rides Their Backs, and Tuft, the Saber-Tooth son she was supposed to marry. She would much rather marry Talon. That thought was buried as swiftly as she had buried her old treasure sack. She fiddled with her neckcloth until she caught Auntie

Birdsong's sharp eyes upon her. Summer picked up the basket she was weaving.

"Give me that!"

Puzzled, Summer handed the bullrush basket to her aunt.

"Not that! The neckcloth. Give it to me."

With a sinking heart, Summer lifted her woman's neckcloth over her head and handed it to her aunt.

Birdsong's eyes narrowed as she peered at the neckcloth. "What shall I sew on it?" she mused.

Tule glanced over. "Oho. You are thinking of the marriage of Summer and Tuft. You must sew something very powerful on it to celebrate such a fine match. Perhaps a Red-Tailed hawk?"

"No, not a hawk. It needs something even more powerful . . ."

"A black wolf?" suggested Summer.

Her aunt's head jerked up. "No! No black wolves."

Summer dropped her eyes to her basket weaving. She would rather her aunt sewed a black wolf on the neckcloth. It would remind her of the man who had taught her to hunt, the man who had given meat for her, the man who she could not forget no matter how hard she tried.

"I will put a saber-tooth tiger on it. That is what belongs on it. A saber-tooth!"

Summer glanced up. Her aunt had no understanding of what Summer wanted. None at all.

"I do not want to marry Tuft!"

"Silence, girl! You will marry whoever your uncle tells you to! I want you to forget about black wolves, and forget about *him*."

Tule glanced in bewilderment from Auntie Birdsong to Summer and back again.

"I do not like Tuft," Summer said. "I do not want to marry him!"

Tule gasped, and Auntie Birdsong glared at Summer. "We have made an agreement with the Saber-Tooths. You are going to marry Tuft. And not another word out of you!" She turned to Tule. "Troublesome girl, that is all she is."

"When I was a girl," said Tule, "I did not have a say about whom I married."

"Nor did I," said Auntie Birdsong. "This girl has too many new ideas. She hunts. She does not want to marry who her parents tell her to . . ." She frowned at Summer.

"My hunting fed you," Summer pointed out.

Auntie Birdsong's breath hissed through her nostrils. A wave of red suffused her face. When she finally addressed Summer, it was through clenched teeth. "I want you to understand that your uncle and I think Tuft will make a *fine* husband for you!"

"You and Uncle are afraid of the Saber-Tooths," Summer shot back. "That is why you will give me to them."

"The Saber-Tooths are fine people," said Tule. "Why, look how fortunate Blue Camas was to marry into them."

191

Summer glanced at Tule. "You gave Blue Camas to them because you also were afraid. We all were. Even Uncle."

"They are a fine people," Tule repeated faintly.

"And when they come for Wren, too? Will they be so fine?"

Tule's eyes sought out her little daughter, asleep on a warm robe. "Y-yes . . ."

Summer thought her voice lacked conviction.

"I am sewing on a saber-tooth design," said Auntie Birdsong and she took out her awl. Summer watched in despair as her aunt began the first few holes that would start the design. To wear a saber-tooth around her neck for the rest of her life seemed too horrible. Quietly she got up and walked away from the fire.

The stars winked in the big indigo sky above her. It was spring and soon the Saber-Tooth People would come for her, just as they had come for Blizzard and Blue Camas. And when they left, Summer would have to go with them. Her aunt and uncle would merely wave farewell as they watched her enter into a miserable life.

Summer's shoulders slumped. She did not want to marry Tuft. She did not want to go and live with the Saber-Tooths. How could she make her aunt and uncle understand? Yet, even if they understood how strongly she abhorred Tuft and the Saber-Tooths, she knew it would make no difference. The Caribou feared the Saber-Tooths and they would give them one more woman to keep the fragile peace between the two peoples. And what was one more woman, after all, when they had already given two?

Perhaps the Saber-Tooths would become less fierce once their blood joined that of the Caribous and they had children and grandchildren in common. But Summer did not want to spend her life appeasing the Saber-Tooth Tiger People. Her life was for *her* to live, for her to enjoy. And she wanted someone to live it with, someone to laugh with, someone to have children with, and a warm hearth to share after a day of hunting together. She wanted—She wrenched her thoughts away from Talon. It did no good to torture oneself with thoughts of what one could not have.

Yet to go quietly and docilely into the fate her aunt and uncle planned for her seemed to be a weak thing to do. Summer was no camp dog, to be eaten whenever its masters decided. She thought of the wolf-dog and how it had fled. She wondered if she should flee. Yet where would she go? She was a woman who had dared to take up a man's weapon, the spear. She had dared to go out into the barren land for a short time and search for game, while those who were supposed to love and protect her starved. She had learned some things about hunting. She could learn more. But she could not go off into the barren lands for a long time alone. She would surely die.

Summer shook her head. How she hated being forced to marry!

"Come back to the fire, Summer," urged Auntie Birdsong. "I did not mean to drive you away."

Summer whirled to face her aunt who had followed her. "You did not drive me away, Auntie. I but needed some time to think."

Her aunt reached out a hand. "Come, come, child. Do not go off like this. We need you at the fire. We need you with us. You are a Caribou. You are one of us."

She took Summer's hand. Auntie Birdsong's workworn hand felt warm. Summer let her aunt lead her back to the fire. "Let us sing some songs," said Auntie Birdsong to Tule. Tule reached for her drum. "The winter is over. We are together. Let us celebrate."

While they sang, Summer tried not to watch her aunt's skillful fingers as the saber-tooth design took shape upon her own woman's neckcloth.

She tried not to remember the spear at Blizzard's back when her cousin was forced to leave with the Saber-Tooths. Summer tried even harder not to remember Blue Camas' sad brown eyes on the day she had left with Spotted Cat. And Summer even tried to ignore the despair that filled her heart.

Chapter Twenty-Three

Summer sat near the outdoor fire with the other Caribou People as they ate. Because it was such a pleasant evening, Uncle Antler had dug a firepit down on the flatlands and now all six Caribou families were enjoying a meal of roasted fish and deer and roots.

She glanced up to see three figures approaching from the east. They traveled beside the screen of trees that grew along the river. Uncle Antler followed the direction of her gaze and squinted. "Must be friends," he said at last. "Enemies would hide themselves. We Caribou are fierce!"

Screech Owl and the other men laughed. They continued to eat and talk, now and then commenting on the advancing strangers.

The gray wolf-dog, still gaunt, had recently returned to the Caribou caves also. Summer tossed him a deer bone that still had marrow in it. She laughed as the skinny beast grabbed up the bone, growled in warning, then slunk off to eat it.

Auntie Birdsong snickered. "Yes, fatten him up, Summer," she said. "Then we will have a tasty stew next winter." The others laughed; Auntie had told them how her family had eaten dog meat during the hungriest part of the winter. But Summer's laughter caught in her throat. She never wanted to eat dog meat again.

She nibbled at the deer rib she held. Finally every morsel of gristle and meat was gone and she flung it, too, in the direction of the wolf-dog. He snapped it up.

Suddenly Uncle cried out in surprise. "Who *are* they?" He half-rose and stared at the strangers who sauntered along between the river and the flatlands. They walked in single file; the leader wore deer antlers on his head.

Summer strained forward, peering to see who they were. Dusk was falling and in the purple shadows it was difficult to see.

Auntie Birdsong put three big chunks of venison onto sticks and placed them over the coals. "We can offer them some meat," she said, and Tule nodded in agreement.

"Pull that meat off the fire, woman," ordered Uncle Antler as he stood up. "We do not know if we will offer these men a single morsel!" He grabbed up his spear.

The other men muttered and reached for their spears, too. All five got to their feet and followed Uncle Antler as he limped forward.

"Go to the caves," Screech Owl ordered the women as he departed.

Summer stood up and peered into the dusk. Should she follow the men or return to the cave?

Several of the other women took their babies, gathered up what they could carry and headed towards the caves.

Auntie Birdsong and Tule stayed near the firepit. "I believe our strong men can drive those strangers away if they need to," said Auntie Birdsong.

"Yes, truly," murmured Tule. She busied herself with placing meat chunks on sticks. "We need not return to the cave just yet. There are only three strangers and we have six Caribou men to protect us." She glanced over at Raw, her son of six summers, and Wren, her youngest girl of three summers, both asleep on a bison robe. "I do not want to awaken Raw and Wren just yet," she added.

Summer picked up her spear. "I am going to follow the men," she announced.

Auntie Birdsong glanced in the direction the men had gone. "No! Do not. Our men travel swiftly and there may be fighting." She eyed Summer. "Return to the cave instead. Some of the women may need help with their children."

Disappointed, Summer wandered off towards the caves. "We will be along very soon," Tule called after her.

When Summer was far enough from the two women that she could no longer see them in the dusk, she stopped. Why could she not follow the men? She wanted to see who the strangers were. She would not get caught up in any fighting. She was simply curious. Who were they? Where had they come from?

As she stood there pondering, she heard a noise behind her. She turned her head to see what made the noise, and a large hand clamped over her mouth. She was yanked up against a hard chest. "Hunting, Summer?"

She recognized that voice in her ear.

She made a muffled sound and Talon's grip tightened. "You must be silent," he warned. "You will not need this." He took her spear from her and threw it away. Then he pushed her ahead of him in the direction of the river, away from the caves, and away from the firepit where Auntie Birdsong and Tule sat talking.

When they had gone a little distance, Talon took his hand away from her mouth.

Summer let out a piercing scream.

He clamped his hand over her mouth again. With his other hand he stuffed a piece of wretched tasting leather into her mouth. Then he threw her over his shoulder. "Now you cannot alert your kinsmen," he grunted. He moved forward but Summer knew he was slowed down by her weight.

To further slow him, she kicked and struggled, trying to free herself, but he held her fast. Oh, where were Uncle and the other men? Had they heard her scream?

Talon managed to reach the shelter of a willow tree near the river before he put her on her feet. The moment her feet touched the earth, Summer tried to run, but he caught her by her leather dress and dragged her back.

By now it was so dark that Summer could barely see her hand in front of her face. Just then the moon came out from behind a cloud.

She tore at the leather binding and managed to pull it out of her mouth. "Let me go!" she yelled.

"Silence," Talon hissed and lunged at her. They fell to the ground, he on top. He grappled with her until he got one hand over her mouth again. He stared into her wild eyes.

His body was heavy on hers, pressing her into the dampness of the grass beneath her. Summer could smell him, and the heady male scent of him added to her fear.

"I will not let you go, Summer," he said. "I am stealing you from your family. You are going to be my wife!"

She went still at his words and her eyes grew huge with fear. At any other time, those same words would have warmed her to her very core,

Theresa Scott

but not now, not like this. To steal her!

She struggled then, with every bit of strength and muscle in her, she struggled. She snapped at him, trying to bite. She kicked. He held her down, and when Summer finally stopped struggling and biting and kicking, wearied from the exhaustion and futility of it all, she thought she saw something like compassion in Talon's dark eyes.

"We go now."

She shook her head. "No!"

"Yes."

"I will fight you with all the strength in my body!"

"So be it. I have chosen you for my wife and you will come with me."

"Why did you not ask my uncle for me?" Summer cringed at the pleading note she heard in her voice.

"Your uncle would never give you to me. Surely you know that."

She thought about that. "He might have."

"After you were promised to the Saber-Tooth cub?" Talon laughed. Then his voice grew cruel. "Your uncle owes me a woman and so I am taking you."

Summer cringed further at his words. They were cold, as cold and hard as the dark eyes that stared into her own.

"I do not want to come with you!"

"I know. You would rather marry the Saber-

Tooth cub. Get on your feet, Summer. We leave."

The howl of a wolf pierced the night air. "Blue Feather," Talon muttered. "Come, we must go." He prodded her to her feet. "I warn you," he said when she stood in front of him, "that if you take one step to run away, or make one cry to alert your kinsmen, I will tie you again and carry you. If you are silent and come with me, I will let you walk."

Summer screamed and began to run. When she got to the river, aspen and alder branches whipped at her face and she put out her arms to protect herself. Talon must have thought her thoroughly cowed because she was able to run some distance before he caught her again.

He threw her to the ground and she felt his hard knee press into the middle of her back to hold her down. The wretched leather gag was forced into her mouth once again. Talon's chiseled face was grim in the moonlight when he turned her over and tied her hands together in front of her. "Now," he said and sat back to look at her. "You cannot escape, so do not even try. Get up."

He pulled Summer to her feet and she glared at him. He smiled back. "Your yellow eyes are very fierce," he said with approval. "You will make a fine mate for a Wolf."

If she could have spat at him, she would have. She had to settle for a low growl in the back of her throat.

"Get going," Talon said. He swung her around and gave her a push in the direction he wanted her to go.

All she needed was a spear at her back, Summer thought in rage. Then she would be in the same state as Blizzard when she was marched off! But this was even worse. At least Blizzard had been married off with friends and family around her. But for Summer, there was no one. A little voice reminded her that once she had wanted this man. And now the very thing she did *not* want was happening: she was being forced into marriage!

Talon and Summer met up with three other men after a long march. One of them wore deer antlers and Summer realized that they were the three she had seen approaching along the river. She wanted to ask what they had done to her uncle and the other Caribou men, but the leather was still in her mouth. Her anger grew until she was suddenly too furious to ask these men anything!

The man with the deer antlers, whom Talon called Blue Feather, walked over to stare down at her. He was a big man, with cruel eyes. Summer had seen him before, when Talon had first visited the cave. Summer refused to quaver under his inspection.

Blue Feather turned to Talon. "She looks better with some fat on her," he said and spat. "Does she have any sisters?"

Talon chuckled and if he had been standing

close to her, Summer would have kicked him.

The men did not tarry long at this meeting place and they were soon on their way, Summer stumbling and Talon prodding her along every now and then. Evidently they expected to be followed, she thought. Good! Perhaps her uncle and the other Caribou men would find her and rescue her!

When they finally reached the Wolves' camp, Summer was taking slow steps. Her breathing rasped in and out, her chest ached from the fast pace she had been forced to endure, her hands throbbed from being tied and her tongue ached from the leather in her mouth. She wanted to fall down and sleep right where she stood. But first she wanted to throttle Talon!

He motioned her over to a wide, skin-roofed lean-to. Summer sank to her knees on a robe that covered the ground. She held herself rigid as he untied her hands, and once the gag was removed from her mouth, and she had swallowed several times to stop the dryness, she managed to snarl, "Let me go! At once!"

Talon shook his head. "I have explained it to you. I stole you. You are now my wife. It will go better for you if you accept that."

"Never!"

His nostrils flared and his dark eyes raked her. Then with a twist of a smile, he picked up a fur and tossed it to her. She caught it. "Get some rest," he advised and sauntered away.

She glared after him, at his broad back, at

his swaggering walk. His wife, indeed!

But he is so much more handsome than Tuft, a little admiring voice whispered in her mind. *If one had to make a choice, this man is the better of the two.*

Aghast at the direction of her thoughts, Summer rolled over and curled herself up in the furs. She closed her eyes. They flew open as she thought, *I could run away!*

She peered out into the dark forest surrounding her. She heard rustles in the night and thought of the wolves, the saber-tooths that roamed. Summer yawned. Perhaps she would have a chance to escape, but not tonight, not when she ached in every place in her body. With an exhausted sigh, she fell asleep.

"It was as you said it would be," said Blue Feather.

Talon dragged his thoughts and eyes away from the woman in his lean-to. The four men sat at the fire, warming themselves after the long march and eating a little dried meat before retiring to their bed robes. "What was that?"

"Antler laughed at our offer for his niece. He said she was promised to the Saber-Tooths and that he would never give her to you."

"He breaks promises when it is easy to do so. Antler is a coward."

Blue Feather said, "He is an old man, trying to appease the Saber-Tooths. Are they truly so fearsome?"

"No."

Blue Feather laughed. "They were fearsome enough when they drove you away."

"They will not do so again."

Weasel nodded. "Think you they will come after the woman?"

Talon shrugged. "Perhaps."

"Would you?" demanded Blue Feather. "If Summer was taken from you, would you go after her?"

Talon pondered. "I did not go after her cousin. But Summer is different. She is not like Blizzard. She is—"

"Softer?"

"Perhaps. Yes, I think I would go after Summer."

Blue Feather yawned again. "We can rest. Whose turn is it to keep watch for the Caribou?"

Sloth volunteered and the others wearily crawled off to their bedrobes.

Talon lay down beside the sleeping Summer. He put an arm around her and settled himself. He sniffed her hair. She smelled warm and sweet. He pulled her to him. She moaned and stirred. He kept his hold on her and she subsided. *My woman,* he thought. *The woman I want. The woman I deserve. My wife.* And he smiled into the darkness, peace in his heart at long last.

Chapter Twenty-Four

Summer woke when the sun was high in the sky. She sat up, dazed, trying to understand where she was. A hide lean-to sheltered her head. She was in a small clearing, ringed by forest. The rushing sound of water nearby came to her ears.

Then she saw Talon. He was sitting on a rock beside the fire and watching her. His eyes held a lively speculation.

She remembered now. She had been stolen! She met those dark eyes with a glare. "I want to return to my people!"

"No."

Summer rose and stalked over to him, not caring that her deerskin dress was wrinkled, that her face felt puffy from sleep, that her hair was tangled. "I do not want to be here. I wish to go home!" She would not cry.

"Have some meat."

She tossed her head and ignored his offer. "Where are the others?"

"Hunting."

Suspicion darkened her voice. "When will they return?"

"When they want to."

"Who are they?"

His eyes held hers. "My people. The Wolves."

She snorted.

Talon's eyes went cold. "They are mother, father, sister, and brother to me. They helped me when you and your people banished me and would have let me die. I would kill for them. You would do well to remember that."

Summer took a step back. She had not meant to rouse such emotions in him. Emotions that, from the angry look of him, made him dangerous to her. She glanced around the little clearing, searching for something to say, anything, to sway him from his anger. Then she scowled. *Let him be angry. It is nothing to me!* "I am no threat to them," she said sullenly. "But to *you*, I am."

He stared at her, then he laughed.

She felt a tiny tingle of relief. "You think I am not, Wolf?" she asked in growing annoyance. "I could kill you."

"I think you would try."

"I could use my knife when you sleep."

He regarded her in amusement and she felt her ire rise. "Think on it, Summer," he said. "If you kill me, you get three husbands: Blue Feather, Weasel and Sloth."

She glared at him. "I do not want three husbands!"

His eyes were mischievous. "Then settle for one: me."

"I could have had a Saber-Tooth for a husband," she pointed out, fingering her woman's neckcloth.

Talon's eyes fell to the cloth and narrowed. He stood up. "What is that?" He walked over and plucked at the cloth. He raised his eyes to hers and she saw fire in those dark depths. "Take it off."

She yanked the soft leather out of his grasp. "No! It is mine. It is one of the few things I have left to remind me of my family. My aunt and her friends and Blizzard each sewed a design on it for my coming into womanhood. I refuse to take it off!"

He glared at her. "I do not like that saber-tooth design in the middle of it."

Neither did Summer, but she would not tell him that. She shrugged and turned away as if she cared nothing about his likes or dislikes.

He reached for her chin and dragged her face around to his. "Your first wifely duty," he said through gritted teeth, "will be to take off that saber-tooth design!"

She gaped at him. Surely such a little thing

could not mean so much to him.

"And you will sew a wolf on it instead!"

Summer felt her face flush. Since his demand was so close to what she had once told her aunt she wanted, she sought refuge in anger. "I will not! I will not do one thing you tell me to do! And I will not be your wife!"

He gripped her arm and held her stiffly before him. "You *are* my wife," he snarled. "You had better accept that!"

"No!"

"Yes!"

They glared at one another. He hauled her closer to him. "I stole you. You are mine!"

"I am not!"

"I can make you my wife. Here. Now!" His eyes blazed with the threat.

Summer did not know what he was talking about. "I suppose *you* will have the ceremony, *you* will prepare the food, *you* will serve the guests, *you* will burn the herbs to the eight directions, *you* will ask the ritual blessings!"

Her voice was raw with anger and pain. All this she was missing. A man who stole a woman did not have to do any of those things that were so important. Summer wanted her aunt, her friends with her. Even Blizzard, traded away as she was, had been accorded that much! Even Blue Camas had that!

But what angered Summer most of all was that she could not make her own choice of man for her husband. So angry she could spit, Summer glared at Talon and to her mortification, tears rose in her eyes. *I should have buried my treasure sack possessions! This is what comes from disobeying the shaman's instructions*, she thought bitterly. *Terrible misfortune!*

Talon saw her tears and remembered barely in time that he had a stone for a heart because of Summer's uncle and her people. He turned abruptly away from her. After several steps and a long indrawn breath, he swung around to face her again. "We disagree on this, I see."

"Yes!"

"Would it have been better for you if we had the ceremony, the friends, the food, the herbs burned to the eight directions?"

"Yes!"

"Would you accept me as your husband if you had all that?"

"No! Perhaps—Oh, I do not know!"

"My friends asked your uncle for you. They talked with him while I circled up behind and stole you."

"My capture was planned?"

"For a long time."

Summer did not know what to say to that. She was surprised he had planned to steal her, although Uncle Antler would never have given her to him. "What was Uncle Antler's answer to your friends?"

"He laughed at them. Said you were promised to the Saber-Tooth and would never be my wife."

Her fists clenched. "I do not want to marry the Saber-Tooth either."

"What you want does not seem to count with your uncle."

Summer glanced away. "What I want does not seem to count with you, either."

Talon frowned. "You are right. What *I* want is what counts. I want revenge on your people. They wronged me."

A shiver went through her. "So that is what I mean to you. That is why you planned to steal me. As a way of revenging yourself."

"Yes."

Summer glared at him. "You have ruined my life just to get your revenge!" she screeched like an owl.

He shrugged. "Your life would have been ruined with the Saber-Tooth."

"Aargggh!" Summer sprang at him in rage. Talon tripped when he caught her and they fell to the ground. He landed on his back with her on his chest. She clawed at his face and he locked both her wrists together with one hand so she could not scratch his eyes out.

"Let me go!" she cried. "I want to go home!"

"Your home is with me now."

"No!" She glared down at him, at those narrowed black eyes, and warned herself she must get away from this man. "Let me go. You have had your revenge! You have proved to my uncle, to my people, that you could steal one of their women. Now let me go back to them."

She hated to hear the pleading in her voice; she felt as though she were begging him but she could not help herself. She had to get away from him!

"I do not want to let you go."

"Why not?"

Talon did not answer this, merely considered her with those obsidian eyes. At last he spoke. "I want a wife. I do not want to live all my days alone."

"You are not alone. You have your friends, Blue Feather and the others."

He shook his head and his eyes perused her face. "They are not beautiful like you."

Talon smiled then and Summer closed her eyes against the onslaught of his blatant male attraction. "Let me go," she whispered.

"Summer," he whispered back. "Look at me."

She opened her eyes a crack.

"I cannot let you go. I want you for my wife."

"You wanted Blizzard once. You let her go."

Talon's smile disappeared. "She was stolen from me."

"So you stole me."

"Yes."

"Why me? Why not someone else?"

He shrugged and she felt it as a tremor through his body. Talon loosened his grip on her wrists. "You are the only Caribou woman of marriageable age."

Summer's fingers curled into claws again.

"*That* is why?" she shrieked. "Because I am the only Caribou woman of marriageable age?"

He grabbed her wrists, one in each hand. "And because," he answered, "you were promised to the Saber-Tooth. It made my revenge all the sweeter."

"Your revenge!" She fought against his grasp. When he would not release her, she arched her back, struggling to rise from his chest.

"It will do you no good," Talon said.

She thrashed about but when her lower torso pressed against his, she froze.

He smiled. "Do it again."

"You—you—!" she sputtered.

"Did your good aunt not tell you about men and women?"

"She had no need to! We—I know—That is, Blizzard told me—"

"Yes?" Talon inquired pleasantly. "What did Blizzard tell you?" His eyes burned into hers.

Summer closed her eyes again. She felt warm and alive from the waist down. "Let me go," she moaned. She felt weak all over.

He let go one of her hands and she braced herself against his chest, her eyes still tightly shut. When he ran his hand along her back, it soothed her.

She felt his hand pushing her down, down against him. Summer wanted to let herself rest against that broad, warm chest, and for a moment she let herself lean on him. The stroking on her back relaxed her. But she dare not do this for long, she warned herself. She opened her eyes.

Talon was watching her and the intensity in his gaze took her breath away. "It will not be so bad being with me," he whispered. "I will be kind to you."

Summer wanted to believe him. She knew he could be kind. He had taught her about hunting, he had given meat to her family through the winter. She knew there was kindness in him, that if she was able to touch that kindness, her life with Talon would go well. Her life with Talon? Was she actually thinking of staying? No! She would not be forced into a marriage! She could not live like Blizzard or Blue Camas.

"I—I cannot," she whispered. "I must be free to choose my husband."

The gentle stroking on her back stopped. "You would go back to your uncle?" She heard the incredulity in his voice. "He will force you to marry the Saber-Tooth. Is that what you want?"

"N-no. I do not want to marry the Saber-Tooth."

"Good."

"But I cannot marry you."

The gentle strokes on her back started once more. "Why not, fair Summer?"

"It was wrong of you to steal me for revenge, to force me to be your wife. I cannot live like that."

215

Talon sat up and pushed her off him. "You had best accept it," he said. "I will not take you back to your people." Then he got up and strode over to the lean-to. He picked up his weapons and gave a shrill raven's cry. A wolf howl answered. "I am going hunting," he said. "Blue Feather will keep watch on you."

He strode off into the forest.

Summer watched him leave. There was an ache in the region of her heart. Something about her troubled him, she mused. Talon would not admit it to himself, but there was something about her capture or his revenge that bothered him. Else why would he run from her just now?

Like a stalking hunter, she was determined to learn what it was and use it against him.

Chapter Twenty-Five

Blue Feather worked stolidly on sharpening the blade of a spear. Summer yawned. Where were the others? Where was Talon?

The day had passed quietly, giving her much time to think about her morning's encounter with Talon. Now night was falling and neither Talon nor the other two men, Weasel and Sloth, had returned to camp.

She sat on a rock by the fire. "When will they return?"

Blue Feather shrugged and kept sharpening the blade.

Summer glanced around the camp. Three lean-to's were set at a short distance from the fire. One of the lean-to's belonged to Talon and that was where she·had slept the past night.

217

The second belonged to Blue Feather, and the third lean-to, the widest one, belonged to the two brothers. She noticed there were no camp dogs—nor a black wolf.

She idly fingered the saber-tooth design she refused to remove from her neckcloth. "Do you think they will be gone long?"

Another shrug.

Summer was getting hungry. There seemed to be little to do in the camp. She rose and wandered to the far edge of the clearing.

"Come back!"

She regarded Blue Feather. "I am only gathering a few twigs for the fire."

He scowled at her. "I said come back."

They held a war of nerves, each glaring at the other, until Summer broke the contact. She turned and sauntered farther into the forest. "No."

Blue Feather got to his feet. He was as big as Talon and for a moment Summer considered him. She did not know anything about him, nor know how he would act if she angered him. Yet she did not feel particularly frightened, because he was supposed to be guarding her. She took three more steps before she was swept up from behind, dragged across the clearing and deposited back on the rock by the fire.

"Stay there," Blue Feather growled. She glared at him. He glared back. "I want you here when Talon returns."

"It is nothing to him if I leave."

Blue Feather snorted. "You are wrong, Caribou woman. He expects you to stay here. You stay here. He expects me to guard you. I guard you." He went back to sharpening the blade.

Summer frowned at him. Then she thought, *Perhaps now is a good time to hunt for weaknesses in Talon's plan for me.*

"Blue Feather?"

No answer.

"Blue Feather, it must get lonely for you here, with only Talon and the other two men for companions. Would you not like to be with more people?"

He lifted the blade and blew dust from it.

"Blue Feather, how would you like to have many fine furs?"

He met her gaze.

She smiled. "A fine man like you should have a wife of his own. Children of his own."

"Hunh." He went back to sharpening one side of the blade.

She sidled a little way off the rock and leaned toward him. "Blue Feather, I can help you win a wife. I can help you get fine furs."

He turned over the blade and began to chip tiny pieces of rock off that side.

Summer took a breath. "Blue Feather, listen to me."

He kept chipping. "I am listening."

"If you help me escape, I will see to it that my uncle gives you a wife and many furs."

Blue Feather laid down the spear tip he had sharpened and reached for his other spear. He drew it onto his lap and eyed the blade.

"Will you help me, Blue Feather?" Summer held her breath. She could feel her heart pounding and leaned forward to hear his answer. "Think on it: furs, a wife, children."

"Will she be like you?"

Summer blinked at the question. "Why, yes, I suppose so, if you want one like me. What am I like?"

"Pretty. Soft. Smart."

Summer smiled sweetly.

"Sly."

"*Sly?*" The word jolted her.

"You are sly. Thinking to offer me furs and a wife if I help you escape is sly, do you not think so?"

Summer almost choked on her words. "You think me sly because I offer you rewards for your help? I do not call that sly, Blue Feather. I call that wise!"

He shrugged and continued to chip at the new blade. When he finished one side, he turned to her and grinned. "I will not help you, Caribou woman. I have no need of furs; I can hunt my own. And as for the sly wife you would find me," he shook his head, "in that, too, I am capable of finding my own."

Enraged, Summer jumped up from the rock. "I will escape, Blue Feather! With or without your help!"

He laughed as she stomped to the edge of the little clearing. He was still laughing when she entered the forest.

She heard his laughter behind her as she strode past the trees. She should be more careful in the forest, she knew, but she was furious at Blue Feather, and at Talon. Blue Feather had no intention of helping her. He had only wanted to tease her, see what she had to say, to offer!

When Summer had stomped through the underbrush, she returned to the campsite and plunked herself down on the rock to await Talon. She ignored Blue Feather.

He chuckled.

She turned her back to him and glared at the fire.

"Hear this, Caribou woman," he said softly. "I will not go against Talon. He is my friend. No, more than a friend—he is my brother. Do not ask those things of me again. You insult me."

"I hope you find a woman, Blue Feather," Summer said through gritted teeth. "And when you do, I hope she breaks your heart!"

There was a silence, then came the reply. "I would never again be so foolish as to trust a woman with my heart, Caribou woman. So your cruel hope is for naught."

Talon arrived back at camp carrying one sage hen.

"That is all you got?" Blue Feather asked in surprise.

Talon threw down the sage hen. "That is all. Game is scarce." In truth, he had done little but think of Summer. Even now his eyes strayed in her direction.

Blue Feather grunted. "Watch out for that woman," he warned. "She is sly. Reminds me of my former wife."

"What did she do?"

Blue Feather glanced at Summer. "She wanted me to help her escape. Said her uncle would give me furs and a woman if I helped her escape."

"You should have taken her offer, Blue Feather," said Talon.

"I was tempted."

Talon chuckled and looked over at Summer who was still perched on the rock beside the fire pretending to ignore them. "I do not know what woman the Caribou People would have given you. They have no young ones left. She is the last."

Summer spun around and glared at Talon.

Her yellow eyes made her look fierce, he thought, as he walked over to where she sat. His eyes dropped to her breasts. He reached out and picked up the front of her woman's neckcloth, letting his hand brush the soft cloth that covered the even softer flesh he knew lay behind it. Talon stared at the neck cloth. The wretched saber-tooth design was still there. He let the cloth drop from his hand. "She is stubborn," he said to Blue Feather.

"All women are stubborn," Blue Feather muttered. "And dishonest. And disloyal."

Summer's eyes jerked to him. "What makes you so bitter?"

Blue Feather did not answer.

Talon sat down by the fire. He supposed he should pluck the sage hen and put it on the fire to roast for the others, but he needed time to think.

He did not know what to do with Summer. Oh, he knew he wanted her in his bed, but she had not cooperated with him since her capture and there was no reason to expect she would cooperate with him now when he wanted her, willing, in his bed.

How did a new husband handle such things? He could not ask Blue Feather. If he listened to Blue Feather, he would soon sour on this woman and all others. "Where are Weasel and Sloth?"

Blue Feather shrugged. "Still hunting."

They would not be much help either, Talon decided. Sloth's wife had died, and Weasel seldom made mention of his three wives.

Talon gazed into the flames. He had his wife, he had his revenge. The Caribou were no doubt searching for her even as he sat here. The thought brought a faint satisfied smile to his lips.

Theresa Scott

He knew Summer was watching him. Out of
the corner of his eye, he saw her occasional,
nervous glances at the darkening shadows in
the forest and then at him. Night was falling
and she wondered what he would do. Well, so
did he.

She rose from her perch on the rock and
walked over to pick up the sage hen.

Talon liked the graceful flow of her movements. He liked her hair the color of dry grass
in the summer. He liked her fierce yellow eyes
that reminded him of a she-wolf. He even liked
her name. It spoke of a happy time, when the
sun shone and the hunting was easy. Yes, Summer was a fine woman, a fine mate for him.
But what should he do about her?

He watched her strong fingers pluck the
feathers off the sage hen. She walked to the
edge of the forest. Talon was about to leap
up and grab her when he saw her bend
down to gut the bird. He sank back on his
haunches.

"Eager?" Blue Feather asked, a twinkle in
his eyes.

"Take a walk in the woods, Blue Feather."

Blue Feather rose and picked up his spears.
He lumbered over to his lean-to and peeled
the large camel skin off the wooden frame. He
met Talon's gaze. "I will give you my advice.
It is this: use her body and enjoy it well. Just
do not give her your heart. Women think a
man's heart is good for one thing and one thing

224

only," he said as he walked to the edge of the clearing.

"And what is that?"

"To stomp on with their dainty little moccasins." Blue Feather disappeared into the forest.

Talon pondered his friend's words. Good advice, he decided. If Summer was at all like the other Caribou People, she would be deceitful and make promises she would not keep. He knew that if he came to love her, he too would be driven to anger as Blue Feather was over his faithless former wife.

Summer returned from the far edge of the clearing. She knelt by the fire and drove a stick through the bird's carcass. She rubbed a handful of aromatic herbs on the hen's fat white breast and placed some in the stomach cavity. Then she positioned a forked stick in the ground at one side of the fire. She propped the spitted bird at an angle on the forked stick so that the hen hung over the bright orange flames.

As the bird cooked, Talon ruminated on how he should behave toward his new, very reluctant wife.

"Would you like to eat?" Summer asked when the bird was done. Talon started, surprised at how swiftly the time had passed.

Later, wiping grease off his fingers with a leaf, he asked, "Would you like to walk down by the river?"

Summer glanced at him in surprise. Was he giving her a choice? Choice was very important to her, she realized. Ever since her parents had died, she had had little choice in her life. She had not chosen who she lived with. Her aunt and uncle had taken her in, and she was grateful, but had she been able to choose, her parents would never have been killed. Had she been able to choose, she would never have been promised to Tuft, and had she been able to choose, she would never have been stolen by Talon. The course of her life had always been decided by others. Summer remembered her vow to herself that she would choose her own husband. How futile that vow seemed now!

Disheartened, she stared at him. "And if I do not want to walk by the river?"

Talon squatted down in front of her and his obsidian eyes held hers. "You are my wife. I want to make you happy."

"Do you think a walk by the river will make me happy?"

He shrugged. "Will it?"

"I do not know."

He watched her, puzzled. Why should it be so difficult to decide if she wanted to walk by the river?

"You say you want to make me happy."

"Yes."

"Then take me back to my people. That will make me happy."

"I cannot do that. You know why."

"Your revenge."

"Yes." But there was more. Talon found he did not want to be parted from this woman. He wanted her in his life. To take her back to her people would leave him lonely, even more lonely than he had been when he had first been banished. "I cannot do that," he repeated, willing her to understand. "I will not do that."

"My people will find me. And when they do, they will kill you!"

"Perhaps. But they have to *find* me first."

"They will."

"Summer, it is not likely your people will find me. Or you. We walked along the river and left few tracks. It will be very difficult for them to follow us."

"It will not! They will look for me. My aunt loves me. My uncle loves me. They will do all they can to find me!"

"If they love you so much, why were they willing to give you to a Saber-Tooth man you did not want?"

"They—they would have listened to me in the end. They would have, I tell you!"

Talon shook his head. "I do not think they were willing to do what you wanted. But you wish to believe otherwise."

She launched herself at him then, and he put up his hands to protect his face from her nails. He grabbed her hands and held them tightly.

"Let me go!" she cried.

He knew if he did so, she would scratch him. "Summer, listen to me."

"No! Let me go!"

He held her in his arms while she struggled.

"You are my wife now. You belong with me. Forget your family."

"No! Never!"

"If I let you go back to them, they will just marry you off to someone else. You would do far better with me. I will treat you kindly."

"No! I cannot stay! I will not! Let me go!"

"No."

She cried then, helplessly, hopelessly.

Talon held her and listened to her sobs, knowing that he was the cause of those despairing cries. He patted her hair, that pale hair the color of sun-kissed grass. He patted her back, soothing her.

He longed to dry the tears from her beautiful yellow eyes because his gut told him, at that very moment, that having a wife who did not want him was far worse than being banished. Far worse than being lonely. Far worse than anything Talon had ever known.

Chapter Twenty-Six

Summer stopped weeping and wiped at her eyes. She did not look at Talon as she pulled away from his arms. He let her go.

Crying was not going to help her get free, she decided, though it did make her feel better. She knew that Talon wanted her to accept her capture and stop fighting him. But she also knew that to be true to herself, she must not give in to him. Once she accepted that she was his wife, she would be lost.

"I would like to walk by the river," she said and rose.

He got to his feet and they walked down to the river in silence. Small birds twittered in the undergrowth and a snake slithered across the path into the sparse grass. When they came near the bank of the river, Summer halted.

A soft breeze stirred the willows. Cottonwood leaves flickered. Purple clouds reflected the last rays of the setting sun. There was a warm freshness to the evening air. Summer inhaled deeply, trying to put her unhappiness behind her.

How she wished that they stood here as a true husband and wife—Talon, chosen by her, and their union celebrated by her family. She remembered when she had watched him so closely during that year after he had come to live with the Caribou People. Little had she known then that he would steal her away.

"Look," said Talon. "Ants." He pointed his spear at a large rotting log that had fallen over in a storm.

Summer squatted, careful not to disturb the tiny black insects that scurried back and forth, each one carrying a tiny piece of wood in its jaws. Each ant would deposit the wood on the pile of sawdust they had made, then hurry back inside the log for more wood. She watched, fascinated, as the ants worked at building up the pile. Larger black ants helped the tiny ones.

She rose. "They are so busy making their home!"

Talon nodded, falling into step with her as she moved closer to the river bank. They stood on the bank for a time, listening to the waves lap at the water's edge.

Talon glanced around for predators, then placed his spear carefully on the ground beside him. Then he stepped behind Summer and enfolded her in his arms. His movement took her by surprise, and she started at his touch, but he held her firmly.

She put a hand on his forearm and felt his strength, his warmth as he stood behind her, looking over her head at the water.

After a while, she sighed and relaxed against him. She leaned her head back against his chest.

He caressed the top of her head with his chin, then buried his nose in her hair. Summer could feel his warm breath on her head. She closed her eyes, remembering that he had given meat for her and pretending, just for the moment, that they were truly married.

Talon lowered his lips to her neck and began kissing his way along her nape. Summer swallowed, but kept her eyes shut. His kisses tickled her neck, and his lips were soft and warm. She felt herself melting inside like a piece of river ice in the spring. His arms were gentle and now his embrace loosened a little. Talon's hands began moving over her body, across her belly, moving slowly, gently. She leaned back into him as his hands dipped lower, soothing her, warming her, touching her in places no man had ever touched her before.

She moaned and reached her hands behind her to hold his head and to keep his lips pressed to her neck. His breathing was coming fast and she smiled a little to herself at that.

231

"Summer," he murmured. His grip tightened on her waist and she felt the strength of him behind her as he pressed into her. "I want you."

She moaned again. His kisses were hot now and frantic on her neck.

"I want you so much."

She tried to open her eyes, but her lids felt heavy; her loins felt heavy.

"Summer . . ."

She liked how Talon said her name. She turned in his arms and then he was kissing her fully on her lips. She felt the strength of him, felt the heat of his kisses and pushed herself further into his embrace.

"Oh, Summer!"

She kissed him back, thrilled by what he was doing to her. His hands were all over her, roving her back, her belly, her breasts. "Summer, I have got to have you!" His breath was coming in quick pants and she grew excited as she listened to him.

Talon raised his head and looked around. "I cannot take you here," he said in a ragged voice. "Come. We will go back to camp."

She felt dazed at the loss of his hot mouth on hers. She pulled his head back down and sought his lips blindly.

"Oh yes, Summer."

They kissed some more and he reached down her leg, stroking her. Talon lifted the hem of her dress and his hand grabbed her thigh. He pulled her closer to him, his hand moving up to grasp her buttocks and press her against him. "I cannot take much more of this," he murmured. "Come with me."

He lifted Summer in his arms and carried her back to the lean-to. The cool evening air on her fevered skin began to revive her. By the time they reached the lean-to, her thoughts were clear again.

Talon laid her carefully down on his bed furs, then lay down beside her. She struggled to sit up, but he met her eyes with a burning look and pushed her onto her back. "Let me," he said, then lowered his head and pressed his lips to hers. He threaded his fingers through her hair. "Oh, Summer," he groaned. "I cannot wait any longer!" He lowered his head and began to kiss the side of her neck.

Yes, the cool evening air had cleared her head. "*I* can wait, Talon," Summer said.

He went still, his face buried in her hair at the side of her neck.

She pushed at him, but gently. "I said, I can wait, Talon."

"I heard you." His voice was almost a groan. Was he in pain?

Summer struggled once more to sit up, and this time she managed to get upright. He lay there, prone, his head in the bed robes.

"What ails you, Talon?"

No answer. Slowly he lifted his face from the fur robes. He looked flushed and disappointed. He gazed at her, then groaned and rolled over onto his back to stare up at the hide on the lean-to.

When he did not move, she said, "Talon?"

"Hmmm?"

"What is so fascinating about the roof of the lean-to?"

He sighed. "It is not easy to explain."

"Please try."

"It is not that the roof of the lean-to is fascinating, Summer. It is that I am trying to control my feelings for you." He gave a shudder.

"I know your feelings for me. You are using me for revenge."

Talon closed his eyes and put a forearm over them. "So I am." He added, "I think, however, that you have your own little ways of revenge."

"Me?"

No answer. Finally, "Go to sleep, Summer."

"Here? With you?"

He sighed again. "With me. Unless you want to sleep out in the forest, prey to the occasional bear or jaguar that might wander by."

His eyes were still covered, and Summer gazed at him thoughtfully. By the fire's light, she could see his burnished skin, the powerful muscles of his arms, his bare chest rising and falling. His black hair looked almost red in the light of the flames, and his lips were quirked as though he were laughing at himself for some reason.

"Talon?"

"Mmmm?"

"I liked your kisses."

He lowered his arm from across his eyes and gave her the full force of his obsidian gaze. "Thank you, Summer. I liked yours also. Perhaps we could do it again. Soon."

She smiled. "Perhaps."

He smiled too, that full grin of white teeth that always dazzled her. "Good night, Summer."

She felt oddly breathless. "Good night, Talon." Summer lay back down.

But for all his readiness to sleep, sleep would not come. Talon finally got up, and stared down at the woman who caused him such physical torment.

She, alas, slept soundly.

He supposed that was as it should be. But he fervently hoped that the next time he touched her, she would let him take more than her sweet kisses.

Chapter Twenty-Seven

"I will weave some baskets," Summer announced the next morning after she and Talon had eaten a meal of fish. Her eyes strayed to Talon's broad back as he bent over the fire, adding wood. She wanted to see his reaction. Not once since her capture had she offered to do any kind of work.

Talon swung around and his eyes met hers. "That would be good. We could use baskets."

She added tentatively, "And some of the hides you brought back should be tanned. Those beaver skins would make a warm bedrobe." She blushed suddenly. Why was she thinking about bedrobes?

Talon's grin flashed.

He left her then, heading toward the river

and singing softly to himself as he went.

Summer hurried after him. "Wait! I will come with you. I must pick some of the bullrush leaves for weaving."

He stopped and waited for her to catch up with him. "Be sure to pick as many as you need," he advised. "We will be moving camp in a few days."

She nodded. Her family, too, had moved often. Only in winter had they stayed in one place: the caves where they always wintered. The rest of the year, the Caribou People kept on the move in their constant quest for food. In the spring, they went to the best fishing spots on the river to catch the spring salmon. In the summer they walked to the camas fields to pick camas bulbs. Autumn found them picking pinyon nuts and gathering seeds, or hunting the huge bison whose meat could feed them through the winter. Sometimes the Caribou People moved every few days, if the animals were few and the snares empty.

Summer and Talon arrived at the river. Taking off her moccasins, she waded into the water. Bullrushes grew thickly in the sluggish, shallow waters near the bank. Summer picked several long green stalks. Spearhead-shaped tule leaves floated on the water and she followed the stems down with her hand until she could feel the long tubers rooted in the mud. She pulled up the tubers. Tule tubers were flavorful and sweet when roasted.

Talon retrieved his spear from where he had left it the night before. He wore a quiet smile as he watched Summer. She knew he was watching her, but she felt more comfortable with him now. Once she even looked up and smiled.

"Do you swim?" he asked. He knew the answer to his question. Memories of when he had seen her naked in the pool in the green glade came back to him.

She nodded. "I like to swim."

He turned away, feeling suddenly guilty, as if she might know he had spied upon her. He shed his clothes and walked into the water.

Summer stared at his well-muscled back and firm buttocks. She swallowed. When the water was up to his waist in the slow moving current, he swung around, calling, "Come in and swim with me."

Mutely, she shook her head. His broad brown chest, his muscular arms, entranced her. He dipped his head in the water and then tossed his head so that his wet hair hung down his back.

Summer's grip on the bullrush stalks tightened. "I—I dare not. I must take these leaves back to camp . . ."

"Set aside the leaves. Come and swim." Talon dived under the water, then came up for air. He splashed around, kicking and swimming and churning the water with powerful strokes. Then he called again, "Come in, Summer. Come into the river and swim!"

She just stood there, mouth agape, and he

started to wade out of the water toward her. When the water lapped at the black hair of his groin, Summer gasped and fled. "The—the leaves must be dried before I can weave them," she cried over her shoulder.

Her heart was pounding wildly by the time she reached camp. She glanced down, to see that she had clutched the muddy tubers so tightly that her soft deerskin dress was covered with brown mud. She threw the rushes and tubers to the ground and darted around the clearing in an agony of indecision. Now she knew how a doe must feel when pursued by a rutting buck.

She wrung her hands. Talon had been naked. *Naked!* Oh, what was she to do? She glanced in the direction of the river, but she could not see him now because of the willows and cottonwoods. What should she do?

Heart pounding, she ran to the edge of the clearing. Should she run into the forest? If she did, would he come after her? Naked?

Calm yourself, she scolded. *He is but a man. Yes, he is naked, but you have seen naked men before. You have seen hunters go naked when they did not want the deer to pick up their scent.*

Yes, Summer had seen men naked on occasion. But it was not the same, she wailed to herself. Talon naked was very different than any other man naked!

Talon, dressed in his tunic and high moccasins, soon returned to camp. She eyed him warily, poised to run.

He eyed her as well. Then he smiled. "I like to swim, too."

Her heart palpitated at that white grin.

"Perhaps next time you will swim with me."

Summer felt her knees grow weak. Visions of them both naked swirled around in her head. "Oh, no!" she gasped. "I could never do that!"

He stared at her in surprise. Then he shrugged. "Very well."

Disappointment filled her that he had accepted her statement so readily. Then she raised her chin. "I am not accustomed to swimming with naked men."

Talon turned away at that and it sounded to Summer as though he choked a little. "I had forgotten," he said at last, "that Caribou women are so innocent."

"Yes, we are! My aunt and uncle were very careful to keep young men away from Blizzard and me."

"Until it came time to give you away to the Saber-Tooths!"

She flushed. She had no answer for that. Although she did not intend to defend her aunt and uncle against Talon's accusations, she ventured, "They allowed you to visit with Blizzard when you came to do bride-service for her." Suddenly Summer was curious. "Did—did you swim naked with Blizzard?" she blurted.

Talon raised an eyebrow. "So inquisitive, Summer!" His grin flashed. "No."

She sagged in relief, then quickly straightened

again and tossed her head. "It means nothing to me if you swam together," she lied.

He shook his head. "Your aunt and uncle guarded their precious daughter most closely, I assure you."

Then perhaps he did not mate with her either, thought Summer.

"But a year is a long time for a man to wait for an attractive woman he thinks he is going to marry," Talon said as though he had read her thoughts.

He stalked over to Summer and halted when his bare chest touched her clothed one. His black eyes flashed as he stared down at her. "I will not wait long for a woman again, especially not for a Caribou woman. Heed my warning, Summer."

She glared up at him, but the memory of his burning kisses last night assaulted her. She wanted to run away, but she stood her ground. "I—I am not afraid of you, Talon."

"No? Perhaps you should be." He stroked her cheek with the backs of his fingers.

Shivers tickled her spine. Then he bent down and kissed her, his lips softly inviting her to kiss him back. She leaned against him, putting her hands on his shoulders, feeling the heat of his skin. She drew him closer. His arms wrapped around her and she clung to him.

When the kiss ended, he shook his head and said, "No, you have nothing to fear from me, Summer. It is I who should fear you."

She stared into his eyes, dazed and struggling to understand his meaning. "Oh, Talon," she murmured, still caught up in the power of his kisses, the scent of him, the feel of his skin under her hands. "I would never hurt you as Blizzard did. I—"

He pulled away from her. "Understand this," he snarled. "Blizzard did not have my heart. She was to be my wife, true, but I had no feeling for her, no understanding of her as a woman. I did not care for her." He glared at Summer. "When she was given to the Saber-Tooth, I knew that she wanted him, not me. It was the public humiliation, the laughter at me, the breaking of a promise by people I had come to love and respect for which I seek revenge, not for some supposed hurt delivered by your cousin's traitorous hand." Talon's broad chest heaved with the passion of his words. "Nor do I care for you," he growled.

A pain, long and deep like that from a knife stroke, plunged through Summer. He did not care for her? He really had stolen her only for revenge? His kisses. . . . She touched her lips. She had been a fool to think his kisses meant anything more than physical pleasure.

With a little cry, she ran from him, but stopped for a heartbeat at the edge of the clearing. Then with a sob, she raced into the forest, disappearing from his view.

Talon watched her go, his lying words echoing in his brain. He must fight this, he thought.

He must fight the tender feelings creeping into his heart, feelings that licked at the cold rock of his heart like flames of a fire. But he knew what rock did when heated by fire: it shattered.

He could not allow this woman to mean anything to him! If he did, his revenge would be for naught. Because then she, and her traitorous people, the Caribou, would have won again. And this time, the stakes were higher than mere public humiliation or the breaking of a promise. This time it was his very soul that might be stolen.

Talon glared into the forest where she had disappeared. He would go after her. Danger lurked in the forest. But when he brought her back, he would not love her. He would use her body, a right he considered he held as her husband, but he would not give her his heart, something he had come perilously close to doing this very morning.

He strapped on his atlatl, grabbed a dart and picked up his two spears. With a low growl he went after her.

Chapter Twenty-Eight

Heedless of direction, Summer ran. She kept her arms up to protect her face from the scrape of low branches as she churned through the woods. She must get away from him, she must!

She plunged on, single-minded, heedless of anything but her need to escape Talon. Anger drove her legs until they ached. Her breath came in great gasps and yet still she ran. When she thought she could run no more, humiliation forced her onward. When she finally could not take another step without her legs buckling, she whirled and leaned against a tree for support. Her eyes strained, searching desperately for any sight of him. Her body throbbed, her legs trembled. The hoarse sound of her desperate breathing echoed in her own ears.

Gradually her breathing calmed and the forest noises came to her—the twittering of birds, the scurry of a mouse, the rustling of a leaf as a snake slithered past. Her heart slowed its drumming and she glanced around. She did not hear his pursuing footsteps. Had she eluded him? Scarcely able to believe her good fortune, she peered through the trees, searching for some sign of him.

Nothing.

Now that Summer had time to survey her surroundings, she found herself wishing uneasily that she had been more alert to where she ran. None of the trees looked familiar. There was no landmark to tell her she had passed this way before. She surveyed the trees once more, hoping to spot something she recognized—a twisted tree, a trail, a rock, anything.

Nothing.

She consoled herself that at least it was daylight. Perhaps the bears and wolves and big cats would be less likely to be prowling for food. She shivered, knowing that the bears and wolves and big cats were *always* prowling for food. The thought of facing a hungry sabertooth with canines the length of her hand set her heart to pulsing frantically once more.

Summer took a deep breath. She was alone. In the woods. With no spear. As she added up the conditions, she felt a tiny frisson of fear, but tried to overcome her fright.

A tentative touch to her treasure-sack reassured her. She had put in it two fire-making rocks, flint and iron pyrite, that she could strike together to start a spark; she could gather dry moss to make a fire to keep the predators at bay.

But a fire would also alert Talon to where she was.

Perhaps a stick then. Summer picked up a stout branch from the forest floor and hefted it in her hands. Yes, it would make a weapon to fight off a wolf or tiger. Not as good as a spear, but a weapon nonetheless.

She scrutinized the trees around her uneasily. Trees were little protection. Over to the west, she spied a pile of large boulders. That would make a good place to hide, she decided. If she stayed in the middle of the boulders, a sabertooth tiger could not creep up on her.

She made her way cautiously to the boulders. Tall and somewhat pointed, each was the size of a mammoth. She walked around the largest boulder, intent on finding a path to the center of the rock cluster.

Suddenly she froze.

The boulders formed a cave—a big cave. And there, slumbering in the doorway, was a giant brown short-faced bear. Its stout nose rested on its huge forepaws as it snored and its tiny eyes were closed. The lair smelled of rotting food the animal had scavenged. The odor made Summer want to gag.

In horror, Summer started to back away. She knew that short-faced bears had unpredictable dispositions, possessed great strength and could run as fast as a man. One swipe from this one's deadly claws and she would join the Great Spirit in His encampment behind the setting sun.

As she backed away, Summer stumbled over a root and fell. The noise of her movements alerted the huge bear. Waking, it spied her instantly. With a roar it got to its feet, then rose on its hind legs.

The shaggy beast towered over her. Pink mouth agape, its sharp yellow teeth held her gaze with a sickening fascination.

Panic surged through Summer and she whimpered, staring fixedly as the glowering bear took a step towards her. Fear spurted an acrid taste on her tongue. Unable to move, she watched helplessly as the beast came on. Her legs felt as though they were made of wood and she could not move.

"Great Spirit help me," she moaned.

Somehow she got the strength to scramble to her feet. Once upright, she backed away from the huge oncoming animal. Summer had lost the stout stick and had no weapon now. But no stick could help her against the huge beast menacing her.

The bear dropped to all fours and lumbered toward her. She whirled and fled. She could hear him padding after her, breaking branches in his path.

Frantic, not knowing what to do, Summer kept her head down and ran. Then a lightning thought went through her brain. She zig-zagged to the east. A large tree with low branches stood in her path, and with a desperate leap, she grasped the lowest branches and scrambled up. She reached for the next branch, then heaved herself to the next branch and brought her feet up under her to the branch just below. She could hear the bear right behind her.

A whistling sound told Summer she had barely missed being clawed by a powerful paw. She reached for another branch and hoisted herself up. A horrible growl reached her ears. She dared not look down, only up.

The bear's next swipe tore off a branch as thick as her wrist.

Branch by branch, Summer climbed out of its deadly reach. When she was far higher than the bear's head, she stopped climbing. Clutching tightly to a branch, she peered down. The bear, enraged at losing its prey, tore up the roots of a small tree next to the one she perched on and tossed it aside. Summer shuddered.

She gasped, awestruck, as the bear tore up three more trees in frustrated fury. Finally, realizing that the bear could not reach her, Summer loosened her hold and watched while the huge animal exhausted itself on the surrounding vegetation. From where she crouched, Summer could see that the bear's head was huge, its raking claws long and sharp. She had never been so close to a short-faced bear before.

At last, Summer's breathing became even. *You are safe*, her mind kept telling her over and over. *You are safe!*

Then the bear started to climb her tree.

Chapter Twenty-Nine

He would give Summer some time to run, thought Talon as he prowled through the forest, following the trail of broken twigs and flattened grass his prey had left behind her. After she wore herself out, she would be tired and docile and return unprotesting to camp.

Breaking into a trot, he saw that she was running blindly. What had he said to upset her so much?

He did not like to think upon her pain, but it was very unusual for a woman to run blindly into a forest. Guilt nagged at him, but he squelched it. She was his mate now; he could say what he wanted to her, even lie to her.

Increasing his pace, Talon was uneasy to see she was heading to a part of the forest he had not visited before. He stopped and sniffed the air. Often he could smell a saber-tooth before he saw one. Good—no such predator was on her trail.

A huge ground sloth moved into a thicket of alder trees. Hunters rejoiced when they happened upon one of the slow-moving animals. Sloths were easy prey and yielded enough meat for several days. But today Talon let it go by unharmed. He was on a different kind of hunt.

Tirelessly, he trotted on.

He found the tree she had leaned against when she had rested for awhile. He touched the bark. Little bits of it had been scraped off here and there by her dress. He smiled to himself. He had chosen a strong mate. Summer had run a goodly distance. But now he was tired of the hunt. Now he would close in.

A low growl reached his ears, and Talon raised his head in alarm. A saber-tooth? A lion? No, not a saber-tooth. And lions frequented only the grasslands, not the forests. Another growl issued forth. He frowned and swung in that direction, slinking noiselessly, careful to use the trees for cover. He wanted no surprises.

Whatever creature it was, it was making so much noise that it did not hear Talon's approach. A shiver of alarm went through him. The hairs on the back of his neck rose when he saw a giant short-faced bear tearing up trees, pulling them out by their roots and tossing them aside. It was the biggest Talon had ever seen. He liked to avoid short-faced bears when he could. They were short-tempered brutes, unpredictable and fast. Their claws were like daggers, and slow poisoning set in when a man was swiped by one of their paws.

Talon had heard of a hunter once who had been mauled by such a bear. So torn and bloodied had he been after the attack that though he had lived another day, the man's wife tearfully begged his brothers to kill him and save him further agony. The brothers had complied.

Talon was about to slink away, content to leave the bear to its strange rage, when a flash of brown in a tall tree caught his eye.

He peered at the tree, trying to determine if the movement came from a perched hawk, or perhaps a saber-tooth.

Then his blood ran as cold as glacier ice. It was Summer!

The bear started to climb the tree, and Talon reached for his atlatl and dart. He did not want to take a chance on wounding the animal. A wounded short-faced bear was even more dangerous. His only hope was to slay it swiftly.

Taking careful aim at the thick fur on the back of the huge animal's neck, he launched the dart. At that moment, the bear moved his head to glare up at Summer and the dart missed, sticking fast into the bark of the tree. The bear resumed its slow climb.

Talon's hand tightened on his spear. Although he had two spears with him, neither one was sufficient to kill this brute. Yet if he did not do something, the bear would kill Summer.

Without further thought, Talon ran up and thrust his spear at the animal's hindquarters. It gave a piercing shriek and swung around. It sniffed the air, its huge head weaving back and forth.

The bear backed down the tree. It had found new prey.

"Talon!" Summer screamed. "Run!"

The bear advanced upon Talon, heedless of the woman's cry. Talon crouched, legs planted firmly, spear pointing at the beast's neck.

The short-faced bear reared up. It towered over Talon and kept advancing.

Talon ran in and threw his first spear at the beast's mouth. The bear caught the spear in his teeth, shook his great head and snapped the spear handle in two. It spat out the spear and kept walking steadily towards Talon.

Talon's last spear was in his hand. Where to hit the beast? The heart was a good spot. The neck, too.

Talon was now only a man's length away from those deadly claws. A calmness settled over him. He had one more chance with his spear.

He waited until the bear came within clawing distance. Then he cast the spear, putting every bit of his strength into the throw. The spear hurtled through the air, the sharp blade slicing into the bear's eye. The beast howled in agony.

"Talon!"

Somehow, Summer had climbed down the tree and pried the dart out of the soft wood. "Here is your dart!"

The bear was howling and pulling at the spear, trying to dislodge the weapon from its eye. Talon took the dart from Summer and slammed it into the atlatl. He swung around just as the bear tossed the second spear aside. Blinded and enraged, the bear charged.

Talon hurled the dart and it slammed into the animal's neck up to the handle. The bear fell to the ground, rolling and roaring.

Talon grabbed Summer's hand and ran, heading for the boulders. "No!" she cried. "He lives there! A mate—"

She did not have to say anymore. Talon understood. The short-faced bear might have a mate waiting at the cave, though surely a mate would have been summoned by all the roaring the beast had done. Still, he could take no chances.

"Come this way!"

They raced through the forest until they could no longer hear the furious bear's roars.

"Enough. I can go no further!" Summer sank to the forest floor.

Panting, he saw that she was pale and worn. She tried to get up, but her legs collapsed under her. He knew she spoke the truth.

He listened. "The bear is dead," said Talon. "I am certain of it."

She shuddered. "I will dream of this for many nights." Her lips trembled. Summer held up her hand and he saw that her hand trembled too.

"I must go back for my spear." Talon could not walk through the forest with no weapons.

Her pale yellow eyes met his. She said, "Go. I will wait here."

He squatted down beside her. "I do not want to leave you alone."

Summer glanced at him shyly and brought out her treasure-sack. "I will start a fire," she said. "I will be safe."

She was still trembling, and Talon wondered what those brave words cost her. He touched her head, the pale blonde hair soft under his hand. "I will come back for you. I will not be gone long." In truth, his legs were still quaking and he did not know if he could still run. But he was glad to be alive, glad Summer was alive.

He embraced her and kissed the top of her head. "I will return," he said. "You will see."

She nodded. Her yellow eyes met his and he saw them shimmer. "I—you almost died— thank you—" Her voice broke and he hugged her to him.

"Shhh. You are safe. I am safe. We will survive," he murmured.

She clung to him and her lips sought his.

Talon tore himself away. If he kissed her again, he would never be able to go and get his weapons. With a wave, he strode off, knowing that her wide yellow eyes followed him.

He returned swiftly, fully armed. Summer was feeding moss to the fire. She looked up at him and smiled.

Talon lowered his weapons to the ground and grinned back at her. He was home.

Chapter Thirty

"I brought the head," said Talon. He deposited the short-faced bear's huge head on the ground. Attached to the head was the pelt. "This will make a warm winter cloak."

"For the Bear People perhaps," Summer joked. "Not for any of the Wolf People."

Talon cut out the bear's tongue and deposited the liver which he had also carried back with him. "The wolves were eating the carcass when I returned to get my spears," he said, pointing to some ragged edges on the skin. "They had torn open the stomach and were feasting on the intestines."

Summer stared at him. "How did you dare to take this away from them? Wolves are fierce and protective."

Talon eyed her. "Yes, they are."

Summer flushed. If Talon had not been fierce and protective, she would not be alive. He emulated the wolves very well.

She busied herself with putting more twigs on the fire. The liver they could eat raw, but the tongue tasted better roasted. She placed the meat on a stick to cook. "You did not tell me how the wolves let you take their food."

He shrugged. "I know them. They are my friends."

When he offered nothing else, Summer accepted that he would say no more about it. But she wondered at a man who could take away the head, skin and liver of a kill that wolves were feasting upon. Such a man was rare indeed. "Did you know those wolves when you came to my people?"

"No."

She sliced through the liver and handed him a chunk of the still warm meat. They ate in silence, and Summer felt her body absorb the nourishment she needed from the meat. Running had depleted her, as had climbing the tree when the bear had chased her. She shuddered as she looked at the giant bearskin stretched out beside the fire. With a tentative finger, she touched one of the long yellow canine teeth.

"I will make you a necklace," she offered and smiled at Talon.

"Thank you." His eyes dropped to her woman's neckcloth. "Perhaps you should wear the necklace. Then you would not have to wear that saber-tooth design at your neck."

She fingered the soft neckcloth. "Does it bother you, Talon?"

"Yes."

Summer wanted to take off the neckcloth then and there, but decided against it. Talon must not think he had so much sway over her. She lowered her hand and smiled. "You have earned the right to wear those teeth, not I."

She busied herself with the fire. When it was crackling, she sat down and said, "I would like to know about you, Talon."

His face was impassive, but his eyes lingered on the offending saber-tooth design. "You already know about me."

The conversation was not going well, Summer decided. "I will tan the bear hide," she said brightly. "The fur is warm and thick."

She thought he had not heard her. Just as she was about to repeat her offer, he said gruffly, "I give it to you as a gift, Summer. You may sleep under it."

She swallowed as a sudden image of sleeping under the bearskin with him crept into her mind. There was an awkward silence.

Thinking of her naked under the bearskin made Talon's body stir. He stood up and stretched. "I will make a shelter for us."

A little shiver ran through her, but she nodded and pretended to feed the fire while she secretly watched him. He gathered branches and laid

261

them in a half-moon shape, big enough for two or three people to fit in. He built up the walls by interweaving branches. Then he placed more branches on the roof to complete the brush shelter.

She watched his swift, economical movements. The man was resourceful as well as brave, she thought proudly. Summer thought of how he had saved her from the short-faced bear and her heart warmed towards him. "Talon?" she said softly.

"Hmm?" His back was to her as he continued to lace branches to form the roof of the abode.

"Thank you again for rescuing me. I do not know what I would have done—That bear—"

He shrugged. "It is good you pried the atlatl dart loose from the tree." He turned and grinned at her. "Thank *you* for that, Summer."

She flushed.

"I chose my mate well," he added.

She dropped her glance to the fire, not knowing what to say and feeling flustered. She liked his words.

Talon carried pine boughs into the structure and laid them on the floor. Summer inhaled the sharp pine scent. "It is ready," he announced with a gesture at the dwelling.

"For what?" But her pounding heart told her the answer.

"Enter," he invited.

"There are no robes," she protested. "We will be cold."

"No, Wolf Eyes, we will not be cold." His slash of a grin appeared. "I will keep you warm."

Summer glanced around at the forest surrounding them, as though she considered running again. Then she looked at the bearskin. He had saved her from the bear. Slowly she rose to her feet. She would not run into the forest this night. She knew in her heart she would not run into the forest any night, for she knew now she wanted Talon. She had wanted him for a long time: when he had done brideservice for her cousin; when he had given meat to her starving people; when he had taught her to hunt; when he had stolen her. Yes, if she was truly honest with herself, she had wanted and desired him ever since she had first seen him.

She smiled up at him when she entered the dwelling.

"You can have the bearskin to keep you warm this night," he told her. "But I am certain I can warm you."

"You warm me, Talon, with just one glance."

"I can do more than that."

He spread out the bear hide over the fragrant boughs so that only the soft fur would touch her skin. She sank down on it and he followed her down, his eyes intense. "Let me show you," he whispered. "Let me show you how good it can be between a man and a woman."

"Yes." Her heart pounding, Summer kept her gaze on his.

Never taking his obsidian eyes off hers, Talon shed his clothes. Then he reached for her. Gently he took off her woman's neckcloth and laid it aside. He lifted the treasure sack over her head. "I am not even looking at it," he assured her as he placed the small sack carefully atop the neckcloth.

"It is all right," she answered. "You have given me the gift of meat the shaman ordered."

"So I have." He reached for her dress and helped her take it off. When she sat before him naked, she heard his breath hiss.

"You are so beautiful, Summer!"

She smiled tremulously. He was beautiful to her eyes too, with his broad chest, his black hair, his intent gaze.

He pulled her against him and she could feel the pounding of his heart against her breasts. When he began kissing her, she thought she would melt like a snowfall into a fire.

"Oh, Talon," she murmured. "What you do to me!"

"What do I do to you?" He nibbled at her ear and then his lips kissed their way down her neck.

She could not speak.

"What do I do?" he prodded.

Now he was—oh, he was licking her skin! "That feels wonderful . . ." she moaned.

"You like that? I can do more . . ." And he did things with his lips she had not even dreamed about. But from now on she would, oh, how she would.

When he was done kissing her, she was as limp as a sleepy bird and as slow moving as a sloth. His hand moved to the very center of her being and he touched her gently, carefully. She felt herself explode. "Talon!" she cried, clutching him. "What—? Ahhhhhh. . . ." A sweet feeling enveloped her, starting where he touched her and swiftly consuming her body.

He soothed her when the spasms ceased. She blinked up at him with lazy eyelids. "Talon." In that one word, his name, was all the love she could not tell him of.

He kissed her and she closed her eyes, unable to bear the sweetness of it. "Summer," he murmured, "I must do this. It may hurt, but I will try to be gentle."

He fit himself to her then and she felt a sharp pang as he surged into her.

"Oh!" she cried out.

He held her then, and she felt their hearts pounding in unison. "Shhh," he soothed. "The pain will be gone soon." He kissed her face, her neck, her breasts. . . .

"Oh, Summer, I cannot—I cannot—it has been too long—" He pushed against her and she felt herself give way to him. He thrust several times inside her. She marveled at his

265

strength, at the feel of him. She gloried in his possession of her.

"Ah, Summer!" he groaned once more before collapsing on top of her as he spent himself in her. Exhausted, he rolled to one side, pulling her with him. "You—are—so—beautiful," he gasped.

She watched him languidly. She felt warm and light all over. She felt—though he had not said the word—loved.

When he opened his dark eyes she smiled at him. She would not tell him just yet of the new feeling creeping into her heart for him. But it was there, oh, yes, it was.

Chapter Thirty-One

The next morning, they made love again. Summer was shy at first, but Talon was gentle and she soon relaxed. Afterwards they lay, spent, in each other's arms.

When they got up, Summer stirred the glowing embers of last night's fire and then picked some berries. They breakfasted on the berries, Summer giving him little sidelong glances. She said, "Tell me more about yourself, Talon." It was important to her to know everything about this man to whom she had given her body and yes, her heart.

He was sitting by the fire and glanced over at her, suddenly wary. "There is nothing more to tell."

Summer smiled and walked over to him. She

squatted down in front of him until their eyes were level. "I want to know all about you," she murmured. "I want to know what your life was like before you joined my people."

Her smile melted something hard inside him. He kissed the tip of her nose. "Truly there is not much to tell. As you know, my mother is dead, my father too." Talon kissed her lips. They clung to each other. "Ah, Summer . . ."

They soon found themselves atop the bearskin again, naked. The morning passed pleasantly in making love. Finally Summer snuggled against him and said, "This is all so new to me." Her face crimsoned as she caught sight of her naked skin touching his. She glanced away.

Talon smiled a lazy smile. "Tell me something about yourself, Summer."

She saw that he truly wanted to know about her. "My mother is dead, my father too. They were slain in a mammoth hunting accident. The wounded animal trampled them before it died. I was but a child and so I was taken to live in the tent of Uncle Antler, my mother's brother, and Auntie Birdsong, his wife."

Talon said nothing. She knew how he felt about her aunt and uncle.

Summer regarded him out of solemn yellow eyes. "How did *your* father die?"

"Hunting. Went out hunting one day and never returned."

"I remember when your mother died."

Talon sighed. "Do we have to talk about this?"

"Not if you do not wish to." But curiosity prodded her on. "Why is it that you do not resemble any of the other Fox people? They are all small and skinny and have reddish hair and green eyes whereas you. . . ." Her eyes ran over his strong naked body and she blushed. Breathless, she continued, "Whereas you are big and strong and your eyes are so dark that I could fall into them and your hair is so long and black . . ." She had to stop, she was blushing so hard.

"My appearance does differ from the Fox People," Talon conceded, then hesitated, feeling himself being dragged into territory he would rather not enter. "Snare, my mother, was not the woman who birthed me, though I considered her to be my mother in every way," he said at last. "She was always kind to me and loved me." He paused. "Thank you for feeding her when she was ill and dying."

Summer stared at him in surprise. "How did you learn that I fed her?"

"She told me. I visited her the night she died."

Summer felt sad for him. "I—I knew she was your mother. I wanted to help her . . ."

"You did, Summer." He kissed her.

"Were you, too, given to your mother's relatives to raise?" she asked. "It is very surprising that such a thing should happen to both of us."

He shook his head. "No, it did not happen that way. Snare had no brothers or sisters."

Talon was silent for such a long while that Summer thought he had forgotten what they were speaking of.

Finally he spoke. "She claimed to have found me in the forest."

Summer stared at him. "She found you? In the forest? That is odd . . ."

"I never asked her about it, but now and then she would say something. Snare told me she found me when I was but a babe. I was alone, crying, near a small pond in a forest. A saber-tooth tiger came down to drink and was just sneaking up on me when she scared it away." He gave her a wry glance. "It seems saber-tooths have dogged me all my life."

Summer felt bewildered. "How strange," she mused. "You were all alone in the forest. . . ."

Talon stared at the brush roof above his head. It *was* a strange story. He himself had always thought so.

"I wonder what happened to your mother, your birth mother?"

Talon shrugged. "Perhaps she had been killed by the saber-tooth."

"If that was so, would not Snare have seen her body?"

Talon's face hardened. "Summer," he said softly, "I am being as kind as I can to the woman who birthed me. It has occurred to me that she did not want me."

There, he had said it. It was something he had always suspected.

Summer was silent for awhile. "Do you think she just went away and left you in the forest to die?"

He shrugged. "It is possible. Such things have happened before to babies who were not wanted."

Summer regarded him sadly. "I did not intend to bring up hurtful memories," she murmured. "I just wanted to know you better now that we have—made love."

Talon's eyes roved over her. Summer blushed, and hot memories of what had passed between them rose in her mind.

"I liked last night. And this morning. Did you?"

She nodded briefly, afraid to do more.

"Summer, is it so bad, being with me?"

There was a yearning note in his voice that surprised her. "If you had wanted me for myself," she said, "perhaps I could bear it. But to know that I am but a means of your revenge does rankle."

He regarded her, his eyes hard. "I will not let you go. Not after last night and this morning when you truly became my wife."

He placed a hand over her breast. She stared down at the dark hand, wondering what might have been between them had he not stolen her. To be his wife had once been her secret fantasy, but now it was as though she was a prize. Summer felt like a caribou doe caught in a hidden pit.

When Talon removed his hand, she got up and slipped into her dress, careful not to look at him.

The silence between them for the rest of the morning was an uneasy one.

Summer gave one last look over her shoulder at the brush dwelling. Then they set out into the forest. She carried the bear hide and skull and they both walked without speaking. Finally they reached the Wolves' camp.

When the sun was low in the sky, Blue Feather returned to camp. By nightfall, Weasel and Sloth had also straggled in and Summer realized there would be no privacy for her and Talon to continue their talk.

The evening meal of horse was consumed in silence. Blue Feather had found a colt wandering down by the river and he had killed it. There were two kinds of horse roaming the land, large and small, and each was a separate tribe and did not mix with the other. Summer seldom ate horse. Her people did not have occasion to hunt the swift animal. Their favorite meat was caribou, hence their name, the Caribou People. She wondered if she would ever see her aunt and uncle and the others again.

Her eyes sought out Talon, the cause of this mess she was in. He was listening to Blue Feather describe his hunt of the colt and so she had a chance to study him when he was not aware of her.

In repose, relaxed and talking with his friends, she could see the strength in his face. And it must have taken great strength, she mused, to survive the banishment time, to gather men about him, to start anew. He bore little resemblance to the young man who had first come to the Caribou camp.

Talon turned suddenly to meet her gaze. Summer glanced away, pretending she had not been watching him, but he was not fooled. He stared at her until she once more met his eyes and without words he promised, "Wait until we are alone in our bedrobes once more."

Summer caught his meaning. She flushed and stood up. She walked to the edge of the clearing, hoping he watched the sway of her hips.

"Hunh, time to leave," said Blue Feather pointedly to the others. "Hunting beckons us once again!"

Weasel and Sloth groaned but dutifully gathered up their weapons and tent skins. In embarrassed silence, Summer watched the three men file off into the forest.

Talon saw she was hesitant to return to the fire once the Wolves had disappeared into the forest. "Come," he insisted, patting the ground beside where he sat.

She walked over to him. "Do they not resent me?"

Talon shook his head and grinned. "I would do the same for them."

"Will you?"

"Will I what?"

"Will you give them privacy with their women?"

"If we find any women for them, I will."

"You make it sound like a hunt," she objected, as she sat down beside him.

"It is."

Living in close confines with the other members of her Caribou people, especially in the winter, had given Summer a keen awareness of when people needed privacy. Obviously Talon's Wolves were also willing to acknowledge when each of them needed to be alone, or with a mate.

"Perhaps they should not have left," she said slyly.

"What do you mean?"

"I do not expect anything to happen between us this night."

"I do."

"You would."

He grinned.

In truth, Summer's heart was beating faster just thinking of the two of them naked. Her face flushed and she scolded herself to stop such thoughts, but it did not work.

She rose, desperate to stop this hunger for him. Yet when had she not wanted him? she asked herself. She knew the answer very well. She had wanted Talon ever since he had first come to woo her cousin.

"Where are you going?" He, too, rose.

"I want to walk this evening," she said brightly. "Let us walk by the river."

He nodded, threw a branch on the fire and picked up his spear. They walked in silence along the path to the water. When they came to the log where they had seen the ants before, Summer squatted down for a better look. The ants were still moving sawdust into a pile. "They are very busy," she murmured. "I wonder when they sleep."

Talon smiled at her, not caring when the ants slept or if they were dead or busily chewing up the other side of the log. He was happy to be with her here, in the cool evening air—with this woman he had won: his wife.

They stayed by the log for awhile, Summer watching the ants, Talon watching her and congratulating himself on his good fortune in selecting this lovely woman for a mate.

At last, Summer had looked her fill and they continued their stroll to the water's edge. Birds called out to warn of their presence. Summer smiled at Talon and pulled off one of her moccasins. She closed her eyes in bliss as she dipped her big toe in the water.

Blue Feather's warning came back to Talon. *Women think a man's heart is good for one thing and one thing only: to stomp on with their dainty little moccasins.* Talon smiled to himself. Summer would not stomp on his heart. He would not let her. Oh, he could make love to her, and appreciate her beauty, but give her his heart? No. It was made of rock and could not be moved.

He smiled at her when she opened her eyes and caught him staring.

"I like to swim," she said simply.

"I know," he answered, again remembering the day he had watched her at the pool in the glade. He no longer felt even a quiver of guilt.

Summer looked surprised, but shrugged it off. She started to peel her dress off. He gaped at her, wondering at this new brazenness, but when he saw her wade into the water, he laid down his spear, undressed, and quickly followed her.

They splashed in the river for some time. The placid surface of the water was warm from the day's heat and felt wonderful as they frolicked and played. Once Talon picked her up in his arms and threw her into the deeper water. Summer laughed as she went under and came up sputtering. He dragged her into the shallows, and then she tried to shove him under. He let her, but he stayed under a long time and Summer began to worry. Then suddenly he surged up beneath her and flung her across the water. She landed with a noisy splash and they laughed together.

Their play created a new intimacy between them, one that Summer became aware of as they were walking back to camp, hand in hand. For a moment she wanted to pull her hand free of his, but she squelched the fear. She wanted him. Why should she deny that she was eager to repeat their lovemaking?

They retired to their robes under his lean-to. And this time when Talon took her in his arms, it felt right and good. They made love and fell asleep clasping each other close.

Summer awoke in the morning looking into his obsidian eyes. Talon kissed her softly and entered her slowly. She arched under him, feeling the strength of him. Together they cried out their ecstasy. When they lay sated, and Talon was falling asleep once more, Summer kissed him awake. "Time to get up," she said.

He yawned and pulled her closer. "Let us pretend we are lazy, sleepy sloths," he said. "Let us lie abed a little longer."

She laughed and rubbed his nose with hers in delight. "Once I daydreamed that you would want to lie with me like this, that you would want to do nothing but kiss me and kiss me and never get up to hunt."

He smiled drowsily, eyes closed. "I like that daydream."

She cuddled closer to him. "Talon?"

"Hmmm?" He seemed to be drifting off to sleep.

"Why me? Was it truly because there were no other Caribou maidens for you to steal?"

His eyes opened and he stared at the hide roof of the lean-to. Then he turned his face to hers and black eyes stared into yellow. He reached for her and kissed her mouth ruthlessly. "I have

277

no soft, sweet words for you, Summer, sweet words that a woman wants to hear. Do not ask them of me."

But protecting his heart of rock was proving more difficult than Talon had anticipated. He must always be on guard. Especially when the woman was crying softly.

Chapter Thirty-Two

Summer dragged herself around the camp the rest of the morning. She should never have asked him, she thought morosely, never pushed him to say that she meant anything more to him than a Caribou doe caught in a pit he had dug. She should have taken his kisses and been satisfied. Blizzard would have.

At the thought of her cousin, Summer became even more morose, if possible. Blizzard would not have been so inept at getting a man to declare his love for her. Why, the Saber-Tooth, Rides Their Backs, had been unable to keep his eyes—or his hands—off her. Except when they departed for Saber-Tooth territory, of course. Then, he had marched her off at the point of a spear, Blizzard plainly unwilling.

She wondered how her cousin fared now and whom she had brow-beaten into doing her sewing. Perhaps Blue Camas.

Summer sighed. How she missed Blue Camas! How she would love to see her friend again, if only for a short while. She even missed Auntie Birdsong. Tough old woman that she was, she was still like a mother to Summer, and Summer would welcome a chance to see her, too. And Uncle Antler. And Screech Owl, and Tule. And Wren, and Raw. Even the shaman. How were they all doing? She wondered sadly if they were still looking for her.

As morning waned, Summer grew sadder and sadder, thinking of her lost people. Talon noticed Summer's lowness of spirit, but he hesitated to say anything. He thought perhaps he had already said enough.

He left briefly and brought back two fat rabbits he had snared and skinned. He was a little surprised to see that Summer had not tried to run away, but then said to himself that she was at last accepting her place as his wife.

Summer prepared the rabbits and when they were cooking, the fatty juices running down and dripping into the fire, she said, "Auntie Birdsong always put special herbs on her rabbits. They always tasted so good."

She sounded so mournful that Talon could not resist asking, "Is that what is bothering you, Summer? Do you miss your Auntie?"

She glanced at him, wondering what he

would say if she told him the truth—that she did indeed miss not only her aunt but her uncle and all the other Caribous as well, and that she wanted to go home because he did not love her and never would. Her lips tightened. She would not tell him of the things dear to her heart. It would do no good.

Talon saw her expression and turned away. There was more to dealing with a wife than he had ever imagined.

He went and sat down near the fire, waiting for the meat to cook, and busied himself twisting a snare to catch birds.

While he worked on the snare, Blue Feather, Weasel and Sloth silently appeared. Talon leapt to his feet. "Welcome, friends."

Summer ignored them.

Blue Feather glanced from Summer's grim face to Talon's eager one. "Oho," he observed, "all is not well in our Wolf camp."

Summer bared her teeth at him.

Blue Feather shook his head. "Women!" he muttered. "You cannot keep them happy."

Summer swung around and turned her back on him.

Blue Feather set down his weapons and roll of skins. So did Weasel and Sloth. "Time to stay awhile. I was getting tired of setting up a new camp every night anyway."

Weasel hooted at this witticism. Sloth nodded agreement with a big grin. Talon frowned

281

at Summer before he returned to his work on the snare.

The acrid smell of burning meat tinged the air, and Summer spun around with a cry. She yanked the meat off the fire.

"Good cook, too," noted Blue Feather. "What else can she do?" He shot Talon a sly look, only to receive a warning glance in return. Blue Feather blithely ignored Talon. "My former wife never burned the meat and she was good in bed. Oho, was she!"

"Then it must have been *you* who was the problem—else why would she have left you?" Summer snarled.

Blue Feather studied her with amusement. "Good in bed, miserable out of it. Like you."

Talon lifted his head, nostrils flared in jealous warning. "How do you know that Summer is good in bed?"

Blue Feather laughed. "Just jesting." He narrowed his eyes. "But if she was not, she would not still be here in our Wolf camp, now would she?"

Talon had nothing to say to that.

Summer got to her feet, her voice shrill. "I refuse to have you discuss me like this! I am a human being and I demand that you treat me properly!"

All four men went silent at this. Three heads swung around to see Talon's reaction. "I agree with Summer," he said firmly.

Silence reigned until Blue Feather began to

tell of his latest hunting trip. He had tried to sneak up on an antelope. He soon had the men laughing about his efforts. When he described how the antelope had started to run, and how he had run after it, the other three men howled with laughter. Every hunter knew not to run down an antelope. The meat was too tough and tasteless after the animal's running juices had surged through its body.

Summer, hearing their laughter, sat down again, but she felt a little better. At least they had listened to her, and Talon had agreed with her. Perhaps there was hope for them all.

She portioned out the rabbit meat. Fortunately, the meat was only singed. With a sweet smile, she handed the most charred portion to Blue Feather. Weasel thanked her upon receiving his share, and Sloth bobbed his head.

"Tasty," said Weasel in shy way of a compliment.

Blue Feather just grunted and peeled off the charred skin.

Talon smiled. His wife was doing well. He was proud of her.

After the meal, Blue Feather took one look at the happy smile on Talon's face as he gazed at his new wife. "Back to the bush," he sighed.

Even Summer had to chuckle as the three men traipsed off into the forest once more.

Chapter Thirty-Three

The stranger had sneaked up on the Caribou camp and surprised the men sitting around the fire. Screech Owl was the first to see him and jumped to his feet, groping for his spear. The shaman rustled to his feet, calling out a chant of protection.

Antler, the headman, slowly rose, peering into the darkness. "Who goes there?" His voice shook.

"A kinsman." The filed, yellow canine teeth of the Saber-Tooth runner gleamed dully in the reflected glow of the fire as he moved silently out of the darkness.

Birdsong grunted and whispered to Tule, "He does not look like a kinsman. I tell you I find it hard to accept that we are related to those Saber-Tooth People."

Aghast, Tule reproached, "Birdsong! How can you speak so? They are our daughters' people now. Do not say such things. Of course they are our people!"

Birdsong muttered under her breath and focused on her weaving, a task her fingers knew how to do without any help from her brain.

"Welcome," Antler was assuring the runner.

Nobody recognized him, but he was dressed in the Saber-Tooth way, with black spots on his clothes and his single thick braid hanging down the left side of his face. And of course, should there be any doubt, there were the filed canines. Oh yes, he was a Saber-Tooth.

"Food," demanded Antler, gesturing at the newcomer. "Wife! Bring some food to our honored guest!"

Birdsong got to her feet and shuffled over to glean some food from the remains of the evening meal. With a sly smile to herself, she shooed away the gray wolf-dog and picked up the deer rib he had been gnawing upon. Brushing off the dirt and flies, she placed the rib carefully on a wooden platter and then added two more ribs that she pried off the roasted deer carcass. Two baked camas roots joined the ribs on the platter. Then she carried this most appetizing meal over to her unwanted guest, saying, "Eat."

He grunted and squatted down to eat. She

smiled as she watched him consume the meal with gusto.

"What brings you to join us this eve?" Antler asked after Birdsong had fetched the Saber-Tooth three more ribs.

The Saber-Tooth wiped the grease from his mouth with a brawny arm. "I, Spit, bring a message from Spotted Cat. He bids me tell you that it is now time to prepare the bride."

"Bride?" Antler repeated.

Spit frowned at him. "The bride for Tuft, Spotted Cat's brave second son."

"Oh . . ." Antler glanced at Birdsong. Every single Caribou suddenly found somewhere to look other than at Spit.

"The bride—she, uh, sleeps," said Birdsong.

"Yes, she is asleep," Antler echoed nervously.

Spit regarded him with suspicion. "I trust that she will be awakened in time for the marriage ceremony." His canines gleamed.

"Oh yes, yes," Birdsong chortled.

"Spotted Cat told me to give her his personal greetings," added Spit.

"Oh, that is quite impossible!" said Birdsong.

"She visits at—at her old grandmother's cave." Antler grinned weakly.

"I thought you said she sleeps."

"Oh, we did. It is just that *where* she sleeps is at her old granny's cave."

"Take me to her."

"It is a long way away," Antler said.

287

"*Very* far away," Birdsong added.

"I wish to see her," Spit said stubbornly.

"We cannot take you to her."

"Why not?"

"She is—uh, there is some sickness. That is it, sickness! You would get sick. We do not wish our esteemed guest to get sick. Oh, no." Antler smiled at Birdsong, proud of his cleverness.

"Sickness! You dare risk Tuft's bride to sickness?" Spit looked horrified.

"Oh, no, no! It is the old granny who is sick," cried Birdsong, glowering at Antler. "Not the bride."

"How could you send her to an old woman who is sick?" Spit demanded. He seized his knife from his belt. Firelight flickered off the sharp blade. "Need I tell you what will happen if Tuft and Spotted Cat arrive for a wedding and there is no bride?"

"Oh, no!" chorused Antler and Birdsong together.

"We understand," Birdsong added miserably.

Spit glared at them. Then, knife out, he padded slowly around the circle of silent Caribou men and women crouched at the fire. He halted in front of Antler and lifted up a thick lock of the old man's gray hair.

Lowering the blade of the knife to Antler's scalp, Spit growled through gritted teeth, "If Spotted Cat finds a single lock of hair on the bride's head missing, it will mean death for you!" His lips drew back to expose his sharp canines in silent threat. "Do you understand?"

Ten Caribou heads nodded.

Spit sliced off the lock of gray hair, and Antler gave a choked cry of dismay.

Spit laughed. "Things will get much worse for you, old man, if the girl is not here when Spotted Cat and his family arrive."

"When—" Birdsong had to swallow suddenly. "When should we expect to see Spotted Cat?"

His attention diverted, Spit prowled over to her, amused when he saw Birdsong draw back. "Prepare the food, woman. Prepare food for many people. We Saber-Tooths love to celebrate!"

"When?" croaked Antler.

"Ten days."

"Ten days? But that is not long enough to—"

"Silence, woman! No one said you could speak!" Spit looked as if he wanted to use the knife again, on Birdsong's throat this time.

Birdsong fell quiet.

"What would you have us do?" Antler's eyes moved from his wife to the man holding the knife.

"Prepare the bride. Make her look beautiful. Get the proper herbs ready for burning." The Saber-Tooth smiled, showing his canines. "Get the gifts ready to give to the groom's family."

"We have the gifts," Antler assured him nervously.

"The herbs, too," added Birdsong. She fidgeted with her weaving, trying to avoid Spit's watchful eyes.

He came closer to her and jammed his knife down into its place at his belt. Then he squatted down in front of Birdsong. "Grandmother," he crooned.

She kept her eyes upon her weaving. "Yes?"

Spit whispered into her ear, and she flinched and drew back, her round face suddenly sickly pale. Spit got to his feet and laughed.

"I will leave you now, esteemed *kinsmen*," he sneered. He sauntered to the edge of the fire's light and swung around to face the cowed Caribou. "Remember. You have ten days. Ten days to prepare the food and prepare the bride!"

Then he vanished into the blackness of the night.

Silence reigned over the Caribou camp. Finally, Antler spoke. "What did he say to you, wife?"

Birdsong shook her head, not wanting to tell him.

"It is better that we know," he said sadly. "Then perhaps we can do something."

"Perhaps." Her shoulders slumped in defeat. "He said, *'Find the bride, old woman. Or I will kill you too.'* "

No one slept well in the Caribou camp that night.

Chapter Thirty-Four

Summer stared up at the lean-to roof. Though the sun had long ago risen, still she did not crawl out of her bedrobes.

"Get up," called Talon. He had just returned from the river and drops of water still clung to his broad shoulders and chest.

She turned her eyes to him. "I do not want to get up." She smiled at him.

He sat down beside her and took her hand in his. "Do you not feel well, Summer?" He pushed a lock of her yellow hair back from her forehead. When she did not answer, only continued to smile at him, he grinned. "You would consume me with your gaze, Wolf Eyes."

Summer blushed and looked away. She had not meant for him to see how much she loved him. She could never forget that he thought her only a prize; something he had wrested away from his enemies, the Caribou and the Saber-Tooths. She gave a tiny sigh. If only they had come together under different circumstances. . . .

Talon lifted her chin with one finger. "Why so forlorn?"

She kept her eyes averted and shook her head. "Not forlorn," she murmured. "Not sad. Only— thoughtful."

He let go of her chin. "That sounds like trouble to me." She heard the teasing in his voice and tried to smile.

Summer raised her eyes to his and saw the warmth in those obsidian depths. If only he loved her, she thought. If only, if only. . . . But he did not. And soon he would know how well and truly she was captured. Every time she looked at him, her heart cried out her love for him. Surely one of these days, Talon would hear.

"Summer," his deep voice was like the caress he gave her cheek, "I must go hunting. We are out of food."

She leaned into his touch, closing her eyes. He was always so gentle with her, so tender. The nights were wonderful. But she knew she had only his body, not his heart. Summer yawned. "I can dig some roots at the river," she offered halfheartedly. This sluggishness was new to her.

Talon shook his head. "I have gathered plenty of wood so that you can keep the fire burning. There is enough water in the water bladders that you should not have to go to the river until the others return."

"You are not coming back tonight?"

"It is unlikely. I may have to hunt farther afield. We have been at this camp for some time and there is little game left."

She nodded. "We were going to move camp," she said drowsily.

"No need to. Not yet." He did not want to move her while this strange lethargy was upon her.

Talon glanced around the camp in satisfaction. The lean-to would keep her dry if it chanced to rain. The fire crackled. There was wood, there was water, and he was leaving her the last of the food. Summer would be safe until Blue Feather and the others returned this night or the next.

He no longer feared that she would run off. He had tested her, leaving her alone for short times and he knew she would be here when he returned. "I do not expect to be gone longer than two nights," he explained, but her eyelids fluttered. He thought she was falling asleep and so he tiptoed away.

"Do come back soon, Talon," she murmured.

Talon walked back and looked down at her. Her great yellow eyes were closed now, but when she was awake, they took in everything around her. *She is a fine mate*, he thought. *Kind, industrious—except for this recent bout of drowsiness—beautiful. Passionate.* He licked his lips. *Very passionate.*

He had done well to steal her from the Caribou. Talon waited for the flash of anger that always accompanied the thought of his enemies, but none came. This time he felt only a slight pang of regret. Regret? Where did that come from? Why regret? Surely he did not regret stealing her?

It was not the stealing, he realized. It was that Summer had not had the chance for the ceremonies that meant so much to her. No chance to receive the accolades from the women, the encouragement from the men, the good wishes of the people she loved.

Talon knew more about the Caribou People now than when he had lived with them. Summer often spoke of them, telling him little things about this one or that one. About how Tule was her aunt's friend and always very proper, always wanting to pretend everything was well. About how the shaman often consulted Auntie for advice on a healing; about how difficult Raw's birth had been and how his parents so doted on him because of it.

Summer told him things about the Caribou that he had not known or observed when he had done bride-service among them. Perhaps, had he known them better, he might have been able to call upon their aid against the Saber-Tooths. He might have been able to tell Screech Owl he needed his help, or asked the shaman to use a chant against the wily invaders.

Talon sighed. There was nothing he could have done, however, about the Saber-Tooths being more powerful than the Caribou. All his knowledge of their personal quirks would have availed him little in that fight. No, what was done, was done. And he was fortunate to have his wife.

He smiled down at Summer's sleeping form. He squatted and pulled the bear hide that she had recently tanned a little higher and tucked it gently under her chin. Still she slept on. He wondered briefly why she was so drowsy. Absently, he touched his new bear claw necklace. Summer had made it for him and he would never take it off.

With one last, longing glance at her, Talon set off into the forest to hunt the meat they needed.

Chapter Thirty-Five

Summer heard the cry of a wolf, far in the distance. She quickly stirred the embers of the fire with a long stick, then leaned forward and dragged more branches onto the coals. The branches and twigs burst into flame and that comforted her. Surely no wolf, or lion, or saber-tooth, or bear would creep up on her when she had such a bright fire for protection—would they?

Her eyes roved the clearing. Beyond the fire's light, she knew the size and appearance of the trees and rocks, familiar landmarks all. She saw nothing out of place and lifted her head, her ears straining to catch any unusual sounds.

Nothing.

This was Summer's first evening alone since

her capture by Talon. She shivered, hearing the wolf howl again in the lonely darkness, and pulled a light, warm fur more tightly around her shoulders. The air this evening was cool. The many furs that the Wolves had accumulated would give a fine warmth this upcoming winter, she thought.

The fire crackled and sparks shot out. Summer hummed quietly to herself as she rose and put more sticks on the fire. She crept around the little clearing, careful to keep within the fire's rosy glow of safety.

Then she heard it. The snap of a twig.

She froze and stared into the darkness. "Blue Feather?" she whispered. "Is that you?"

No answer.

"Who goes there?" Her voice trembled.

Silence.

Summer hurried back to the fire and stood as close to it as she dared. She picked up a long thin branch and shoved the tip into the flames. Holding the branch aloft like a torch, she moved it in a circle around the tiny clearing, searching in dread for some sign of who—or what—was out there.

Nothing.

"Weasel?"

Another loud snap. Someone—or something—was nearby.

She swallowed. "Sloth? Is that you?" Her voice sounded shrill to her own ears.

"So this is where you are, girl!"

She whirled. "Uncle Antler!" she gasped, dropping her torch. "What are you doing here?"

He marched forward, Screech Owl right behind him. The shaman and four other Caribou men followed them into the tiny clearing. Summer stared at them as though they were strange spirits of the forest. "Where—what—how did you find me?" she gasped.

Her uncle shuffled over to the fire and reached his hands out to warm them over the flames. "We have been looking for you day and night, girl."

Gratitude rushed through Summer. Her uncle and the Caribou People had not forgotten her! They had been searching for her ever since her capture! That it had taken them so long to find her was no reflection on their love for her. They had done what they could.

She ran up to her uncle and threw her arms around him.

He unclasped her arms and set her aside. "Yes, we found you, girl. We are all glad about that!"

There were murmurs of agreement from the other men.

Summer took a step back, trying to control her excitement at seeing her relatives. Evidently Uncle Antler thought it unseemly for her to hug him. She must remember that she was a woman now and not an impulsive child.

"Get your things," said Uncle Antler. "We must leave."

"But you just arrived," Summer cried in dismay. "Stay! Talon will return soon. You can talk with him, make him understand that he must marry me in the Caribou way, with herbs and gifts and ceremony!"

Her uncle looked at her as if she had become deranged. "Girl, I have no time for this. We must leave before that man returns."

"Wait, Uncle! Talk with him," pleaded Summer. "Tell him you will accept him as my husband if we have the proper ceremonies."

"That is not what I wish to do," Uncle Antler answered. To Screech Owl, he said, "Get her things."

Screech Owl looked befuddled as he glanced around the clearing. Then he spied the lean-to and wandered over to it.

"I do not want to go with you," said Summer. "You will."

She crossed her arms. "I will not!"

"Summer!" snapped her uncle. "Your aunt is waiting for you. The Caribou People are waiting for you. Do not act like this. You only make it more difficult for yourself!"

"I am not going anywhere with you!"

"You are!"

Screech Owl came back with several furs bundled in his arms. "Let us take these," he said, his voice muffled by the pile of furs.

"I am not going anywhere with you," Summer repeated stubbornly. She would not leave this camp. Talon was due back the next night, or even sooner, and she intended to be here to greet him—with or without her relatives! "Talon will return soon, I tell you."

"He does not want you," her uncle said.

"What do you mean?"

"That man does not want you."

"How do you know?" Summer demanded.

"If he did, he would not make it so easy for us to find you. He leaves you alone," said her uncle. "He leaves a huge fire burning. Those are not the things a man does when he wants to hide a woman away for himself."

Hands on her hips, Summer shouted, "You know nothing of what Talon does or does not want!"

Uncle Antler shrugged, unmoved by her anger. "We have come to take you back."

"I do not wish to go back with you." She glared at him. "I am happy here with Talon."

A lie, Summer thought. She *could* be happy here with Talon, if he loved her. But even though he did not, she would still stay with him because he treated her kindly—and because she loved him and knew it was better to have part of him than none at all.

"What took you so long to find me?" she demanded.

Her uncle would not meet her eyes. "We—uh, we looked and looked for a very long time,

301

for days and nights. But it became difficult to follow the trail . . ."

"We gave up," said Screech Owl heavily. "We did not know where to look for you after awhile."

"So you stopped searching for me." She glared at her uncle. "How did you find this camp? Why did your tracking skills improve so suddenly?"

Uncle Antler shook his head. "It is not that, girl. It is that we missed you so. Your auntie longed for you. She cried at night for you. To stop up her tears, I was forced to come and find you."

Summer wanted to believe him, wanted to believe that they all cared about her.

She glanced at the other men; they were all watching her. "Your auntie wants you to come home," said Screech Owl.

Her shoulders slumped. "I would like to come home for a visit," she admitted.

"Good," grunted Uncle Antler.

"But not to stay!" Summer warned, meeting his gaze fiercely. "I would only come for a visit. Then I would return to Talon."

Her uncle shrugged his shoulders.

"We must wait for Talon, or Blue Feather, and explain to them," muttered Summer. "They would worry about me otherwise."

Uncle Antler said impatiently, "I do not wish to wait. We must return at once."

Her suspicions roused, Summer asked, "Why must we hurry?"

"Your aunt—uh, she has been crying for a long time. She must see you soon, or I fear—"

"She is not near death, is she?" cried Summer as fear suddenly gripped her.

"Oh, no." Her uncle shook his head sadly. "But she has been grieving for so long. Perhaps her death is closer than I thought . . ."

"Do not say so!" cried Summer. "I do not want her to die! Oh, no!"

She ran over to the lean-to and hastily gathered up a dress and knives and a packet of food. She snatched up the bearskin Talon had given her and running back to the men, she threw it on top of the pile of furs that Screech Owl already staggered under.

"There! I am ready!"

"We will leave then, the sooner to get back to your poor aunt. I pray that she still survives," said her uncle. He turned to the shaman. "You must sing a chant to see that she does."

The shaman obligingly shook the caribou hoof rattle that he always carried and began to chant.

Uncle Antler nodded in satisfaction. "Come, men."

The small party of Caribou men and one woman left the Wolf camp. By the time the fire had burned down to mere embers, they were back in Caribou territory.

Chapter Thirty-Six

"Auntie!" cried Summer, running towards her bulky aunt. "You have recovered!"

Auntie Birdsong rose from her place near the fire. "Recovered, girl? Whatever are you talking about?" She returned Summer's hug. "How good it is to see you! So beautiful you look too! The Saber-Tooths will be—"

"Summer is tired from her travels," Uncle Antler cut in. "She needs to rest!" He glared at his wife meaningfully.

"Rest?" Auntie Birdsong looked from her husband to her niece. "Oh. Yes. I can see that rest would be a good thing for you." She smiled. "Come."

Summer was watching her aunt and uncle closely. "What goes on here?" she demanded.

"I return to find that my aunt, who I thought was dying, looks marvelously well." She glared at her aunt. "Were you ever sick, Auntie Birdsong?"

Auntie turned to her husband. "Was I?"

"Yes. You were."

Summer whirled to face her uncle in disgust. "I was tricked! You lied to me again, Uncle Antler!"

"I had to get you back here, girl."

"The Saber-Tooths!" said Summer, understanding suddenly dawning. "It is for them, is it not?"

"Why, yes, child. Did your uncle not mention them?" Auntie Birdsong looked upset.

Uncle Antler muttered, "I forgot."

Summer howled in outrage. "You did not forget! You never intended to tell me!"

"Now, girl," he soothed. "What is done, is done. You are here, back home with your people. That is what is important."

But Summer was too furious to listen to his words. She stalked away from them both and marched over to a bubbling creek a little distance from the Caribou camp. Sitting on a rock, she took off her mocassins, plunged her feet into the cold water, and kicked. She muttered to herself for a long while. When her seething anger at her aunt and uncle gradually faded, she marched back to the encampment.

She passed the eight tents that were set up and marched up to the biggest one covered with drawings of a caribou herd on migration. It was her uncle and aunt's tent. Dropping to her knees, she pushed aside the door flap.

"I wish to speak with you both."

"Not now, child," came her aunt's voice. "Your uncle is very tired. It was a difficult journey for him." There was reproach in her voice.

"Auntie," Summer said sternly, "I must speak with you. This is too important to wait."

"Just let us rest a little," pleaded Auntie Birdsong. "It has been difficult for both of us. We are getting old."

Summer refused to be turned away by guilt.

"I will not go away, Auntie," she answered. "I want to talk with you and Uncle. It will be best for all of us if we talk about this now."

She heard movement inside and finally her aunt crawled out, followed by her uncle. They both had wrapped themselves in furs. Summer frowned, recognizing the furs as some of those carried away from the Wolf camp by Screech Owl.

"Those are my furs!" she exclaimed.

"Very pretty they are, too," said her aunt approvingly. She pulled a fur off her shoulders. "Here."

Summer took the proffered garment and wrapped it around herself. A cool breeze was blowing and the fur *was* warm.

"Did you tan them yourself, child?" Birdsong asked.

"Yes, but I am not here to talk about tanning furs." Summer crossed her arms and glared at her aunt and uncle. "I have decided to return to my people."

"Good, good!" said her uncle. "That was all we wanted. For you to return to us, the Caribou People—"

"Not the Caribou People. The Wolf People."

"The Wolf People?" Auntie Birdsong repeated faintly, looking bewildered.

Her uncle looked angry. "Enough of this, girl! You will stay with us!"

"But not for long, Uncle. I know you only brought me here to marry me off to Tuft!"

Uncle Antler glanced at the ground. "I was going to tell you about it, girl. But I did not think you would come with me, if I were to mention it at that man's camp."

"How right you were! Had I known what you planned, I would have kicked and screamed and yelled until Talon and the others came and rescued me!"

"Ah, but you are here now, so they cannot— uh, 'rescue' you. Though of course you do not need to be rescued from your own loving relatives." Uncle Antler gave her an earnest glance.

Summer smiled humorlessly. "Do I not?"

"No!" huffed Auntie Birdsong. "Now, child," she soothed, "you are tired. You have had a long journey, and what you need is rest. We can talk about all this in the morning."

Suddenly Summer did indeed feel tired. Having to fight her relatives, the realization that her aunt was not deathly sick and that her uncle had deliberately lied to her, the knowledge that they planned to marry her off to the Saber-Tooths, the return journey—all of it had truly drained her. "Very well," she muttered. "Tomorrow morning we will speak."

Her aunt smiled. "Tomorrow. I promise."

"Me, too." Uncle Antler yawned. "Now I too must get my rest."

He crawled back into the tent, hastily followed by the bulkier Birdsong.

Summer marched to Tule's and Screech Owl's tent which was decorated with a painted design of owls and tule leaves and tubers. Without ceremony, Summer ordered Screech Owl to give her some of the furs he had taken from the Wolf camp. He swiftly complied and helped her set up a rough lean-to. Soon she was sound asleep under the bearskin robe.

Summer awoke to loud cries.

"Where is the bride?"

"Gifts! Beautiful gifts!"

"Gifts for the Caribou! Expensive gifts!"

Dread seized her. She recognized those voices. It was the Saber-Tooths!

Chapter Thirty-Seven

Talon sauntered along beside the river. He had not seen any animals he wanted to hunt, but he knew he eventually would. The weather was warm, he had his spear at the ready. It was a good day.

He peered ahead, looking for a deer shape or even an antelope silhouette amongst the willows. Sometimes they came to drink at the river's edge, though not often in the heat of the day.

He smiled to himself. Just ahead was a choke cherry thicket and he knew that beyond that thicket was the glade where he and the black wolf had spied upon his woman swimming on that long-ago day. Was it only a summer past?

Talon quickened his pace and moved quietly

through the brush. He parted the thick leaves of a choke cherry branch and peered. Yes, there was the glade. The white waterfall splashed onto black rocks, down, down until it churned into the deep green pool.

He entered the green glade, walking with silent feet upon the springy moss. There was something about this glade that called to him. Always had. He shrugged. No doubt it was the beauty of the place; it was a feast for his eyes. The summer light looked green filtering through so many leafy branches. Bursts of flowers in yellows and reds and purples were sprinkled through the moss.

Taking a deep breath of the fragrant air, he felt the quiet beauty of the glen soothe him. It was truly a serene place.

He took off his moccasins, shed his clothes, and laid his spear aside. Wading into the pool, he swam for awhile, but swimming was not the same without Summer. If she were with him, he would want to stay in the water longer.

Shaking the wet droplets off himself, he waded out of the pool. He pulled on his leather trousers and glanced at his spear, ready to take it up again. Then he thought, *It is the quiet part of the day, the time when the animals seek shelter from the hot sun and sleep. Why should the hunter not take a rest also?*

He lay down on the soft moss, crossing his arms behind his head, and looked up at the patch of blue sky overhead. He would just close his eyes and think about Summer while the hot sun dried the water from his body.

Warmth from the sun penetrated his skin. The heat felt good to him. Talon yawned and closed his eyes.

What a fortunate man he was! He no longer had to live alone. Like the wolves he sought to emulate, he had gathered around him three good hunters: Blue Feather, Weasel and Sloth. The four of them were truly like a wolfpack, he thought, pleased. They hunted together, camped together, fought off predators together. Captured mates together.

And best of all, what a fine mate he now had! There was not a man anywhere that could claim a lovelier, more intelligent, kinder, more passionate mate than he. And some day the Great Spirit would give them strong, healthy children. Life was very good in his world and Talon knew it.

He opened one eye. Everything was quiet and green. He closed his eye. Sleep came easily to a hunter in this beautiful, serene glade. . . .

He awoke to a spear at his throat.

Chapter Thirty-Eight

The big man holding the spear to Talon's throat grinned. Keeping the spear steady, he lazily kicked Talon's own spear out of reach. "Easy," he said. "You make it too, too easy!"

The exquisitely sharp spear point stayed right where it was—at Talon's throat. The young man laughed and shook his long black hair as though at a joke.

Obsidian eyes met obsidian eyes. Talon understood the man though his words were clipped.

"It is a rare treat to catch you off guard, Jrow! But I did it!" He laughed again. "Chuckchuck!"

Talon tried desperately to read meaning into the incomprehensible words and actions. What was wrong with this man?

A large dog came ambling up, his tongue lolling out of his mouth. He resembled a brown wolf with silver on his nose and belly.

"Sit!" said the stranger.

The dog sat.

"Chuckchuck found you," the man said.

Talon remained silent. He did not want to say anything that would force this man to pierce his throat with that spear and end his days.

Suddenly the man whipped the spear away and grabbed Talon's right arm. He hoisted him to his feet. "Come, let us go back to camp. The others are in a hurry. Come, Chuckchuck!"

But the dog did not move. Instead, he looked at Talon and growled deep in his throat.

"Chuckchuck?"

Another low growl was followed by a lift of the upper lip and a savage snarl.

The man stared at Talon. "What is it, Chuckchuck?" He was not laughing now. Not grinning, either. Eyes narrowed, he moved closer to Talon.

There was a flash in the man's black eyes, then his spear pricked Talon's chest. "You are not Jrow!"

Talon wished he had his spear. He did not like this man who acted so strangely.

The stranger peered at him, more curiosity than hostility in his eyes. "But, by the spear of my father, you *look* like Jrow! Resemble him enough to be his twin!" He leaned even closer. "But now I see that your eyes are set deeper, and your nose is more hooked." He laughed. "Who are you?"

The dog stalked over on stiff legs. He sniffed at Talon. Then he growled.

"Chuckchuck does not know you either. Who *are* you?"

Talon could not fathom the sudden bewilderment and anger in the other's voice. "If you will take away your spear, we can talk," he suggested.

"You even sound like him!" the other exclaimed, incredulous.

Talon slowly raised one hand to push away the spear that was still touching his throat.

"Do not!" warned the other. "Though you look like Jrow, know that I will still kill you!"

Talon lowered his hand.

"Much better. Turn around."

Talon slowly turned around. He could hear the other man move and guessed that he had bent down and picked up Talon's spear.

"Move." The prick of a sharp spear tip on the skin between Talon's shoulder blades gave his movements added impetus. "Chuckchuck."

Talon could hear the dog padding after them. "Where are we going?" he asked. They had left the glade and were following the river east. He glanced at the sun. It was high in the sky. How could he return to Summer and their camp if this stranger forced him away?

"Quiet!" snapped the man. They followed a small creek that branched off the river. Soon they were walking along a forested ridge above the creek. After awhile, the stranger said, "Tell me your name."

Talon shook his head. He would tell this man nothing.

The dog growled.

Talon pretended to stumble over a root and lurched to one side. "Hurt," he muttered, holding his ankle. He winced with fake pain.

When the other knelt down to look at the ankle, Talon grabbed at the spear with both hands.

"*Haaiiiy!*" cried the stranger in surprise.

The two men wrestled for the weapon. The stranger yanked it out of Talon's grip, Talon grabbed it back. Over and over they rolled, down a small cliff to the creek, each one trying desperately to wrench the spear from the other's grasp. They were the same size and evenly matched in wrestling skills. Talon began to tire, as did the stranger. But they still struggled on. The dog ran alongside them, growling viciously.

They were fighting in the creek now. The cold water revived Talon, but it revived his opponent also. With gritted teeth, Talon succeeded in climbing atop the man. Somehow the spear had been lost, no doubt in their tumble down the cliff.

The water was too shallow for Talon to hold the stranger's head under; he would not drown, though that was a trick Talon would have liked to try. Just when Talon thought he had succeeded in besting his opponent, the man gave a great heave and rolled over, forcing Talon off. Now Talon was on the bottom.

"Tell—you—this," panted the stranger. "Aaayyy—you fight—like—a mad dog!"

Talon glared up at him.

"What say—we stop the fight?" The man's breath was becoming even again. "Neither of us is going to win this one—too evenly matched! Besides, I have little wish to kill you because you so resemble Jrow."

Talon frowned. "Why should I trust your words? I do not know you. You held a spear to me. I think you want to kill me."

The other threw back his head and laughed. "I tried to! But I did not succeed, did I?" He laughed again. Then he got up. His leather trousers were soaked with mud from wrestling in the creek. Talon rose and his hide pants were wet and muddy, too. The stranger ambled over and picked up his spear. Shaking his head, he muttered, "Chuckchuck, we are going to have to fight better than this if we are going to beat Jrow!"

He saw Talon watching him suspiciously and pointed to the top of a small grassy ridge. "Your weapon is up there, where I dropped it." He grinned at Talon. "I liked your trick."

"What trick was that?"

"Pretending to have hurt your ankle. I will have to remember that trick and try it on Jrow."

"Who is Jrow?" Talon asked.

The man shrugged. "My cousin." Then he met Talon's eye and his grin disappeared. "But why should I tell you anything? You have not answered *my* questions."

Talon regarded the man for some time before finally saying, "You are the only man I have ever met that looks like me."

It was true. The Fox People did not have black hair like this man, or the black eyes that he and Talon shared. The Caribou People had brown or blond hair and eyes the color of leaves and grass and sky. None of them had black hair and black eyes. And most of the Saber-Tooths and the Camel People had light colored hair and eyes. Talon wanted to learn more about this man.

The stranger shrugged. "All my people look like me," he said with complete indifference.

Talon wanted to fight the man again. How could he explain to a man who had been surrounded all his life by people who looked like him what it was like for a man to be alone, in the midst of many?

His frustration must have shown on his face for the other said, "My name is Krae. My people and I come from the northlands. We are called the People of the Sun. Come and meet my people."

Talon glanced up at the sky. This man's people came from the sun?

Krae laughed. "We call ourselves that because the sun once ruled the land of our ancestors for many, many sleeps. Then the sun went away and our ancestors lived in darkness for many sleeps. The women fretted, the babies cried, the men could not hunt. Nobody liked the darkness, day upon day. Finally, Jrowonn, a wise man whose name means 'out of the darkness,' led our people into a new land where they found the sun once more. Our people were happy again." He regarded Talon solemnly. "The old ones still tell stories about that time. Have you not heard?"

Talon shook his head absently and noted the position of the sun in the sky, thinking of the time. It was his first day away from Summer, but he had not expected to return to their camp until the morrow's evening.

"How long does the journey to your people take?" he asked.

"Half a day's travel."

Although Talon would have time to visit the stranger's people who reputedly looked so much like him, he would much rather return to Summer. He was uneasy about leaving her for a long time. He thoughtfully regarded the grinning young man while he searched for the right words of refusal.

At last he said, "Thank you, but no. I will not come with you this day. I have someone who waits for me."

A frown crossed Krae's face, though he kept his grin. Talon understood his disappointment. It had been a sincere invitation, kindly meant.

"Perhaps I will visit your Sun People another time."

The grin disappeared from Krae's face and his sharp spear came up and pricked Talon's breastbone once more.

"You leave me no choice," Krae said, real regret in his voice. "I must force you to come with me."

Chapter Thirty-Nine

Krae's sharp spear now pricked the skin between Talon's shoulder blades and he quickened his pace. The smell of smoke reached Talon as he was marched through a cold, shallow creek and then up a small hill. On the other side of the grassy hill he could see many round dwellings made of brown hide dotting the brush here and there. Each dwelling had a fire burning nearby and it was the smoke from those fires that put a blue haze in the late afternoon air and assaulted Talon's nostrils.

As they came closer to the encampment, Talon saw men and women going about their everyday tasks. Women cooked and scraped hides, men sat talking and sharpening weapons. He expected Krae to tell him that this was the Sun People's camp, but Krae said nothing. He only pricked Talon with his spear when Talon stopped once to stare at the strange round dwellings and even stranger people.

They passed a big, black-haired man, who glanced up at them from where he sharpened a spear. Another man sat outside a hide dwelling and polished an atlatl handle. He regarded Talon, then muttered something to his neighbor, whose long black hair fluttered in the breeze as he wound sinew around the base of a spear tip, attaching it to a spear shaft. All three men, their weapons at the ready, rose and followed Talon and Krae.

Two black-haired women were scraping hides as they watched Talon's progress from under their long lashes. They halted their work to stare and whisper to each other. They, too, rose and threw their scraping rocks to the ground. They followed Talon and Krae, leaving behind two stretched hides that would soon dry and harden in the sun.

Another dark-haired woman, her spoon lifted to her mouth, stopped and simply stared at Talon, her jaw still open to receive the food.

Children playing a happy game of "Sabertooth tiger stalks a bison" paused in the dirt where they crouched. One black-eyed little boy got up and ran over to poke at Talon with a tiny spear.

These people are going to kill me, thought Talon. He clenched his fists, angry that he had been so easily taken and had allowed himself to be brought to this enemy camp. He should have killed Krae when he had the chance, but he had believed the man meant him no harm. For that foolishness he would now pay with his life.

A sudden silence fell over the camp as he and Krae approached one particular dwelling. The large tent was decorated with red ochre paintings of giant beavers and ground sloths. The dwelling itself was large and smoke drifted lazily out of an opening in the top. As Talon waited, he heard a low murmuring sound behind him. Questions from the crowd of men and women swirled around him.

"Jrow? Why do you do this, Krae?"

"That is not Jrow!"

"Who is he?"

"What family is he from?"

Talon's fists relaxed a little when he heard them speak. Perhaps they did not plan to kill him, after all.

Krae called out and a middle-aged man emerged from the large dwelling. His long hair was streaked with gray, but his muscular body was that of a man many years younger. Behind him came a woman, shorter, also middle-aged, with gray wings of hair drawn back from both sides of her face. When Talon met her dark eyes, he felt unaccountably drawn to her.

The middle-aged man straightened and gazed first at Krae, then at Talon. His breath hissed between his teeth.

They do not like me, Talon thought.

The woman, whom Talon guessed to be the man's wife, hid behind the man. She seemed unable to take her eyes off Talon, and he saw her reach for the man's arm as though seeking support.

"Who—who is this man?" the middle-aged man asked Krae. He cleared his throat. "Who—who does he say he is?"

Talon was puzzled by the man's hesitancy.

"I do not know his name. He will not tell me." Krae nudged Talon and added softly, "But look at him."

Talon could feel the middle-aged man's intent gaze.

"Why do you hold him at spearpoint?"

Krae grinned. "It was the only way he would visit us, Uncle Shrond."

Talon maintained his silence while Krae's uncle studied him keenly. Finally Shrond addressed him. "Who are you?"

Talon's eyes hardened. He did not like the man's intent gaze. Indeed, all the watching Sun People were oppressively silent, and seemed excessively interested in him. "I do not wish to say. I do not know you. I was forced to come here. I do not like that."

Shrond nodded, and Talon released his breath.

"We mean you no harm. We are but curious. Where do you come from?"

Talon shook his head, his lips tight. He would not tell this man anything. He did not want the Sun People to seek out the Wolves or Summer and try to harm them.

Shrond turned to Krae. "Where did you find him?"

"In the green glade, the one with the pool and the waterfall."

There was a loud gasp and suddenly the woman who was standing behind Shrond crumpled to the ground.

Shrond bent over her in consternation. "Fleet, Fleet, wake up! Help me wake her," he said to several women who ran over to him.

Talon was forgotten. He could have run, but he did not think he would get far, even with the Sun People distracted by the woman on the ground.

After a short time, she revived and her husband pulled her gently to a sitting position. "Fleet?"

"I—I am well again, Shrond," she said. Her voice was warm and low. Again, Talon felt strongly drawn to her. At that moment, she met his eyes.

"It is the stranger," she said and swallowed.

The crowd murmured at her words.

Talon's jaw tightened. Would they kill him because this woman feared him? He swung around and glared defiantly at the men and women. The murmuring increased.

Shrond held up a hand. "My people, I must ask for silence while we decide what to do."

"Where is Jrow?" asked a man.

"Still hunting," answered Shrond. "But he is due to return this eve."

"This will be a surprise to Jrow," Krae chortled.

"I am afraid the surprise has been to Fleet," Shrond said.

Krae fell silent, even looked crestfallen. Talon felt a moment's pang of sympathy for the youth whose spear was still at his back. He straightened his shoulders to shift the point away from his skin.

"Krae, do not hold our guest at spearpoint any longer," said Shrond.

Talon felt the speartip leave his back, and he breathed easier.

"Will you join us for our evening meal?" Shrond asked Talon politely.

The woman, Fleet, was peeking from behind the man's shoulder. Her dark eyes seemed to devour Talon. He wondered if she would crumple to the ground again and blame him for it.

He felt the press of the Sun men and women, breathed the smell of their close-packed bodies. There were many more of them than there were of him. He had little choice. "Very well."

He followed Shrond and Fleet into the hide dwelling. Inside it was tidy and surprisingly large. Sewn hides had been draped over a frame of willow branches which formed the bones of the tent. An aromatic scent came from an assortment of baskets, filled with dried leaves and packages of dried food, that lined half the curve of the hide floor. Fur robes were spread out to make a sitting area, and glowing embers burned in a rock circle in the center. Smoke drifted out of a blackened hole in the top of the dwelling. "Our homes are round, like the sun," explained the woman, following Talon's gaze.

Talon nodded shortly and sat down, well away from her. He did not want to be the cause of another faint.

"You have many people in your camp," he observed dryly after a lengthy silence.

Shrond nodded. "We have as many people as five men have fingers," he answered.

That was a goodly number. Talon's Wolves, counting Summer, were only five. These Sun People had more people than the Caribou and the Saber-Tooth put together!

"You look very much like one of our people," the woman observed.

Her husband shot her an unreadable glance.

Talon shrugged and answered warily, "Perhaps."

"Do you—" the woman hesitated, "—have family nearby?"

Talon shook his head. "My father is dead. My mother too. No brothers and no sisters."

"Ah," said the woman sadly, or so it seemed to Talon.

"But I have my own people." Talon was not going to let these strangers think that he had no people he could call upon. That had happened with the Saber-Tooths and it would not happen to him again.

"Where do they live?" asked the woman.

Talon shook his head and tightened his lips.

There was another lengthy silence. "We have not been in this territory for many seasons," observed Shrond in his deep voice. Talon could feel the intensity of his gaze. "Not since our son Jrow was born long ago," he murmured.

Talon felt uncomfortable again. The man and the woman were eyeing him. He was almost relieved when Krae came sauntering through the doorflap. "Where is the food?"

The woman named Fleet rose to her feet. "I will get some," she answered.

She left the hide dwelling and returned moments later with a large bowl that exuded a wonderful fragrance. It smelled like juniper berries and meat and Talon's mouth watered. In his enthusiasm to return to the Sun camp, Krae had not stopped even once for food and so Talon had not eaten since daybreak. Dusk was now falling.

Fleet ladled stew into wooden bowls and handed them around. Talon was surprised that she served him first. He forced himself to wait until the others started to eat. It would not do for them to think him ill-mannered.

The stew meat tasted as if it had come from a plump doe that was caught sleeping. The tender meat floated amidst pieces of camas and wild onion and chunks of thick tule root. The taste of juniper berries mingled with other herbs. Talon closed his eyes in bliss, holding the meat in his mouth, savoring it, not wanting to swallow just yet, so delicious did it taste. But he consumed it all.

Later, he waved away Fleet's beaming offer of a fourth bowlful.

His stomach full, Talon began to feel hopeful about the circumstances in which he found himself. Things could be worse—he was still alive. These Sun People had fed him and treated him well. All except for Krae. Talon eyed the young man as Krae slurped up more stew.

Just then there was a loud cry outside the hide dwelling. "Jrow is back!" exclaimed Fleet.

Shrond rose to his feet and left the tent. Krae hastily followed him.

Talon heard the murmur of deep voices outside the dwelling, then the doorflap was pushed back and Shrond re-entered, followed by Krae.

Behind Krae came a large young man, whose dark eyes fastened upon Talon. Talon kept his face impassive. Though this man had black hair and black eyes, Talon saw no strong resemblance such as Krae had spoken of. Krae was mistaken.

"This is my son Doan," said Shrond. Doan took a place beside Fleet, his mother.

Another dark head filled the opening of the dwelling. Dark eyes pierced the gloom and stared at Talon. This man had a flattened nose and a scar along one cheek. Talon did not think he looked anything like himself. "My son, Lawt," said Shrond as Lawt took his place next to Doan.

When the next black-haired man walked through the entrance, Talon was prepared. He peered at the man, finding him to be about his own size, but he noted that the man's eyes were of a lighter brown and his nose strongly resembled the beak of an eagle. No, this person did not look anything like himself. These Sun people were badly mistaken. He would thank them for their hospitality and leave. As the man started to take his place next to Lawt, Talon rose to go.

"My son, Shelt," announced Shrond.

Talon frowned and glanced back at the man taking his place in the row of sons.

When Talon turned toward the tent's entrance, his way was blocked by a fourth man coming through the door. They met, piercing black eye-to-eye.

Yes, this man had black hair. Yes, his big, muscular body was of similar size, but it was at his face that Talon stared the longest. It was like looking at himself in the still waters of a pond on a sunny day!

Shrond announced, "My son, Jrow."

Chapter Forty

Talon opened his mouth to say something, but no words came out so he closed it. The two men faced each other for several heartbeats.

Puzzlement showed in Jrow's dark eyes. "Who are you?"

Talon could only shake his head. He slid his hand down his own face, surreptitiously feeling his cheekbones, the cleft in his chin. True, he had spent little time examining his reflection on the surface of ponds, but he had done so a time or two, enough to feel confused now. Krae had been correct. This man closely resembled himself, and Talon had no explanation as to why that should be.

Somehow, Talon's legs carried him back to his place on the furs once more, but his eyes sought out Jrow. How uncanny that the man should so resemble himself!

Silence lengthened in the crowded tent as Talon and the four young men stared at each other.

Talon rubbed his chin uneasily. It *was* unusual that he and this other man should look so much alike. But, he told himself, such things happened upon occasion. No doubt the Great Spirit, using dark hair, dark eyes, a nose, a mouth, occasionally painted one man's features similar to another man's.

Jrow addressed Talon. "Who are you?"

Talon shook his head and did not answer.

"Do you not think it is strange that we should look like one another?"

Talon shrugged. Just because there was a strong resemblance between Jrow and himself was no reason to believe that he shared anything more with these people.

"Who are your people?" asked Jrow.

The Wolves, thought Talon. Aloud he said, "I come from the Fox People."

"What do they look like?"

Talon described them. He saw Fleet whisper something to Shrond and the man nodded.

"Do they treat you well?" asked Shrond.

Talon shrugged again. "I no longer live with them. But yes, they treated me well when I was with them."

A speculative silence filled the tent. "Among the Sun People," ventured Shrond, "it is unusual for a man to leave his people."

"Even upon marriage?" Talon asked. "Does a man not leave the Sun People when he marries?"

"Sometimes," Shrond acknowledged. "But usually his wife joins us."

"It was different for me," said Talon stiffly. "My Fox People arranged that I would marry a Caribou woman. Because there were so few Fox People, they agreed to join up with the Caribou People for protection,"

"Where are these Caribou now?"

Talon shrugged. "I care not. They gave my woman to another man and banished me."

The youngest brother, Doan, gasped. Shrond frowned. Jrow demanded, "Did you kill the man?"

"No. He was of the Saber-Tooth People and he had many men to help him fight. I did not get the chance to kill him. I *did* manage to fight him before I was banished."

"Did you win?" Krae asked.

"No."

Four frowns met this answer.

"His brother joined the fight," explained Talon.

The four brothers nodded in unison. "I would have done that!" exclaimed Doan. "Brothers always help brothers!"

The others laughed.

Talon suddenly felt curiously bereft, knowing that·these men approved of an action that had gone so badly against him. But all four brothers were staring at him, so he added, "Their father, headman of the Saber-Tooths, feared I would cause further harm to his sons and he demanded that the Caribou banish me."

"And the Caribou did so." Shrond sounded angry.

"Yes."

"What happened to the men who fought with you?" asked Jrow. "Were they banished also?"

"No one fought with me," answered Talon, and he felt his face redden in shame.

After a long silence, Shrond said, "These Saber-Tooths must be greatly feared."

"Yes, they are."

"Where do they live, these fierce Saber-Tooths who took your woman?" asked Jrow.

"The Saber-Tooth Tiger People live far to the west, along the river."

"It seems to me, young man," observed Shrond, "that you have no people, and no woman."

Talon's jaw tightened. "Not so! I went back and stole a Caribou woman, one who had been promised in marriage to the Saber-Tooths."

The four brothers and Krae hooted in glee. "I would have done that!" exclaimed Doan.

Lawt, the brother next to him, slapped him on the arm. "You would not!"

The two got into a brief mock tussle that halted when Shrond said sternly, "Sons."

Abashed, the two sat up straight. Talon had

to hide a smile. Apparently Lawt and Doan sometimes found it difficult to act with the necessary gravity expected of full-grown men.

He found himself envying these Sun People. There were so many of them. It brought home anew to him his own lack of support. He had never belonged to a large group of strong men such as this.

How wonderful it must be to have so many men to call upon to help one hunt, to help one fight, Talon thought. If he had had brothers like these, the Saber-Tooths would never have been able to take Blizzard and drive him away!

Hard on that thought came: *But then I never would have had the opportunity to steal Summer, either. And I certainly do not regret that!*

I have my Wolves, Talon told himself, trying to staunch the lonely feeling that threatened to overwhelm him. *And I have my wife. My people will grow.*

"I want to tell you a story, my sons," said Fleet gently. She had been silent for so long that Talon had almost forgotten her presence. "It is a tale that your father knows, but it is not known to any other of our people."

Shrond nodded. "We never thought it necessary to tell you before. Now we do."

"Ah, Mother, could you not wait awhile? We want to ask this man more questions." Doan was watching Talon with interest.

"I think not," she answered firmly. "It is best

if you hear what I have to say."

She was silent for a time, and Talon had the impression that she was gathering her strength.

"When you were born, Jrow," she began, glancing at her oldest son, "I was alone. At the shaman's request, I had gone alone to seek the herbs that I would need for your birth in a month's time.

"Unfortunately, while I was in the forest, my birth pangs came early. I knew that I must go through the birth very soon. And alone. So I sought out a private place. I discovered the green glade, where the waterfall slides into the deep pool."

Jrow nodded. Evidently he had heard this part of the tale before. "And there you gave birth to me."

"Yes, I did. But I gave birth to you on the second day. I have never told you that you were actually born second."

"Second?" Jrow leaned forward. "What are you talking about, Mother? I am the oldest!"

"Listen, my son. On the first day I gave birth to a boy, my firstborn," Fleet said. A serenely happy look came over her face. "He had deep black eyes and black hair. His body was long and strong. He was a beautiful child." Her face fell. "I fell asleep with him in my arms and when I awoke he was gone."

There was a collective gasp from her audience. Talon leaned forward. He felt a tightening in his chest as Fleet continued.

"I wept many tears, at first fearing I had but dreamed my child. Later I wept more tears when I realized it had truly happened. Then to my astonishment, I went into labor a second time, and a day later I brought a second baby boy into the world. That was you, Jrow, my dear son." She glanced at Jrow. He was staring at her, open-mouthed.

"Why do you tell us this now, Mother?" demanded Shelt.

Fleet met Talon's eyes. "I believe this man to be my firstborn son."

At her words, Talon felt as though he were suddenly spinning round and round in a whirling pool. Fleet's son! Such a thing could not be! He met her eyes, his own wide in disbelief.

Her sons were equally disbelieving. There were cries of, "No! No!"

"It cannot be!"

"Mother! You know not what you say!"

But Fleet tightened her lips and remained silent, as did Shrond.

"It does make sense," Krae observed after a moment. All four brothers glared at him and he grinned. "Look at him. Your eyes do not lie to you."

Four incredulous pairs of eyes turned upon Talon.

He glared back.

"I thought he was Jrow when I first saw

339

him! I sneaked up on him and caught him unawares!" Krae crowed. "He was asleep in the green glade. Snoring like a fat saber-tooth that has just feasted upon a ground sloth!"

Talon flushed in embarrassment.

Jrow began to laugh. Finally, Lawt, Shelt and Doan started to chuckle, too. Soon, all five men were laughing loudly, and it shook the hide walls of the tent.

Shrond, Fleet and Talon, however, did not join in the hilarity.

Fleet looked at Talon shyly. "Is there anything you can tell us of your birth?"

Talon regarded this woman who had just claimed to be his mother. His mind still reeled from the thought, yet some part of him seized on the idea and held it tight. If this were true, suddenly everything was explained for him: the strange birth story of his Fox mother, and the fact that he did not resemble in the least any of the Fox people.

He asked, "Did—did you look for your baby?" Unaccountable, how his throat thickened and he wanted to weep.

Fleet said sadly, "Yes. I told Shrond what had happened. We decided not to tell the other people—it was too strange. Shrond searched for our child, but there was no one nearby. Whoever took my baby moved away very swiftly." Grief crossed her face. She brushed at her eyes and rose slowly. She went over to where her baskets were lined up against one wall, picked up a basket and handed the basket to Talon. "This is all that Shrond found in his search."

Talon stared at the basket. It was a simple berry basket, old and tattered. The handle had unravelled. Inside was a single dried yellow violet. He turned the basket round and round in his hands. On it was painted the design of a red fox running. Talon had seen similar designs in the home he had shared with Snare.

He closed his eyes tightly, then willed himself to open them. He handed the basket back to Fleet without speaking.

"After Shrond searched and searched and could not find you," continued Fleet, "I asked him if we could move far away. I did not want to be where such a thing could happen to my other precious son. I did not know if spirits had taken you, if a wolf had taken you. . . ." She shook her head. "I just did not know. . . ." She began to cry softly, the fear and loss of many years echoing in her sobs.

Talon's throat thickened. His mother, his mother! He was finally willing to believe that Fleet *was* his mother, and the terrible loss of her love for all those years, the loss of this family for all those years, overwhelmed him.

"I must be alone," he said abruptly and left the tent.

No one came after him. Left alone, Talon wandered around the quiet camp, unseeing of the hide tents with the flickering fires lighting their walls. His family, his mother, his father, his brothers. . . .

He wandered far from the settlement until he was alone under the vast night sky. When Talon came to a huge pine tree, he leaned against the rough bark and he wept. He wept for the loss of his mother, for the loneliness, for the pain of his youth. All those years he had known himself to be unlike those around him. He knew deep down that he did not fit in with the people he lived with. All those years. . . . ! In an agony of pain, he staggered to his feet. He raised his head to the moon and howled out his anguish. The howl ended with a hoarse cry of rage. All those years!

And his Fox mother! What about Snare? Why the lies? Ah, but now Talon knew why she had lied. She knew he would hate her if he knew the truth, that she had stolen him from the loving arms of his own mother! The storm of his rage and anger renewed itself in him and Talon grabbed up a dead limb from the ground. With the limb he beat the ground, beat the trunks of trees until his arms ached from exertion.

At last he threw down the limb. All his howling and raging and beating could not bring back those lost seasons, could not give him back any of that precious time with the family he had been meant to have.

He had only now. Only this time, only this day. Perhaps he could make a new start, with his true family.

Quiet now, the storm of his grief swept away, Talon wondered what it would have been like to grow up with brothers who looked like himself, with the father who had sired him, the mother who had borne him. With the many Sun People.

Weary and exhausted, he made his way back to the hide tent where he had learned the news that had shaken him to his very core.

Fleet looked up when he entered.

Her story also explained why Talon had never come upon his own parents in the many seasons since his birth. They had left because of Fleet's grief over the loss of her baby son. *Oh, Mother,* he implored silently. *Why could you not have kept searching for me?*

Aloud he said, "My name is Talon."

Chapter Forty-One

Seven pairs of expectant black eyes stared at him.

"Well? Do you believe that you are our missing son?" asked Shrond, giving voice to the question that hovered in the minds of all in the tent.

"Do *you*?" countered Talon.

"Yes," answered Shrond.

"Yes," said Fleet firmly.

"Yes," echoed Krae.

The three younger brothers, Lawt, Shelt, and Doan, were silent.

Jrow shrugged. "Perhaps, perhaps not. I will wait and see before I decide."

"I would say the same," said Doan. "Although you do look like Jrow . . ."

Talon nodded. "It is reasonable to wait," he agreed. "I myself know not what to think. But I will tell you what my Fox mother told me."

With seven pairs of eyes avidly watching him, Talon began the strange birth story Snare had always told him. "When I was a little baby, my mother found me in the forest near a pond."

"That would have been the green glade!" exclaimed Krae.

Talon nodded. "She told me that she rescued me from a saber-tooth who was just about to eat me."

"That would have been you, Fleet," said Krae wryly.

Fleet's eyes flashed but she kept silent.

"My mother, Snare, took me into her home. She and my father, White Belly, raised me as their only son. My mother had other children, but they all died at birth before I was born. White Belly died when I was but five summers old."

Unbidden came a memory of Snare as she herself was dying, lifting up her arms to her unseen children.

"Was she kind to you?" Fleet sounded as if she were forcing the words out.

Talon nodded. "She was. She always told me stories and sang me songs when I was little. When I was older, she took me with her to find plants. She cooked my favorite foods . . ." He felt himself flush. "And did all the motherly things," he muttered. "I know she cared about me."

He glanced at Fleet and continued, "I think she loved me very much. I loved her too and I was grateful to her for taking care of me."

Fleet's lips were so thin they almost disappeared. "But you did not know the truth: that she had stolen you!"

"No," Talon admitted. "I did not know that."

There was a throbbing silence in the hide tent. "He does not have to choose mothers, Fleet," Shrond reminded his wife gently. "Snare is dead."

"She died shortly after I was banished from the Caribou People," Talon said. "It was Snare's idea to join up with them and to get me a fine bride at the same time."

"Her idea did not work, did it?" Fleet pointed out.

"No, it did not, but she meant to help me."

Shrond said, "Fleet, the more you attack the woman, the more he will defend her. She was the only mother he ever knew." Fleet stared at the ground, her shoulders slumped in defeat. "But you now have the chance to be the mother of his later years," Shrond added earnestly.

"He does not need a mother now," she muttered. "He is already full-grown. He does not need me now." Fleet turned her face away.

Pain lanced through Talon, but he said nothing. He had been alone too long, been betrayed too many times, to expose his innermost thoughts and feelings to these people who, though he was willing to accept them as family, were still strangers to him.

Shrond took a deep breath. "You do not know that, Fleet. Perhaps he does not need a mother to do everything for him as a little child does, but he will need wise counsel upon occasion. You could supply that."

Jrow burst out laughing, as did his brothers.

Fleet's eyes flashed. "None of my other sons come to me for wise counsel!"

"Oh, but we do," said Jrow, his dark eyes twinkling. "We come to you to find out what maiden said this, what maiden did that. To find out who wishes to marry Doan, who sneaked away with Lawt in the night . . ."

"Oh!" Fleet looked exasperated and swatted her hand through the air as though at a pesky mosquito.

"But Talon is married," objected Krae. "He has no need to know what the young maidens are doing!"

His cousins laughed at his seriousness.

Talon found himself relaxing under the rough camaraderie of the family. As he observed each brother, he marvelled to himself, *Here is my brother Lawt, here is my brother Shelt, here is my brother Doan and here—* He stopped. Jrow was frowning at him. *Here is my brother Jrow.* The last thought was defiant.

Then Jrow slowly smiled at Talon. "I think,"

said Jrow, rising to his feet, "that this man *is* my missing brother."

He walked over to where Talon sat, reached down, and grabbed his hand. With a hard tug, he pulled Talon to his feet. Then he threw his arms around Talon and hugged him.

Talon found himself hugging Jrow back. Then Lawt was hugging him, and Shelt was hugging him. They were laughing as they embraced him. Doan and Krae joined in, each trying to outdo the other in giving Talon great hugs. Next came his father, Shrond. He pounded Talon's back and Talon could tell the old man was very strong.

Lastly came Fleet. She smiled up at him and then reached up and put her arms around him. "My son," she whispered, her voice breaking. "My beautiful son."

Talon had to bend down to embrace his mother. Tears were running unashamedly down his face, but his heart was singing. *I have come home. I have come home. At long last, I have come home. . . .*

Chapter Forty-Two

"Are you certain you cannot stay another day?"

Talon looked into Fleet's pleading brown eyes and smiled. "Yes, I am certain. I have already stayed a day longer than I expected."

"But I have just found you," protested Fleet. "I do not want to lose you again!"

Talon gave her a hug. "You will see me soon," he promised. "And I will bring my new wife with me."

Fleet smiled, recognizing her firstborn's determination and yielding to it. "I will be happy to have Summer visit my home," she said graciously. "You may both stay as long as you wish. You may even," she raised her voice to make certain Shrond overheard, "join our Sun People, if you wish."

Talon grinned. "I have my Wolves. We would have to talk about it amongst ourselves first."

Fleet's face fell.

"I have been alone for a long time, Fleet," said Talon. He was not ready to call her "Mother." Not yet, perhaps never. He felt towards her as he would a favorite aunt. "The Wolves helped me when I needed it. I will not turn my back on them now, even though I have other people and other resources."

He picked up his spear and hefted his pack onto his back. "I am a rich man," Talon said. "I have so many new relatives, powerful relatives. I do not know what to do with all my wealth!"

Shrond came up to him and crammed one more piece of dried meat to the bulging food bundle atop Talon's pack. "Remember, my son," he said, "we will remain here for half a moon. Then our people will move east towards the bison hunting grounds." He pointed at the rising sun. "We would welcome you to join us for the fall hunt."

Talon smiled. "I will discuss it with my wife," he said. He was very eager to get back to Summer. He knew that Blue Feather and the others would protect her while he was gone, but he longed to see her lovely face.

Krae came up to join them, followed by Jrow, Lawt, Shelt, and Doan. Krae looked particularly downcast.

"What is the matter, my sister's son?" Fleet asked.

He answered, "I lost the gamble."

"What gamble?"

"To see who accompanies Talon back to his camp."

"But I am going alone," said Talon in surprise.

"No," answered Jrow. "You are not. You have company." He grinned and thumped his chest with his thumb. "Me!"

Talon opened his mouth to protest but Lawt interjected, "We decided. One of us goes with you. We did not find you only to lose you."

Talon nodded, humbled and touched by the affection surrounding him. When he could finally speak, he said, "I will be glad of your company, Jrow."

"I thought you would be," said his twin arrogantly.

Talon's lips twitched as he tried to stifle his amusement.

"I am glad you are going with Talon," murmured Fleet. "You will both look out for each other."

"As brothers always do," Doan added.

There were more hugs at the parting and then Talon and Jrow headed into the forest. They planned to take a trail that followed the river so that they would reach the Wolves' camp sooner.

"We will reach my camp by late tomorrow," said Talon. "And wait until you meet my wife! She is beautiful."

"Of course," said Jrow. "I would expect no less."

They reached the Wolves' camp before the sun set. Talon was pleased with the time they had made. Jrow was an expert hunter and good companion and Talon was glad of the opportunity to get to know this brother who so resembled himself.

The appearance of the two startled Blue Feather and Weasel. Sloth dozed by the fire.

After introductions, Talon glanced around the camp. "Where is Summer?"

Blue Feather stared at him. "What do you mean?" he asked slowly. "I thought she was with you."

Dread coiled in Talon's stomach, and he felt Jrow stiffen beside him. "I left her here," Talon said, as evenly as he could.

Blue Feather got to his feet. "She is not here. When we returned, she and her things were gone . . . I—"

Talon whirled on Jrow. "We must find her!"

Jrow nodded grimly. "We will!"

His twin's confidence gave Talon new heart.

"When Weasel, Sloth and I returned," said Blue Feather, "Summer and her things were gone, but there was no sign of a struggle. We thought you and she had decided to go off together for a few days."

Talon's scalp tightened in fear. "How long ago?"

"A day," answered Blue Feather. "We came back here yesterday."

His heart pounding, Talon cast around for signs that would tell him something, anything, about what had happened to Summer.

"It rained two nights ago," said Blue Feather.

"No tracks then," gritted Talon.

"No."

Weasel woke Sloth and explained the situation to him. Sloth looked worried and hurried to join Talon and Jrow who were bent over the ground searching for a footprint, or any other sign that would tell them in which direction Summer had gone.

"Did you see anything at all unusual when you came back?" Talon asked.

Blue Feather shook his head. "Nothing. We even looked around, just to make sure that she had gone with you. There were no signs of struggle. Everything looked fine."

Talon groaned. "She was tired. I left her here. I needed to hunt and I knew you would return in the next day or so . . ."

Weasel said, "She knows better than to go off alone, does she not?"

Talon did not want to consider that Summer might have run away again. He remembered how it had been between them, how he loved her. "No," he answered tersely, "she would not run away. Not now."

Blue Feather raised one eyebrow at that but mercifully kept silent. Talon was in no mood to hear about former wives or faithless women.

"Do you have enemies?" asked Jrow.

Blue Feather laughed. "A few."

Weasel said, "The Caribou People."

"The Saber-Tooths," added Blue Feather.

"No struggle, you said," mused Talon aloud. "Then she must have gone with someone she knew, trusted."

"Or it could have been a saber-tooth cat, or a bear," added Weasel solemnly.

Weasel continued, "She could have wandered off and a bear—"

Talon gritted his teeth, remembering the bear that had chased Summer. He held up a hand. "Do not say it, brother!"

He felt Jrow stiffen beside him. "You call this man 'brother'?

"These men are all my brothers," Talon answered. "These are the Wolves who stood by me when I was alone and banished."

Jrow nodded. "You are fortunate to have them."

Blue Feather shot him a glance. "Jealous?"

"No." Jrow smiled. "Grateful."

Talon glanced around the clearing. "It is dark," he muttered. "But I must leave you now."

"Where are you going?" Blue Feather asked.

Talon glanced at him. "To find Summer."

"And where do you think she might be?"

"It is either the Saber-Tooths or the Caribou who have her," answered Talon. "I will track down both bands until I find who has taken her."

"There was no sign of struggle. That tells me it might be her people, the Caribou," suggested Blue Feather.

"It might."

Talon walked over to his lean-to and picked up his wolf cloak, a plain leather tunic and a camel hide to keep him warm at night on his journey.

Suddenly out of the darkness came a loud shout.

Chapter Forty-Three

The hairs on the back of Talon's neck rose. He dropped the wolfskin and grabbed up his spear. He prowled to the edge of the camp. "Who goes there?"

A slim brown youth stepped into the circle of light thrown by the fire. "It is I," he said shyly.

"And who are you?" Blue Feather's voice was gruff. He, too, had been caught off guard.

"I am Sparrow Hawk, of the Caribou People."

Talon's breath hissed in. He peered at the youth, realizing suddenly that the lad did indeed look vaguely familiar. Not wanting to be recognized, Talon stepped back into the shadows.

Blue Feather raised his spear, but Talon said,

"No spear, Blue Feather. He is but a boy."

The youth stuck out his chin. "I am a runner," he said proudly. "I bring a message from Antler, the mighty headman of the mighty Caribou People."

Blue Feather raised his spear again and snorted in disgust. "And what does the *mighty* headman of the *mighty* Caribou People have to tell us?"

Sparrow Hawk glanced uncertainly at the men standing around watching him. "You are not the Wolf People, are you?"

Before Talon could answer, Blue Feather cut in, "No. We are the Mice."

"The Mice People? I have not heard of them." The boy looked uneasy.

Blue Feather nodded solemnly. "We were about to have a mouse dance, just before you called out to us."

"Oh." The boy thought about that. "The Mice People? A mouse dance?"

Blue Feather nodded enthusiastically. He held up his big hands curled into paws. "We dance like this." He gave several little hops around the clearing. Sloth and Weasel started to imitate him.

Jrow leaned on his spear and watched the proceedings, grinning. But Talon glared at Blue Feather. Levity was out of place. Summer was missing!

"We eat mouse food," said Blue Feather, warming to his role. He plucked up a stalk of grass and nibbled on it. "Like this."

The boy stood staring, open-mouthed.

"We scurry through the forest like this," added Blue Feather, clearly enjoying himself. The sight of the big, strong Blue Feather tiptoeing along the edge of the camp clearing was utterly ridiculous.

"You are awfully big for mice," Sparrow Hawk observed.

"We are actually *big* mice," said Jrow. "Rats."

Blue Feather nodded. "You may join us, if you like."

"Uh—no," answered Sparrow Hawk. "I am bringing a message," he repeated, as much to remind himself as to tell the others. "As long as you are not the Wolf People, I can tell you."

"Wolf People? Us?" scoffed Blue Feather. His paws were curled and he was tiptoeing again.

Sparrow Hawk smiled and relaxed. "No, I can see you are not Wolves!" He snickered.

"What is the message?" Talon's voice from the shadows was curt. He had to find Summer, and a sickening feeling in his gut told him that the youth's message might taunt or even threaten him.

The youth swung to peer through the darkness at Talon. "It is this: You are invited to the marriage feast of Antler's daughter."

"I thought he married off his daughter many seasons ago."

The boy looked relieved. "Ah, so you know the Caribou People then."

"Yes," said Talon.

"Marriage feast?" asked Blue Feather. He scurried over to the boy, but he did not succeed in looking like a mouse. "What marriage feast?" He hopped about. "We Mice greatly enjoy marriage feasts."

"Oh, you will enjoy this one," the boy said earnestly. "There will be mouse food for you there. I am certain of it."

Jrow gave a strangled cough.

"The Caribou People," the boy went on, "are marrying off their most beautiful daughter, Summer, to the younger son of powerful Saber-Tooth headman. Perhaps you have heard of the Saber-Tooth People?"

Talon stiffened. So that was what had happened! The Caribou had taken Summer back so that she could marry the Saber-Tooth cub! His fingers gripped his spear handle so tightly he thought it would snap.

Blue Feather hopped closer to Sparrow Hawk, his big hands still curled into paws. "Do tell us more. We Mice are very curious people."

Sparrow Hawk took a step back suddenly when he realized that every one of the big Mice men was listening intently to his every word. "We are inviting all the neighboring people," he said nervously. "I was told to invite everyone I came across. Except for the Wolf People, you understand."

"Oh, yes," answered Blue Feather, Weasel and

Talon. Sloth nodded sagely.

"Would not want them," agreed Jrow with a grin.

"No." The boy glanced at him. "No, we certainly would not!" He looked around the clearing. "May I sleep here?" he asked. He gave a yawn and stretched. "I have been traveling all day and I am very tired."

"Yes," answered Blue Feather. "Wherever are our Mouse manners?"

The boy shrugged. "I do not know what kind of manners Mice have." He yawned once more.

"Dainty manners," Blue Feather assured him, leading their guest over to Talon's lean-to. "You may sleep here," he said, generously indicating Talon and Summer's bed.

Talon glared at him. Blue Feather gave a silent laugh.

"Thank you," muttered the boy, sinking down onto the pine boughs. He stretched out. "Good night."

"Good night," cooed a deep-voiced chorus of well-wishers.

"Dream happy mouse dreams," added Blue Feather in a squeaky voice.

The boy looked up at that. "What?"

"That is the way Mice People say goodnight," explained Blue Feather kindly.

"Oh." Sparrow Hawk sank back down. "Dream happy mouse dreams," he repeated drowsily.

"We will," the Wolves chorused, then were

363

silent until they heard soft snores coming from Talon's lean-to.

"Now that I know where Summer is," murmured Talon, "I will get some rest and leave in the morning."

"We will come with you," Blue Feather said, and the others nodded.

"I will go and get my brothers," Jrow added.

Talon shook his head. "Do not involve the Sun People. It is not your fight." He was grateful for his twin brother's offer, however.

Jrow said, "It *is* our fight. I will get them to help."

Blue Feather asked, "Do you ever just accept 'no'?"

"No." Jrow grinned. "Do you?"

Blue Feather sighed. "Sometimes I have to."

Jrow shrugged, amused. "I have never had to."

"Then you have not met the right woman."

Jrow looked puzzled. "Woman?"

"Do not get him started on that," warned Talon. "He will tell you all about his former wife."

"I have listened to all your complaints about the Caribou," said Blue Feather. "Why cannot you listen to mine about my former wife?"

"What complaints?" Jrow asked.

Talon shook his head. "I have heard enough. I am getting some sleep," he said. "Good night."

"Dream happy mouse dreams," said Blue Feather in that squeaky, high voice.

*   *   *

They broke camp as the sun was rising. Sparrow Hawk readily agreed the Sun People should be invited, and told Jrow how to get to the Caribou camp.

Then Jrow set out for his people's camp to fetch his brothers to the "marriage feast," and Sparrow Hawk led Talon, Blue Feather, Weasel and Sloth on the trail to the Caribou camp. And Summer.

Chapter Forty-Four

Another morning crawled by like a groundsloth eating his breakfast of leaves as Summer sat sewing in the hot tent. Auntie Birdsong and Uncle Antler had confined her to the hide dwelling as her punishment for refusing to marry the Saber-Tooth. When Summer had the temerity to speak Talon's name, Auntie Birdsong had thrown up her hands and clucked like a sage hen. Uncle Antler had frowned and told Summer that she was annoying him. Then he had rushed off to speak with Spotted Cat, the Saber-Tooth headman.

She peeked out of the tent and saw black-spotted Saber-Tooths wandering past the little dwelling. The sun beat down on the whitened hide; its heat brought a red flush to her face.

Summer opened the skin door wider to let a breeze cool the tent. Taking a drink from the bison bladder refreshed her, and she nibbled at the last roasted tule root left on the platter her aunt had brought her.

Summer could see Tuft talking with his brother and father down by the river. A brisk breeze sprang up and carried the sounds of Rides Their Backs' and Spotted Cat's jocular laughter to her ears. She wondered if they teased Tuft about the marriage that was to take place on the morrow.

With a groan, Summer sank back on her haunches and stared dully out of the tent. How she wished she had never left Talon's camp!

She buried her head in her arms. Her uncle had lied to get her to come back to the Caribou camp. Her aunt's reported sickness, her uncle's search day and night for her—all lies, nothing but lies. Oh yes, they wanted her back, but only to marry her off to the Saber-Tooth! Summer closed her eyes in agony. She had been so foolish to believe her uncle!

And where was Talon? What would he think when he returned to the Wolf camp and found her gone? Would he look for her? Would he think a tiger or wolf had eaten her? Worse, would he think she had run away? *Ah, Talon! Where are you?* she cried inwardly.

Then she lifted her head as a new thought struck her. She placed a hand on her stomach to soothe the queasiness there. She was beginning to suspect that she carried Talon's child.

And to think her foolish aunt and uncle wanted to marry her off to Tuft, the Saber-Tooth! A mere day after she had returned from Talon's camp with Uncle Antler, the Saber-Tooths had arrived and pitched their black-spotted tents on the dry yellow grass field where the marriage celebration was to take place.

Her friend, Blue Camas, staggered past Summer's tent. A huge bundle of sticks bent her back like that of an old woman. In the time since Blue Camas had arrived at the Caribou camp, there had not been a single chance for the two friends to visit alone.

"Blue Camas!" hissed Summer. She fluttered her fingers outside the tent, with little hope that Blue Camas would see her, bent over as she was. "Come here!"

The young woman in the spotted leather dress looked up. Pleasure lit her face. "Summer!"

Glancing swiftly to left and right, she quickened her pace to the tent and swung the heavy bundle off her thin frame. Dropping to her knees outside the tent door, she embraced Summer. The two women laughed and wept.

"Blue Camas!"

"Oh, Summer!"

"How good it is to see you!"

"And you!"

They hugged again and then Summer urged, "Come inside. Visit with me for a little while!"

With a hasty glance over her shoulder, Blue Camas crept into the tent.

"Now," said Summer, smoothing a place beside her, "tell me how it has been for you. What is it like to live with the Saber-Tooths?"

Blue Camas' face fell. "You will find out soon enough. Let us speak of happier things."

Summer did not like the ominous sound of that. "I would never find out," she said, "had I a choice in the matter."

"What are you saying?" asked Blue Camas, her brown eyes wide. "That you are being forced into this marriage just as I was?"

"You know that," chided Summer. "I never wanted to marry Tuft!"

Blue Camas sighed. "Yes, I know that," she admitted. "But I had hoped that, with time, you might change your mind." She looked hopefully at Summer.

"No. I have not."

Blue Camas bowed her head. Both women were silent. Finally Blue Camas offered, "Perhaps—perhaps Tuft will make a good husband." But she would not meet Summer's eyes.

"You know Tuft better than I," Summer said. "What is he like?"

"Oh . . ." Blue Camas shrugged. "Like most of the other Saber-Tooths . . ."

"Blue Camas, I do not think you are telling me what you truly think. Are you?"

Instead of answering, Blue Camas peeked out of the tent. "I must go. They might come looking for me."

"Who? Spotted Cat?"

"Him, or one of his other wives. They watch me like a family of red hawks watch a squirrel."

"Spotted Cat has them spy on you?"

"No. But they are jealous and look for any chance to speak against me."

"Oh." Summer cast around for something else to say to keep her friend a little longer. "I have not seen Blizzard," she began. "Uncle Antler and Auntie Birdsong were particularly upset that she does not seem to want to leave her husband's tent. It is odd, do you not think?"

Blue Camas glanced nervously out the tent doorway again. "I really must leave, Summer." She rose.

Summer put out a hand to stop her. "Wait! Tell me who it is you fear. Is it Spotted Cat? Is it Rides Their Backs? Who?"

Blue Camas stared at her friend. She opened her lips to speak, then snapped her mouth shut. "I cannot tell you." She pushed past Summer.

"Do not run off!" Summer pleaded. "We have hardly had time to visit!" Seeing the hesitation on her friend's face, she promised, "I will not talk about the Saber-Tooths anymore."

Blue Camas swung around, a sad look on her pretty face.

"Unless you want to," Summer amended.

Blue Camas gave a tiny smile. "You have not changed, Summer. Not at all." She crossed the small space and sank down beside Summer again. "How I have missed you!"

Summer nodded. "It has been lonely for me, too."

After a long silence, Blue Camas murmured, "It is just that I do not wish to frighten you, Summer."

"About what?" Summer held her breath.

"About the Saber-Tooths. About what they are like."

Summer waited, not daring to interject a single word lest she drive her friend away.

Blue Camas leaned forward and her troubled eyes met Summer's. "Rides Their Backs does not treat Blizzard well."

Summer's stomach clenched. "What does he do? Does he beat her?"

Blue Camas shook her head. "No, he does not beat her. He has no need to."

Summer frowned. "Whatever do you mean?"

Blue Camas glanced out the tent's opening. Satisfied that no one could overhear them, she leaned even closer and whispered, "He has made her a slave to his new wife!"

"A slave?" echoed Summer, shocked.

"The Saber-Tooths wanted the rich fishing territory that belongs to the Greenhead Duck People. So they arranged a marriage with the daughter of the Greenhead Duck leader. Rides

Their Backs was supposed to take her as a second wife, but she would have none of it. She insisted she be his only wife. Rather than send Blizzard back to her people and offend your Uncle Antler, Rides Their Backs made her a slave to his new wife."

Summer was stunned. "How humiliating for Blizzard!" She thought of her proud, beautiful cousin. "Uncle Antler would be far *more* offended to learn that his beloved daughter is a slave!"

"Yes," agreed Blue Camas quietly. "That is why she stays in the tent. She fears that your uncle will hear of her plight and try to fight the Saber-Tooths to free her." Blue Camas stared at the ground. "The Saber-Tooths would surely win and many Caribou would die."

"How unlike Blizzard to think of others," Summer mused aloud.

"She has changed, Summer."

Summer pondered. "If the Saber-Tooths wanted an alliance, why not marry the Greenhead Duck woman off to Tuft instead? He has no wife."

"That was suggested, but the Greenhead Duck woman would not take a second son. She wanted a firstborn son. More power," said Blue Camas.

"How do you know this?"

"As one of Spotted Cat's wives, I learn much that I am not supposed to know." She picked up the discarded wooden platter and pretended to serve Summer a piece of meat from it. "Another tasty morsel of antelope, O Greenhead Duck Leader?" she asked in a high voice.

Summer shook her head.

"No? Then perhaps you would enjoy the finest, tastiest camas bulb our camp has to offer?"

Summer smiled and shook her head again.

"O Greenhead Duck Leader, do not let me interrupt your important conversation about how you truly do not wish to marry off your daughter. Or you, dear Spotted Cat, of how your son *must* have his daughter, else you will sneak up in the middle of the night and burn all the Greenhead Duck tents. Oh, no, I do not hear such things, not I, your lowly fifth wife. Here, have a roasted grasshopper!"

Summer laughed.

Blue Camas' smile was sad as she replaced the platter. "The Saber-Tooths get most of their women by taking them from weaker people, I have found."

"And so they think that I am just one more woman to be taken away from my people!"

Blue Camas nodded.

Summer's eyes sparked. "Blue Camas, I will tell you something." She leaned forward. "I am not going to marry Tuft. I told Auntie Birdsong and Uncle Antler this. They insist that I marry Tuft, but I will not do it!"

Blue Camas frowned. "Spotted Cat will not like it."

"Surely you will not tell him!" cried Summer, fear starting in her. Perhaps she had misjudged her old friend. Perhaps Blue Camas' loyalty was to the Saber-Tooths now.

"No, I will not tell him," Blue Camas answered. "But I know how he thinks. He will not like it that you protest this marriage to his son. He wants to call upon the Caribou People for help on the hunt when the caribou herds migrate."

"I will not protest the marriage. I will simply avoid it."

"How?"

Summer hesitated. She would not join the Saber-Tooths, not ever. But how was she going to avoid marriage to Tuft? "I—I must think on it."

Blue Camas narrowed her eyes. "You had better think swiftly, Summer. You are supposed to marry Tuft on the morrow."

Summer winced at the reminder. "If only Talon—" Aghast at what she had almost said, she clapped her hand over her mouth.

Blue Camas pounced like a wolf on a rabbit. "Talon? The man who did bride-service for Blizzard?"

Summer nodded reluctantly.

"What about Talon?"

"I do not want to say."

"Summer, I told *you* about the Saber-Tooths!"

Summer pondered this. "Mmmhmmm," she muttered at last.

"Yes?" Blue Camas smiled encouragingly.

Summer took a breath. "Talon stole me away from my people."

Blue Camas' eyes bulged like a frog's. She sputtered, "How—? Why—why are you here then?"

"My uncle tricked me into returning in order to marry me off to the Saber-Tooth. He made me believe my aunt was very sick and dying." She frowned. Her uncle's betrayal still angered her. And it hurt her, too, that he would rather sacrifice her than stand up to the Saber-Tooths.

Blue Camas nodded slowly. "There was talk among the Saber-Tooths that your uncle might have tried to hide you away. So they warned your uncle ahead of time that he must produce you." She shook her head. "But Spotted Cat did not guess that you had been stolen." She smiled. "He and Tuft *will* be angry."

"Not as angry as they will be when they come for me and I am not here!"

Blue Camas had a sly little smile on her face, a new smile that Summer did not recognize. "What amuses you?" she asked cautiously. Had she been wrong to trust Blue Camas? Blue Camas would not repeat Summer's words to Spotted Cat, would she?

"I would like to see the Saber-Tooths thwarted," whispered Blue Camas. Then she lifted her head suddenly. "Hsssssst!"

Several people walked past the tent. Summer peeked through the narrow opening and saw

Rides Their Backs, followed by a tall, arrogant-looking woman whose light brown hair hung in a thick Saber-Tooth braid to the right of her strong-boned face. Her finely tanned yellow leather dress was decorated with painted ducks in flight.

"The Greenhead Duck wife," whispered Blue Camas.

Behind them trailed another, shorter woman, her head bent as she though she dared not look a person in the eye, so humbled was she. To Summer's consternation, she recognized the woman. Blizzard! Oh, how she had changed! Her long brown hair—the hair that she had so proudly spent so much time combing—was now dirty and tangled with moss and leaves. Her antelope-thin body, once so firm and lithe, was now scrawny. Her ragged leather dress hung on her. Black bruises dotted the backs of her legs.

"*That* is Blizzard?" breathed Summer, looking for any recognizable vestige of the once proud cousin she had known and feared.

"That is Blizzard," Blue Camas said sadly.

Summer swallowed. "I see now that these Saber-Tooths are truly dangerous people. They can destroy a woman's very spirit." Her insides went cold and still at the realization.

"They can," agreed Blue Camas.

"Never have I seen a woman so changed, so, so—" Words failed Summer at the sight of Blizzard. She shivered.

Blue Camas turned to Summer with that same sly smile. "I want you to escape them, Summer. Tell me what I can do to help you." There was a ferocious gleam in Blue Camas' eye. "It is too late for me. But it is not too late for you. Tell me what you want me to do."

Summer tugged nervously at her woman's neckcloth. "I must make a plan. I do not know yet what it will be, Blue Camas," she said earnestly, "but I will think of something!"

The ferocious light faded from Blue Camas' eyes. "Do not tax yourself, Summer." She sighed. "The Saber-Tooths are very strong. Too strong for one woman." She smiled sadly as she rose to leave. "Tomorrow morning will soon be here. I bid you farewell."

Chapter Forty-Five

Summer placed her ear against the side of the tent. She could hear the loud talking and laughing of the feasting Caribous and their guests. All afternoon, her aunt and the other Caribou women, laden with bowls of stewed meat and roasted roots and fresh berries, had hurried back and forth serving their many ravenous guests.

The tent flap was back in place and she pushed it aside to peek outside. There he was: the black-spotted, leather-clad man that the Saber-Tooths had set to guard her. As she watched him lazily swat at a fly, she wondered if Blue Camas had betrayed her despite her promise not to.

As the afternoon shadows lengthened Summer's anxiety increased. More times than she could count, she glanced out the narrow opening of the tent, only to see her guard still there, sometimes lounging, sometimes yawning, now sitting, now standing, but always *there*.

To pass the time, Summer pulled out all the stitches of the saber-tooth design on her woman's neckcloth. What should she sew in its place? She remembered that she had once wanted to sew a black wolf design on her neckcloth. Her fingers fell idle as she pondered.

Ever since becoming an adult woman, Summer's one vow had been to choose her own husband. She had thought that her aunt and uncle would let her choose, but now she knew how foolish she had been. They would never allow her to choose her own mate. They had not even allowed their beloved Blizzard a true choice.

Summer sighed. She had been living on dreams, false dreams, to think her aunt and uncle would ever let her marry whom she chose. Now they were insisting that she marry Tuft—she needed only to look outside the tent at the guard for proof of that. They had not listened to her pleas or demands. No, there would be no help from Auntie Birdsong and Uncle Antler.

What should she do?

She must take her life into her own hands, Summer decided. That was what she must do. To stay in this tent any longer would mean to accept a marriage that would destroy her very spirit, as it had destroyed Blizzard's.

Only she, Summer, could help herself. She must escape. But where would she go?

Her heart immediately supplied the answer: to Talon. Although he had stolen her, he was the man she loved and wanted.

Yet if she went to him, would he see her love as a gift? Or would he continue merely to regard her as a prize that he had succeeded in wresting away from his enemies?

Talon did not love her as Summer loved him. Desperate, the only thing she could do was present herself to him, tell him of her love, and hope that he would accept her, not as a Caribou daughter, not as a Saber-Tooth bride-to-be, but as herself, the woman Summer.

Yet she risked much. This time, if she fled the Caribous and the Saber-Tooths, there would be no returning to them. They would not want her back and she would truly be alone. She would have banished herself from their presence. What if Talon did not want her anymore?

Summer did not know, but she knew she had to find out. She must escape, find Talon, and tell him of her love.

As she listened to the deep voices of the singing Saber-Tooths, her resolve to escape hardened. But to do so, she must outwait the guard. Once he fell asleep, she could tiptoe past him. Yet every time she peered out of the tent, there he was—wide awake, upright, and alert.

She sighed. The moment he fell asleep, she vowed, she would slip out the back of the tent and run away. While Summer planned, her fingers flew over the neckcloth, sewing on the new design that was true to her heart.

More time passed. She had finished the neckcloth and now braided her hair to occupy herself, wondering if she should try to make her escape while the guard was still awake.

Voices! Summer perked up. He was talking with someone. It sounded like Blue Camas.

Cautiously, Summer got to her feet, fingering the little packet of dried meat she had sewn to the underside of her woman's neckcloth. It should be enough to feed her until she could find Talon.

Her heart beat faster at the thought of him. Talon! How wonderful he was compared to Tuft and the Saber-Tooths. She must be with him! She must find him! He, not Tuft, was her choice of husband. Even if Talon rejected her, Summer knew that she must make the attempt or die. She belonged with the dark renegade who had stolen her heart.

Blue Camas was laughing with the guard now, and Summer frowned at her friendliness to the Saber-Tooth. She suddenly had the sinking feeling that she had been wrong to believe Blue Camas' offer to aid her escape.

She risked another peek out the narrow opening. Blue Camas was offering the guard a morsel of meat from a wooden platter. Summer was reminded of Blue Camas' clowning earlier. Perhaps her friend truly *was* trying to help her. Perhaps she meant to distract the guard with conversation and food so that Summer could creep out the back of the tent.

But no, Blue Camas was leaving, giving a friendly little wave to the guard. "Goodbye, Spit," she called sweetly, and Summer felt her newfound hope drain away.

She sat back down and began braiding her hair again. As she did so, she worried that she had waited too long to make her escape. Oh, why had she waited until the very eve of the wedding to run? Now it might be too late! Yet she knew she had waited so long because she had not known what else to do.

Once, going alone into the forest had been Summer's greatest fear. Every instinct told her that to go off alone into the land meant death. She remembered the day when Talon had been banished. How she had wanted to go with him! But stronger than her desire to be with him had been her fear of a lonely, hungry life away from her people. So she had allowed her aunt to sway her.

And then, after he had captured her, it was only when anger drove her that she had run heedless into the forest. The bear had taught her what could happen to a lone woman.

But this past winter, Summer had hunted alone and found that she could survive. She could do it again.

She was risking everything to go and find Talon: life, limb, heart and soul. She risked a bloody death if she crossed the path of a bear, a saber-tooth tiger or a pack of wolves in her hunt for him. And if she never found him, there would be a deep, abiding loneliness for however long her life lasted. Yet despite the risks, it was that call inside herself to be free, to find love, that drove her.

Now a practical problem arose in Summer's mind. When she escaped, *how* would she find Talon? Both times, on the trip to Talon's camp and away from his camp when she had been tricked by Uncle Antler, she had been so upset that she had not noticed any landmarks that would point her the right way.

Summer said a prayer to the Great Spirit to guide her to Talon's camp. When she had finished her prayer, she felt better.

As dusk descended, she yawned and peeked out of the tent again, peering around for the guard. To her surprise, he was sprawled on the ground—snoring!

Summer leapt to her feet. Blue Camas must have put a sleep-inducing herb in his meat!

Summer poked her head outside the tent and saw the merry-makers dancing and singing. Auntie Birdsong and Tule were bringing out their drums. Summer smiled to herself. Once the drumming began, the revelers would sing and dance long into the night, forgetful of the lone woman in the tent.

She waited until the throbbing of the drums told her that everyone was dancing. Then she grabbed up the bearskin and crept from the tent.

She stood still a moment, memorizing the scene in front of her: the blazing fire, the shadowy dancers, the drumming, the singing. She would never see her Caribou people again and she wanted to carry away this one last memory of them.

The scene emblazoned in her brain, Summer wrapped the bearskin over her shoulders and raced for the black rocks that bordered the forest. No one saw her or cried out. Encouraged, she darted behind boulder after boulder until she reached the safety of the pine trees. She ran deeper into the forest, listening for any outcry, but all she heard was the singing and drumming, fainter now that she was farther away.

She had done it! She had escaped! Jubilation made her heart race.

Summer traveled in a large half-circle through the woods until she could hear the sounds of the river. Then she stopped and tried to remember the way back to Talon's camp. She hoped that if she followed the river, it would lead her to the Wolves' territory.

After much pondering, she told the Great Spirit of her troubles. "Please guide me," she whispered. "Please help me find Talon." No answer came that she could tell, so she followed the river in the direction where the sun would rise in the morning. *Yes,* she encouraged herself, *if I but follow the river, I will come to Wolf Territory—and Talon!*

Chapter Forty-Six

The Great Spirit had done it! The Great Spirit had guided Summer back to Talon's camp! She recognized the rock near the river and the place where she and Talon had played and frolicked in the water. She was very close to his camp! She began to run along the river bank, heedless of the sharp stones that hurt her feet.

"Talon! Talon!" she cried.

The lack of answer did not disturb her. She halted and peered through the trees. There was his lean-to with the skin draped over the frame! Her heart pounding in joy and relief, she ran, ignoring the slapping branches. "Talon!"

She sped into the clearing and stopped, glancing around. "Talon?"

There was the frame of Blue Feather's lean-to, and there, the lean-to of the brothers. "Weasel? Sloth? Talon? Where are you?"

That weak little quavering cry did not come from her, did it?

"Talon?"

Somehow the camp did not seem as reassuring as Summer had thought it would be. She had walked for part of a night and then slept, then walked through the next day, following the river. It had taken one more day before she had come into territory she recognized. Now she was home. But where were Talon and the others?

"Talon? Where are you?"

Dismayed, Summer realized that he was not here. He was not anywhere within the sound of her voice.

Fear rolled over her—fear of the saber-tooths that came to drink at the river, fear of the bears that lurked along the forest trail. Summer had eaten the last of the meat the night before and had only berries for breakfast. She was out of food and out of ideas. And the thing she feared the most had happened. She was alone. Summer sat down and wept.

When she had dried her tears with the back of her hand and wiped her nose with her fingers, Summer walked back to the river and splashed her swollen eyes with the refreshing, cool water. Should she wait for Talon? Surely he would return. His lean-to was still here. Surely he intended to return . . .

She wandered back to his lean-to, hungry for the sight of anything that belonged to him. Summer touched the hide roof, remembering how they had lain together under it. New tears sprung up and she dashed them away. Then she wandered over to the ring of rocks that framed the fire pit. The ashes were cold.

She searched the ground for Talon's tracks, wondering if they would tell her where he had gone. To her increasing dismay, she saw several sets of tracks, not just Talon's. She also saw that Blue Feather's belongings were gone. So were Weasel's and Sloth's.

She counted six sets of men's tracks. Six? How could that be? There were only four Wolves. Pondering this, Summer walked in ever-widening circles, wishing she were better at following tracks. If only Talon were here, he could read the tracks and tell her what had happened. But then, if he were here, she wouldn't be desperately searching for him. . . .

Summer wiped at her brow. Fear and weariness were causing her to think strange thoughts. Oh, what should she do? She sat down under Talon's lean-to.

Suddenly a frightening thought occurred to her. What if Talon had been attacked by enemies? What if he had been taken away? She did not know enough about tracks to know if some of these were Blue Feather's,

Sloth's and Weasel's, or if they belonged to aggressive strangers. What if Talon had been in camp alone, waiting for her to return, and other hunters had come and taken him away?

Summer rubbed at her eyes, not knowing what to do. Uneasily she thought that it might not be wise to stay in the camp. Whoever had taken Talon away might come back. No, her thoughts were going in circles. Maybe she was just imagining the danger to him. Summer did not know what to think . . . Lying down at last, she wrapped herself in her bearskin and fell asleep.

She lingered at the camp another day, living off snared grouse and a single rabbit she had been fortunate enough to catch. But she could not relax. She did not feel safe. Summer decided she must leave and find a safer place to stay. She would return to the Wolves' camp now and then, to see if Talon had returned, but she did not like being here alone with only her memories for company.

She rolled up Talon's lean-to hide to take with her and picked up the bearskin. At least she would have something to remind her of Talon. Carrying the rolled hides, she set off to find a new place to make camp.

Chapter Forty-Seven

The Saber-Tooth guard awoke, sat up, glanced around. He rubbed his stomach and got unsteadily to his feet, staggered a few steps over to the tent and pushed aside the hide flap.

He froze, staring inside. Blinking several times, he tried to make his eyes focus. The Caribou woman had disappeared!

Worried now, Spit saw that the roaring fire the guests had been dancing around had burned down to mere embers. Here and there on the grass lay dark shapes. The wedding guests were sleeping.

"I think," muttered Spit to himself, "that now is a very good time to visit old Grandfather's people. Far better to risk my life with the forest predators than with Spotted Cat! And that second son, Tuft, gets mean, too!"

Spit slipped into the quiet pine forest, ignoring the rainbow-colored dewdrops that winked on spider's webs lacing the needles.

Some time later, yawning Caribou women crawled out of their tents and began to make the morning meal.

Auntie Birdsong laid some sticks on the fire and prodded the embers into a blaze. Abruptly, she remembered Summer. The bride would be hungry on this, her marriage morn. Auntie Birdsong felt a little quiver of guilt—she had forgotten to send any food to Summer last night.

Ah, well. Auntie Birdsong shrugged. There had been so many guests expecting her attention. It was a fine thing that so many guests had arrived for the wedding—a great honor for Antler and the Caribou People.

She hurried over to Summer's tent, carrying a wooden bowlful of last night's stew. The girl would have to be satisfied with that.

When Auntie Birdsong reached the hide dwelling, she frowned and glanced about for the Saber-Tooth guard. Spotted Cat had feared the bride would run away and Antler and Birdsong had agreed a guard was needed. But where was he?

Perplexed, she set down the bowl, dropped to her knees and peeked into the tent.

Then she let out a shriek.

Chapter Forty-Eight

"Oh, Sparrow Hawk, what have you done?" moaned Uncle Antler.

The youthful runner gazed at his headman in astonishment. "Why, I but brought more guests for the wedding feast. As you told me to do."

"These men are not guests, you runt of the herd! These men are the—"

"I know who they are, O Headman. They are the—"

"Wolves," said Talon pleasantly as he moved the youth aside and stood facing Antler, wearing his snarling wolf's head cloak. "We thought we would join you in celebration." His handsome face hardened. "Where is the beauteous bride?"

Antler sighed and his round shoulders slumped. "Birdsong," he called. "Get over here!"

Auntie Birdsong came at his call, puffing from her run. "What is it, husband?" She stopped short upon seeing Talon and fingered her woman's neckcloth nervously. "What are *you* doing here?"

"He has come to celebrate Summer's wedding," snorted Antler. "Why else would he be here?"

"Very good," said Spotted Cat heartily, striding up to see why the crowd was gathering. "The more guests, the better—" He frowned. "Who is this man? I think I have seen him before."

Tuft wandered up behind his father. He stared at Talon for a moment and then bared his sharp canines. He hissed in his father's ear.

"Oh," grunted Spotted Cat. "The man we banished."

Talon had to smile at the disparagement in his enemy's voice.

"Who are these men with you?" demanded Spotted Cat.

Beside Talon, Blue Feather moved his sharp spear to his right hand. Weasel and Sloth grimaced and stepped closer to Talon and Blue Feather. All four looked imposing in their snarling wolf headdresses.

Before Talon could reply, Antler muttered wearily, "They call themselves the Wolves."

"Antler, my husband," Birdsong whispered, "we must talk!"

"Not now. I have something more important to talk about with these men."

Birdsong snapped her mouth shut in disgust.

"Well," said Spotted Cat to Talon, "I care not what you call yourselves. You cannot attend my son's wedding. You are not wanted."

"We have been invited," said Talon smoothly.

"By whom?" demanded Spotted Cat.

"By Antler." Talon's narrowed gaze dared the Caribou headman to deny it. "This past winter we became good friends."

Antler wanted to object, Talon could see it in the struggle on his lined face. Before the Caribou headman could say a word, Talon added, "There may be another harsh winter coming. One never knows."

Antler's shoulders sagged further.

Spotted Cat whirled on him. "Antler, you did not tell me you invited this—this—renegade!"

"I forgot," Antler said weakly.

"Well, get rid of him!" snarled Spotted Cat and turned on his heel.

Talon stood, legs apart, hands on his hips, defiant. "I will not go."

Spotted Cat swung around with a ferocious frown on his face. His upper lip lifted to reveal his sharp canines. He prowled slowly over to face Talon. "If I tell you to go, you go!"

"No! I want to see the bride."

"Tuft," ordered Spotted Cat. "Get Rides Their Backs and the other men. Now!"

Talon, Blue Feather, Weasel and Sloth stood their ground, glaring at the Saber-Tooth headman.

All waited in tense silence until Tuft returned with Rides Their Backs and eight more men. When Spotted Cat saw them, he gave Talon an ugly smile. "*Now* you and your Wolves will leave!"

"No. I will not be driven away by you again."

"You wolf scat!" sneered Spotted Cat. "Antler?"

"Yes?" came the reluctant answer.

"How many men do you have?"

"Six," Antler sighed.

"Tell them to get over here."

"Birdsong, go and get them," Antler ordered.

"But husband, first there is something I must tell you."

"*Get them!*" yelled her husband, relieved to be able to yell at someone in this situation. As she hurried away, he shook his head. "Women! All they do is talk!"

Spotted Cat counted on his fingers. "We have more men than you do, Wolf. You leave!"

Talon knew that he and his Wolves were badly outnumbered. But he refused to run from this man ever again. He would stay and claim Summer. He wanted to marry her in front of her Caribou people and drive this interloper away. That was what he wanted.

Blue Feather regarded Talon keenly and muttered, "I think we should do as he says."

Talon felt a hopelessness rising in him. He tried to stave it off. "No! Summer is mine! I will not be driven away a second time. I will die first." He met Blue Feather's eyes. "If you wish to leave, do so."

Blue Feather glanced at the growing crowd, then at Weasel and Sloth. He raised an inquiring brow.

"We stay," said Weasel. Sloth nodded.

Blue Feather shook his head. "I have no desire to be Saber-Tooth prey," he said at last, "but I will stay too."

"Good," grunted Talon. He scanned the tents. Where was Summer?

Birdsong returned with five men behind her. "Here, husband," she said to Antler. "Here are your precious men!" She spat on the ground and stomped off. The men ignored her departure.

"We beat you once," Spotted Cat said. "We will beat you again." His sharp canines glistened in the morning sun. "I would like that."

"So would I," said Tuft.

Rides Their Backs stepped up to Talon and pushed him.

Talon stood his ground. "I will give you one

chance to leave," he said evenly.

The Caribou and Saber-Tooth men laughed at him. "We are not going away," snarled Tuft.

"You are!" He shook his spear. "I will be happy to kill you!"

"I have killed many men!" Rides Their Backs said through gritted teeth as he, too, shook his spear in Talon's face.

"How many of those did you kill in a fair fight?" muttered Antler.

Spotted Cat whirled upon him. "Do not speak to my son that way, Caribou turd!"

"Hiy-yi-yi," a Caribou man growled. "Do not talk to our headman that way, Saber-Tooth louse!"

The eight Saber-Tooth men moved to form a tight circle around Spotted Cat and his sons. One shouted, "We will beat you Caribou men if we have to!"

Antler regarded Spotted Cat and Talon speculatively. The Saber-Tooths had mistreated his daughter. He had seen Blizzard's bruises and ragged clothes. If Antler were to swing his men over to the Wolves' side, they might be able to defeat the Saber-Tooths. He flushed at the heady thought.

Then Spotted Cat said, "If you think to throw in your lot with him, think again, Caribou vermin! I will not rest until I revenge myself upon you. That is how I deal with Saber-Tooth enemies!"

The Saber-Tooth men were all showing their

sharp canines and growling now, a low, menacing sound meant to terrify their enemies.

Antler went pale and his voice trembled. "My men fight on your side, Spotted Cat."

Talon was not surprised. The Caribou headman was brave only with women.

The Caribou men began stamping their feet and bugling, imitating the fighting sounds of Caribou bucks in rut. Like the Saber-Tooths' growling, the clamoring noise made by their bugling was meant to unnerve.

And it did. The Wolves moved closer to each other for support and reassurance.

The Caribous moved in a herd to surround the Wolves, while the Saber-Tooths pressed forward in a growling, snarling mass.

"We will kill you! We will kill you!" yelled Spotted Cat, and his men took up the chant.

Talon felt surrounded by a thick evil that he had never known existed before. Men on every side of him were calling for his blood. Blue Feather's arm was pressed against Talon's by the crush of the people around them, and Talon felt even stalwart Blue Feather tremble.

He raised his spear to threaten the attackers, but he might have been waving a thin willow branch for all the fear his gesture inspired in his enemies.

"Get back! Get back!" he shouted, but the

growling and bugling drowned out his warning.

Then someone swung a heavy stick. It thudded against human flesh. The terrible fight had begun.

Chapter Forty-Nine

It was fortunate, thought Talon, as he ducked and fended off a vicious blow from a maddened Saber-Tooth, that he and his Wolves wore heavy wolf furs. The thickness of their garments protected each man from the heavy blows that rained down upon them.

But not even thick furs could protect them indefinitely. Sloth was the first to fall, tripped by a cunning Caribou. Weasel fought as though deranged to protect his brother, but the two spear wounds he sustained, one to an arm, one to his belly, bled so heavily that Talon feared he would swiftly weaken.

Blue Feather was bellowing heartily and swinging his spear about as though it were a club. He managed to knock down several

opponents and Talon rejoiced that he had such
a good man at his side.

Because there were so many men milling
about in such a small area, it seemed as though
they formed one great, many-legged, growling,
shuffling animal.

Tuft and Rides Their Backs singled out Talon, driving him from the comparative safety
of the crowd. Talon could read in their cloudy
green eyes their grim determination to kill
him. They separated, Rides Their Backs cir-
cling behind Talon, Tuft shaking his knife in
Talon's face. Talon heard snarled words over
the bugling and growling, and he saw the hate
on Tuft's contorted face.

Rides Their Backs jumped on Talon's back,
the way the Saber-Tooth tiger attacked its prey.
He thrust one muscular arm under Talon's
chin and yanked back on his throat. Tuft
prodded Talon's hide-covered chest with his
knife, searching for the best place to sink the
sharp blade.

Talon fell over backwards onto Rides Their
Backs. Tuft jumped on top of him. Talon
desperately tried to shake off Rides Their
Backs' hold on his neck while at the same
time writhing and bucking to protect his
belly and face from Tuft's deadly, seeking
knife.

Tuft raised his knife. "Now you die!" he
screamed. His blade plunged down towards
Talon's heart.

Suddenly a spear intercepted the downward thrust and Tuft's knife was knocked aside. He whirled in astonishment to face a naked, ferocious, dark-haired, hulking man painted in red mud.

"Jrow?" Talon regarded his twin in disbelief.

Jrow did not answer, but launched himself upon Tuft. They fell to the ground in a tangle of arms and legs.

Rides Their Backs' grip on Talon's neck loosened for a moment and Talon was able to grasp his arm and roll over. The two wrestled on the ground, each seeking a death grip on the other's throat. Talon's knife was lost in the fight but Rides Their Backs' deadly blade found its way between them.

"Now," panted Rides Their Backs, holding his knife to Talon's throat, "I will send you to the Land of Darkness. I will cut you into such tiny pieces that you will never find your way to the Great Spirit!"

The awful threat sent a shudder through Talon. He grabbed Rides Their Backs' knife hand and pulled the Saber-Tooth's tight fist away from his neck. They rolled over once more, and this time the knife pricked Rides Their Backs' neck. Talon swiftly killed him.

Shaking his head to clear it, Talon rose to his feet and glared down at Rides Their Backs, expecting the Saber-Tooth to rise and lunge for him. When his opponent did not move, Talon took a step closer.

Killing a man such as this is like killing a bear or a lion, he thought, as a surge of triumph rolled through him. He put one foot on the dead Saber-Tooth's neck and gave a howl of victory.

A hoarse cry caught his attention.

Tuft had Jrow down and was choking the life from him. Talon grabbed Rides Their Backs' knife and ran to aid his brother. He threw himself on Tuft. Tuft whirled, too late, and Talon's weight carried him smashing backwards into the dirt. Jrow scrambled to his feet and with a roar, pushed Talon aside and sank his blade into the Saber-Tooth's heart. Tuft gave one last snarl and died.

"He is dead!" Talon's voice rang with triumph. "And so is his brother!"

He looked at Jrow suddenly, glad that he and his own brother lived. "My thanks for arriving when you did, brother."

Jrow, painted red and covered in dirt, grinned back. "We Sun People like to fight."

"You have killed a man before?"

Now that Tuft and Rides Their Backs were dead, Talon felt both relief and a sense of awe at what he had done. He had killed a man. The surge of triumph was wearing off and a feeling of remorse was beginning to take its place.

Jrow shook his head. "We fight, but we do not usually kill. Our enemies run away from us because we are so fierce and so many."

All over the grassy field where the Caribous and their guests had set their tents, Talon could see his brother's dark-haired Sun people. "It is good that you brought so many men," he said. "My thanks."

Jrow nodded. "I must find Doan and Shelt and Lawt and see how they fared."

"Where is Shrond?" Surely Jrow's father— Talon still had difficulty thinking of the older man as his father, too—would not join in such a deadly fight.

Jrow pointed with his spear. Shrond, a spear in each fist, was talking with some of his men. Talon saw with relief that the older man was uninjured.

Talon scanned the field to see how his Wolves had fared. Everywhere he looked he saw big, black-haired men, the Sun men. His brother's people were now his people. They had fought for him. Despite his bruises, despite his sore muscles, Talon felt a quiet pride radiate from his chest. He was no longer alone—he had men who would come to his aid!

But women's shrill wails filled the air, and Talon thought their mourning cries sounded far worse than the growling and bugling that had commenced the fight.

Talon came to a halt beside two mangled bodies. Two wolf hides lay ground into the dirt beside the bodies. On one of the wolf-head masks, the jaws had been smashed and broken.

Talon forced himself to stare at the torn and twisted bodies. White-haired Weasel lay atop a now forever silenced Sloth. Weasel had been faithful to the last, defending his brother with his own body.

Talon turned away and wiped his eyes. They had been good men, faithful helpers, good hunters, and their deaths would leave a great gap in his life.

Jrow walked up to Talon. He too looked down at the broken, bleeding bodies. He said nothing, but put his arm around Talon's shoulders.

Talon's throat was thick with unshed tears, making it difficult to speak. "Brothers," said Talon hoarsely. "Wolf brothers."

Jrow nodded. "We will give them a dignified burial," he said sadly. "That is what brothers do for one another."

Talon tightened his lips. He would weep later for his dead Wolf brothers. Now he must find Summer. On legs that trembled, he staggered past groaning, moaning injured men, and came to a tent. He peered in. She was not there. He stumbled to the next tent. Not there. Where was she?

Talon passed to the edge of the field and began the slow trek back. Had he missed a tent?

And where was Blue Feather? After seeing what had happened to Weasel and Sloth, both good fighters, he feared how he would find Blue Feather.

He felt grateful for Jrow's silent presence. When they returned to the place where Talon had killed Rides Their Backs, there was a small crowd gathered around a keening woman. Her face was ravaged by tears and her mouth contorted by her highpitched cries of sorrow as she clutched Rides Their Backs' dead body.

Jrow walked over and pulled her off the dead Saber-Tooth, but she collapsed on top of him again. "I loved him! My husband! Oh, my husband!"

Talon felt remorse chewing at his vitals. He had been the one to kill her husband. He tasted bitter saliva in his mouth. Killing men, however cruel they were, was *not* like killing bears or lions.

Jrow joined him. "Who is that woman?"

Talon shrugged. "One of Rides Their Backs' wives. I do not know her."

Two Saber-Tooth women dragged a dead woman past them. Her ragged clothing rode up her long, thin legs to expose black and blue bruises, and her tangled brown hair dragged in the dirt. They were dragging the body in the direction of the Caribou tents. "A woman died in the fight, too," observed Talon in surprise. "Come," he said to Jrow. "We must find Summer and Blue Feather."

They started the search once more.

Then he saw a wolf hide on the ground, covering a man. Talon suspected the worst. Running up to the body, he reached out a trembling hand to lift the wolf's head off the face.

Blue Feather lay very still. Talon dropped to the ground beside him and put a finger to the side of his neck, hoping to find a pulse. He felt the faint tremor. "He is alive!"

"He has lost much blood," Jrow said, gently touching Blue Feather's torso. Blood seeped from several wounds.

"But he is alive! Come, we must find the Caribou shaman. He will know what to do!"

Jrow put out a hand. "Wait, brother. Is it not better to use a Sun shaman? The Caribou might revenge themselves upon your Wolf brother." He pointed at the dead and injured Caribou men and the women weeping beside them.

"Yes. Call your shaman," Talon said. "I want this man helped. But we must get help for him now!"

Jrow ran to get the shaman. He returned with a thin, short man who carried a rattle of dried bird claws that he shook every few moments. Atop his head, the shaman wore a nest of white and black feathers. Half of his wrinkled face was painted in purple berry juice, the other half in red mud. Over his thin chest he wore a vest of finely tanned grey birdskin. A circlet of white and black feathers surrounded each ankle. One leg was painted purple to the knee, the other red.

Before Talon's startled eyes, the man suddenly fell to the ground. His eyes closed and he lay very still. Then his body began to twitch and convulse. He rolled onto his back and stared at the sky. His eyelids fluttered closed again and he went very still, as though in a deep sleep.

"Our shaman," said Jrow proudly.

After a little while the man awoke from his trance and Jrow explained that he wanted Blue Feather cured. He helped the shaman to his feet and set his feather nest back on his head.

The shaman blinked several times and then crouched down beside Blue Feather. He shook his rattle to the eight directions and waved Jrow and Talon away.

"Our shaman will help your brother," Jrow told Talon. "You will see."

Talon did not want to leave Blue Feather alone in the care of the Sun shaman, but he decided he had to trust Jrow's judgment in this. He felt a little easier when he heard the Sun shaman begin to chant.

Jrow led Talon past a large, black-spotted body that lay face-down in the dirt. Five women sat around the corpse, each one wailing louder than the last, except for the youngest woman, who sat silently. The silent woman was Blue Camas. Jrow ignored the women and rolled the body over with his foot.

"Spotted Cat," Talon grunted. "The Saber-Tooth headman." But there was no rejoicing in his heart. His enemies were dead, but so were two of his Wolf brothers and no Saber-Tooth deaths could bring them back. Ever.

His only consolation now was Summer. "Summer," he muttered to Jrow. "I must find her."

He glanced around. Wherever he looked, wounded Saber-Tooths were dragging themselves back to their tents. Black-haired Sun People lounged in small groups, gesturing and animatedly refighting the battle. Here and there, Caribou women aided a wounded Caribou to a dwelling.

Talon spotted Sparrow Hawk, the runner who had first invited them to the Caribou camp. He ordered, "Find the old woman—Birdsong, she is called. She will know where Summer is." The youth hurried off.

Birdsong sobbed over Blizzard's body. Tears streaked the dirt on the old woman's face. Antler sat beside her, ignoring her sobs. His eyes held a lost look, his face drooped in sorrow. Flies landed on an open gash on his arm.

When Birdsong was done with her tears, she began digging a shallow grave. "Help me," she grunted. Antler did, his wounded arm dangling uselessly at one side as he helped his wife bury their dead child.

After they spread dirt over the shallow grave, Birdsong placed two rocks on top of it.

"I must find the shaman," said Antler and tottered off. Birdsong stood by her daughter's grave and stared unseeing at the gravel mound. Her only, beloved child was dead!

The youth Sparrow Hawk came running up and took her arm gently. "Come, grandmother. The Wolf People want to talk with you." He led the unprotesting Birdsong over to where Talon and Jrow stood.

Talon was unmoved by the woman's disheveled appearance. "Summer, your niece. Where is she?" he demanded.

Birdsong looked at him and her wide eyes seemed dazed.

"Where is she?" Talon repeated.

The old woman frowned and shook herself.

Talon's ire rose. He had lost two Wolf brothers this day and was not in the mood for her strange behavior. He gripped her upper arm firmly.

Birdsong's mouth pursed and she stared down at his hand but he did not remove it.

"Where is she?"

Birdsong looked at him and saw his dark hair and hard, dark eyes. This was the man responsible for Blizzard's death! Because of him, her beloved daughter had been taken away by the Saber-Tooths. Because of him, the Saber-Tooths and Caribou had fought the Wolves. Now Blizzard was dead. And *he* was to blame!

"I will show you where she is." Birdsong's face split in a hideous grin. "Come with me."

Talon and Jrow followed her past the Caribou tents. She led them over to a mound and pointed at it.

"There!"

Talon stared. Two large rocks sat atop the fresh burial.

"There is your precious Summer," Birdsong announced. "Dead!"

Chapter Fifty

Talon wandered along the river. Days had passed, days in which he had wandered, lost in grief. When the old woman had pointed out Summer's grave, he had acted as one demented. It had taken Jrow and his three brothers to hold him down. Once his anger had passed, grief had set in. His brothers had let him go then, seeing his need to be by himself.

Never had Talon known such sorrow and anguish. Days were seen through a dull haze, nights spent in restless sleep until dawn heralded another day of aching loss. That was what his life had become. He had lost her, lost the woman he loved. His time with her had been as fleeting as the season for which she was named. His loneliness and sorrow was far worse than when he had been banished.

Talon wandered into the old Wolf camp, but only silence and memories greeted him. He picked up a dead coal from the fire circle, rubbed the ash between his fingers and sniffed. It was old. Rain had come since the last time a fire had burned here.

The three lean-tos still stood, though the hide skins were gone. Talon prowled around the camp, looking for signs, but the rains had washed everything away, leaving nothing on the ground for him to read.

Dully, he sat down on a rock by the fire pit while he pondered what to do. His life had lost meaning. With Summer's death had come the death of hope. Oh, he had the Sun People, he had a living, breathing body, but the spark of life in him had been extinguished.

The next day, Talon rested atop a rocky hill. Below on the grassy plain, a pack of wolves were running down an antelope. When one wolf tired, another took up the chase. The third wolf to run, a big, powerful black animal, finally brought down the antelope.

Talon remembered the wolf pups he had seen that late Spring day long ago. He thought that this black wolf might be the elder brother who had guarded the pups, but though Talon narrowed his eyes and peered through the distance, he could not be certain it was the same wolf.

The sound of the black wolf's triumphant howl drifted to Talon's ears. The rest of the wolf pack converged on the antelope carcass. Talon saw that the black wolf, though the largest, deferred to two other, older wolves. He counted five wolves in all. If these were the pups Talon had seen, then two pups had died.

Talon shook his head sadly. The black wolf had lost two of his brothers, just as Talon had lost two Wolf brothers. Life was hard in this land, he thought. An antelope carcass made a good day.

He watched as a sixth wolf, a slender gray, trotted up and nosed at the black wolf's jaw.

Talon rose and stretched, standing on the hilltop. The waters of the river wound off to the east. Trees grew alongside its banks and Talon knew that deer and other game hid in those cool dark depths of shade.

He said a prayer to the Great Spirit, telling Him of his despair, of how he mourned Summer's death. The Great Spirit did not answer and Talon felt more alone than ever.

Was this what his life had come to? He had his people now, but the most important part—a woman he loved and who loved him—was gone. He was alone, so alone. How he missed Summer! Her laughing face, her wide yellow eyes—he turned away and wiped at his own eyes.

Some time later Talon wandered down to the river, only half-alert in his grief to the danger of saber-tooths and other predators. Once he smelled bear and halted, keeping very still. He heard brush crackle and saw the dark shape of a bear. He held his breath while he counted two cubs with a large sow. He waited some time, until they moved off. Once they had gone, he too continued on his way.

He was sitting by the river when he heard some leaves rustle. Talon turned his head slowly, so he would not scare off whatever animal had come to drink, and found himself staring into the yellow eyes of the black wolf. Talon watched the wolf, whose tongue lolled out of his mouth, and whose manner seemed relaxed. *A bellyful of antelope meat will keep a wolf calm,* thought Talon.

After staring at him awhile, the wolf padded over to the water and drank. Then to Talon's surprise, from out of the bush behind him came another wolf, the smaller gray he'd seen earlier. Her yellow eyes focused on Talon and she gave a low growl. The black wolf lifted his head, then went back to drinking. The female eased from the bush and joined him, but she lifted her head every now and then to watch Talon.

"You have found a mate," Talon whispered softly to the black wolf. "You are most fortunate."

The wolf stopped drinking and swung his head to look at Talon.

"I wish I had my mate with me. But she is dead."

The wolf glanced away from Talon and stared across the river.

Talon followed his gaze. "Yes, I wish I could look across the river and see her. But I cannot. You see, she has gone far away, to the Great Spirit's camp." His voice dropped. "I never told her how much I loved her."

The black wolf lowered his head and lapped at the water once more. When he was done, the female pretended to bite his muzzle, but he moved away, not wanting to play. He stared at Talon one last time, then slipped away into the bush, the female trotting at his heels.

"Since I have no mate and nowhere to go, I will follow you, black wolf."

Talon rose and followed the wolf into the cool green forest.

Chapter Fifty-One

Talon recognized familiar landmarks on the riverbank where the black wolf and his mate traveled. When they passed a huge patch of choke cherries, Talon knew they were near the green glade where he had first seen Summer naked. A tiny shiver went through him. It was also the glade where Fleet claimed she had birthed him.

The black wolf plunged into the choke cherry patch, his gray mate sliding silently through the bush behind him.

"Yes, you have been to this place of green glade and waterfall before," Talon muttered.

He had seen both the black wolf and Summer in this glade when Summer had been swimming. How his heart longed for her! He felt a stirring. His body did, too.

Talon followed the wolves into the glade. It was as he had remembered it, except that the green willows and cottonwoods had turned yellow. The thin white waterfall cascaded over black rocks and pooled into green, silent depths. Ah, the beauty, the peace. . . .

The black wolf turned to gaze at Talon. His yellow eyes seemed to be telling Talon something. Then he and his mate slipped back into the brush.

But Talon did not see them go. His heart pounded suddenly in his chest and his breath labored.

A hunger like that in a starving man after a long, empty winter rose up in him as he stared at the woman who slept on a brown bearskin on thick green grass. Her long hair, the color of grass in the dry autumn, fanned out around her head. Her leather dress, hiked up high as she slept, exposed enticing naked thighs.

"Summer?"

Talon dropped his spear and walked toward her as one in a daze. "Summer? Can it be? Is it—?" His hands grasped blindly at the air in front of him as though by doing so he could keep her from disappearing.

"Summer?"

The woman awoke and blinked. Her yellow eyes focused on him and she sat up. "Talon?"

His eyes widened, his pulse pounded. A cry caught in his throat, joy filled his soul. "It is you!" He ran to her. "Summer! I have found you! You are alive!"

She reached out for him. "Talon! Oh, Talon!" Tears pooled in her eyes at the sight of him. Her heart raced, her breath caught, she could barely speak. "Oh, Talon! I thought you would never come!"

"Ah, Summer," he exclaimed. "I know not the word, so full is my heart, but I am most happy!" He sank to his knees beside her and scooped her up in his arms. "Ah, Summer! I will never let you go!"

Summer pressed herself to him, trying to become as one with him. "I missed you so," she cried. "I was so alone, I did not know where you were, what had happened to you! When I came to the Wolf camp—"

He kissed her on the lips to silence her. "I am here. We are together. That is all that matters."

She clung to him, their lips meeting again.

Talon ran his hands over her body, down her long legs, stroking her arms, assuring himself that she was truly here, alive, with him. "Ah, Summer." He laughed suddenly, elated with her, elated with his life. "You feel so good in my arms!" He kissed her again. "The black wolf led me to you!"

"What black wolf?" She drew back, bewildered, glancing around the glade.

"He is gone. Do not think on it," Talon knew he was not making sense, but he was too happy to care. "Oh, Summer, how good it is!" He crushed her to him again and started covering her sweet flesh with kisses.

She leaned into his kisses and his love. Her own hands were busy, never still, searching, finding, all her yearning for him expressed in her caresses. "Oh, Talon!"

He laughed in sheer joy. He was kissing her everywhere, on the nose, on the cheeks, on the mouth, everywhere his lips could reach. Finally, he murmured, "But how is it that you are here? I thought you were dead!"

"Dead?"

She laughed and lay back down on the bearskin, pulling him down with her. "I am alive. Come, I will show you!" she murmured.

He laughed and kissed her again. She snuggled close to him and sighed happily.

Then he suddenly grew sober, holding her tightly in his arms.

"Summer, I must tell you what happened."

"Yes, Talon?"

He hugged her close. "I went to the Caribou camp to find you. But the Saber-Tooths were there and wanted to fight me. They knew I wanted you for my wife. We fought. Two of my Wolves died."

She sat up, aghast. "Who?"

"Weasel and Sloth," he said. "Blue Feather was badly injured, but they died fighting for me; they were all true brothers."

Summer touched his face gently, stroking his cheek and strong chin. He turned his head and caught her fingers and kissed them.

"I am sad you lost your Wolf brothers," she murmured.

"I, too."

They were quiet, holding each other.

"But I am so glad you are alive," Summer said at last. "I could not bear it if you had been killed!"

He kissed her forehead. "After the battle, I searched for you. I searched in every tent but I could not find you. Finally, I called your aunt to me, to demand that she tell me where you were." His arms tightened on her. "She led me to a grave and told me that you were buried there."

"No!"

"Yes. Your aunt lied to me, a lie that has caused me much pain. When I thought you were dead, I—" He swallowed as he remembered his despair, his loneliness.

Summer met his eyes. "That lie was extremely cruel," she whispered. "I do not understand why she said such a thing."

He pulled her to him and kissed her again. "I am so glad you are alive!"

She laughed. "So am I!" .

They kissed some more and then Talon said, "I have something else to tell you. I have a family."

She leaned back, and her hand went to her belly. She peeked at him through the waterfall of her long hair. "How did you know?"

"What are you talking about?" Talon asked, bewildered.

Summer patted her belly. "We have a babe growing."

"Summer!" He hugged her to him. "Any more joy and I will burst!"

She laughed and kissed the cleft on his chin.

He moved his head and caught her lips. "I am very happy that you carry my child!"

He kissed her again. When the kiss ended, he said, "The family that I was speaking of is my birth mother and father, and my brothers."

Summer stared at him. "I fear the battle you fought has addled your brain!"

He laughed. "My new family are of the Sun People. They helped me. They fought against the Saber-Tooths with me."

"Talon, the Saber-Tooths! What of them?" Summer glanced nervously around the clearing, prepared to leap up and run.

Talon smiled. "Do not worry, Summer. They are no longer a danger to us. Spotted Cat and his sons are dead."

"Tuft, too?"

"*Both* his sons! Dead. Very dead."

Relieved, she snuggled against him. "Tell me about these Sun People."

He kissed her neck. "Do you remember how my mother always told me she found me in a glade?"

She nodded. "You kiss *soooo* well, Talon . . ."

"Mmmhm, so do you . . ." He nibbled her neck. "Well, it seems that was partly the truth. Fleet, my Sun mother, birthed me in this very glade." Summer's eyes widened. "My Fox mother stole me from her." He kissed the tip of Summer's nose. "And I have a twin, Jrow, and three other brothers. There are many Sun People. They number more than the Saber-Tooths."

Summer patted his cheek. "You are a wealthy man to have such a large family to call upon." Then she sat up, her expression serious. "Talon, now there is something else I must tell you." How wonderful he was to look upon! Summer thought she would never get her fill of looking at this renegade she loved.

"Talon, you must know that my uncle lured me back to his Caribou camp," Summer explained. "He led me to think that Auntie Birdsong was dying, but when I arrived there, she was not dying at all. The real reason he wanted me back was so I could marry Tuft, the younger Saber-Tooth son. They kept me in a hot little tent so that I would not run away before I was married off." A shudder went through her. "I am glad Tuft is dead!"

Talon nodded solemnly.

She gazed into his obsidian eyes. "I did not want to marry Tuft. Never! It is you I want. I want to be with you always, to be your wife."

He began to speak, but Summer would not let him. "Hear me out, Talon," she said. "This is difficult for me to say. I have to tell you that I want to be your wife. But I come to you as Summer, a woman. I am not Summer, a Caribou daughter, or the bride-to-be of a Saber-Tooth. I will not help you avenge your enemies. I am here only as a woman. A woman who loves you."

Talon could not meet her eyes.

She saw him look away and her heart fell. "I know that it is very important to you to defeat your enemies, but I will not be part of that victory. I will not be a living reminder of your hate for them. I bring only love in my heart for you, Talon," she said, opening both hands, palms up. "I have nothing else to give you—no people, no victory. Only my love." She took a breath. "Is it—is it enough, Talon?" She swallowed. "Knowing all this, do you want me?"

A wave of deep sadness threatened to engulf him. He had thought he had lost Summer to death. Now that he had found her again, he never wanted to lose her. But he now realized that in his vengeful theft of her, and in his hard-won victory over her people, he had almost lost something far more valuable: her precious love.

Talon's eyes fastened on the black wolf sewn on her woman's neckcloth. He cleared his throat and met her eyes at last. "Yes, I want you, Summer. I love you!" He held her tightly. "I want you to be my wife, to be my mate. I want you at my side for the rest of our lives."

She went limp in his embrace. "I thought—"

He kissed her temple. "Thought what?"

"I thought you wanted me only for your revenge . . ."

Pain lanced through Talon at his own selfishness. "I did, Summer," he confessed. "I was like a wounded wolf that seeks its den, licks its wound, and snarls at everything, so full of its pain. Such a wolf cannot sniff a deer scent, run through the tall grasses, or sing with the pack.

"I was such a wolf. All I knew was my own pain." He kissed her. "I have been a wounded wolf. Oh, Summer," he murmured. "I want you so badly." He kissed her. "I love you. I want another chance to earn your love."

"You need not earn my love. It is already in your keeping."

He stared down at her lovely face. Then he kissed her gently, a kiss of regret, remorse and hope. He lifted his head. "I know you wanted to choose your own mate. Are you certain you want to stay with me? Perhaps your uncle will find a good man for you, a fine hunter . . ."

She shook her head. "Uncle Antler will never let me choose my own mate. You told me that once, but I did not want to hear your words. But I had time to think while sitting in that hot little tent. I realized that I *thought* what I wanted was the right to choose my own husband.

"But even when you were doing bride-service for Blizzard, what I *truly* wanted was you. Only I felt guilty and ashamed of my desire for the man who was betrothed to my cousin."

"I am no longer betrothed," Talon reminded her. "Have not been for some time. Did you forget?"

She smiled. "No, I did not forget. But I knew it was wrong to want another woman's man, especially my cousin's. Auntie Birdsong thought it was shameful, too."

Talon snorted at that. "Yes, well, Auntie Birdsong has little right to tell others how to behave! She must see to her own behavior. That is what I think!"

Summer smiled wanly. "Yes, that is true. I think now that she was just shaming me to keep me with her. When you were banished, I wanted to come with you—"

"Ah, Summer!" He pulled her closer to him "Would that I had known." He kissed her. "Had I known you wanted to come with me into my banishment, I would have let you. All that lonely time—" He shook his head sadly.

"I tried." Summer bowed her head and wiped her tears. After a moment she looked up at him. "But you did not see me. And Auntie put her

hand on my shoulder to keep me with her."
Summer smiled through her tears. "I was too
young then. I needed to grow up some more.
I knew what I wanted, but I did not know how
to get it." She kissed him. "Now I know."

"Think you?" he growled playfully as her
hands again began to wander over him, seeking, finding, caressing.

"I ventured into the forest lands, alone, to
find you, Talon! I braved bears and wolves and
saber-tooths for you! That is how much I want
you. There is not another woman I know who
would do that!"

Gently he kissed her forehead. "I love you,"
he murmured.

"You are the only man I want, Talon! The
only man I ever wanted! No other will do."

He liked the low growl in her voice when
she said that. Talon kissed her again. "And
you are the only woman for me, Wolf Eyes,"
he murmured. "Let me show you how much I
love you."

"How strange," she murmured. "I was just
about to show you."

And she did.

Epilogue

One year later

"Would you like another roasted grasshopper?" Auntie Birdsong's trembling hand shook the platter she held out and the grasshoppers rattled.

"No, thank you," Summer answered. "I have already eaten several and they were truly delicious."

"And you, son-in-law? Would you care for another tasty grasshopper?"

"No, thank you."

Summer gave a silent sigh of relief that Talon's tone was polite. She turned to him. "We must leave now."

Auntie looked forlorn. "Must you? There is

plenty of room for you to sleep in our tent. And do you have to take the baby?"

Summer glanced down at her fuzzy-haired son, asleep in her arms. "It is night, time for him to sleep in his own tent, Auntie."

Auntie pouted. "Your visit is so short," she complained.

Summer felt Talon stiffen beside her.

"Our place is with my husband's people," Summer said gently. "But we are enjoying our visit with you. We still have many days left to visit with you." She held up five fingers.

Uncle Antler spoke up from beside the fire where he sat wrapped in the new bison robe Summer and Talon had given him. "We are most fortunate that you are visiting us, daughter. We are glad that you bring your husband and child, also." He frowned at his wife.

Auntie Birdsong caught his look. "Yes, oh yes," she said hastily. "That we are. Most glad!" Her eyes dropped to the little bundle snuggled against Summer's breast.

After Summer thanked them again for a delicious dinner, she and Talon left the tent.

The evening air was cool and bright stars winked above their heads. Smoke from the Caribou camp fires scented the air. As they walked toward their own tent which was set at some distance from the Caribou tents, Summer observed, "It must have been difficult for Auntie and Uncle when we suddenly just appeared in their camp."

Talon snorted. "No more difficult than it was for me to come here!"

"I think Auntie deeply regrets lying to you about my death," said Summer. "I believe it truly was her grief over Blizzard that made her strike out to hurt you, as she said."

"That may be. But it does not sit well with me that she lied and told me *you* were dead."

"No, that was not right." After a little while Summer said, "I think she truly regrets lying to you."

Talon was silent for awhile. "And what about your uncle? Does he regret his lie to you that your aunt was sick and dying?"

Summer shrugged. "He has not said as much, but I noticed he tries to behave in a more kindly fashion towards me. He even made a little spear for our son to hunt with when he is older."

They walked along for awhile longer, breathing in the fresh, moist air near the river. "Your kinfolk cause much grief," said Talon.

"They do," Summer acknowledged. "But I love them. I am the only daughter they have now. And they are still the only relatives I have."

"Has it been good for you, living with the Sun People?" Talon stopped walking and waited for her answer.

"Yes. And the magnificent marriage feast your family gave us when we arrived among them greatly endeared them to me."

Talon chuckled. "Even Blue Feather likes living with the Sun People."

The baby whimpered and both parents' eyes were drawn to him.

"Your aunt and uncle seem fond of the baby," observed Talon.

"Yes. I think it was Pup that won them over so swiftly. They were most anxious to make amends when they saw our beautiful son." Pup was his baby name. Later he would receive his adult name. Summer kissed the top of the slumbering child's head.

Talon kissed the top of Summer's head. His voice was warm and deep as he said, "Our lives are full of love. We have each other and our baby. The animals come easily to my spear. We live with a powerful people, the Sun People." He grinned. "And we make short visits to see your family."

Summer elbowed him in the side and they both laughed.

From somewhere far off came a single wolf howl. Before the howl died away, it was joined by an answering howl. The two cries held and blended together, rising and falling, in a joyous song to life. The wolf had found his mate.

References

Anderson, Elaine and John A. White 1975 "Caribou (Mammalia, Cervidae) in the Wisconsinan of Southern Idaho" in *Tebiwa, The Journal of the Idaho State University Museum*, Vol. 17, #2. Pocatello, ID. pp. 19–37.

Butler, B. Robert 1969 "More Information on the Frozen Ground Features and Further Interpretation of the Small Mammal Sequence at the Wasden Site (Owl Cave), Bonneville County, ID," in *Tebiwa*, Vol. 12, No. 1, Pocatello, ID. pp. 58–63.

Butler, B. Robert 1972 "The Holocene or Postglacial Ecological Crisis on the Eastern Snake

River Plain" in *Tebiwa*, Vol. 15, No. 1, Pocatello, ID. pp. 49–63.

Butler, B. Robert 1978 "A Guide to Understanding Idaho Archaeology (3rd Edition): The Upper Snake and Salmon River Country." Idaho State Historic Preservation Office, Boise, ID.

Cahalane, Victor H. 1961 "Mammals of North America." The Macmillan Company. New York.

Dort, Wakefield, Jr. 1968 "Paleoclimatic Implications of Soil Structures At the Wasden Site (Owl Cave) in *Tebiwa*," Vol. 11, No. 1. Pocatello ID. pp. 31–36.

Dort, Wakefield, Jr. 1975 "Archaeo-Geology of Jaguar Cave, Upper Birch Creek Valley, ID," in *Tebiwa*, Vol. 17, No. 2. Pocatello, ID. pp. 59–65.

Dort, Wakefield, Jr. and Susanne Miller 1977 "Archaeological Geology of Birch Creek Valley and the Eastern Snake River Plain, Idaho." The Geological Society of America. First Annual Field Trip. November.

Driver, Harold E. 1969 "Indians of North America." Second edition, revised. University of Chicago Press. Chicago, IL.

Furlong, Marjorie and Virginia Pill 1974 "Wild Edible Fruit & Berries," Naturegraph Publishers Inc., Happy Camp, CA.

Gruhn, Ruth 1961 "The Archaeology of Wilson Butte Cave," South-Central Idaho. Occasional Papers of the Idaho State College Museum, #6. Pocatello, ID.

Gulick, Grover C. 1971 "Snake River Country." The Caxton Printers, Ltd. Caldwell, ID.

Hall, Roberta L. and Henry S. Sharp 1978 "Wolf and Man: Evolution in Parallel." Academic Press, New York, NY.

Kurten, Bjorn 1972 "The Ice Age." G.P. Putnam's Sons. New York, NY.

Kurten, Bjorn and Elaine Anderson 1972 "The Sediments and Fauna of Jaguar Cave, II. The Fauna" in *Tebiwa*, Vol. 15, No. 1. Pocatello, ID. pp. 21–45.

Lawrence, R.D. 1990 "Wolves." Sierra Club Books, Little, Brown & Co., San Francisco, CA.

Lopez, Barry Holstun 1978 "Of Wolves and Men." Charles Scribner's Sons, New York.

Lyttle, Richard B. 1983 "Birds of North America." Gallery Books, New York.

McDonald, H. Gregory and Elaine Anderson 1975 "A Late Pleistocene Vertebrate Fauna from

Southeastern Idaho" in *Tebiwa*, Vol. 18, No. 1. Pocatello, ID.

Meatte, Daniel S. 1990 "Prehistory of the Western Snake River Basin," Occasional Paper of the Idaho Museum of Natural History #35, Pocatello, ID. Northwest Printing, Inc.

Miller, Susanne J. 1982 "The Archaeology and Geology of an Extinct Megafauna/Fluted Point Association at Owl Cave, the Wasden Site, Idaho: A Preliminary Report," in *Peopling of the New World*. Edited by Jonathan E. Ericson, R.E. Taylor & Rainer Berger. Ballena Press Anthropological Papers. #23. Los Altos, CA.

Miller, Susanne J. 1983 "Osteo-Archaeology of the Mammoth-Bison Assemblage at Owl Cave, The Wasden Site, ID" in *Carnivores, Human Scavengers and Predators: A Question of Bone Technology*. Edited by G.M. Le Moine and A.S. MacEachern. Proceedings of the 15th Annual Chacmool Conference, Archeology Association, University of Calgary, Calgary, Alberta.

Miller, Susanne J. and Wakefield Dort, Jr. 1978 "Early Man at Owl Cave: Current Investigations at the Wasden Site, Eastern Snake River Plain, Idaho," in *Early Man in America: From a Circum-Pacific Perspective*, Edited by Alan Lyle Bryan. Occasional Papers of the Dept. of Anthropology, University of Alberta. #1. Published by Archaeological Researchers International, Edmonton, Alberta.

Parker, Rev. Samuel 1846 "Journal of an Exploring Tour Beyond the Rocky Mountains." Fifth Edition. Auburn: J.C. Derby & Co. New York.

Sadek-Kooros, Hind 1966 "Jaguar Cave: An Early Man Site in the Beaverhead Mountains of Idaho." PhD. Thesis. Harvard University, Cambridge, MA.

Sadek-Kooros, Hind 1972 "The Sediments and Fauna of Jaguar Cave, I. The Sediments" in *Tebiwa*, Vol. 15, No. 1. Pocatello, ID. pp. 1–20.

Schlesier, Karl H. 1987 "The Wolves of Heaven: Cheyenne Shamanism, Ceremonies, and Prehistoric Origins." University of Oklahoma Press, Norman, OK.

Stevenson, Marc 1978 "Dire Wolf Systematics and Behavior" in *Wolf and Man: Evolution in Parallel*, Edited by Roberta L. Hall and Henry S. Sharp. Academic Press. NY. pp. 179–207.

Sweet, Muriel 1976 "Common Edible and Useful Plants of the West." Naturegraph Publishers, Inc., Happy Camp, CA.

Theresa Scott loves to hear from readers. Please send an SASE to her at P.O. Box 832, Olympia, WA 98507.

FORBIDDEN PASSION

THERESA SCOTT

Bestselling Author of *Bride of Desire*

"More than Viking tales, Theresa Scott's historical romances are tender, exciting, and satisfying!"
—*Romantic Times*

Ordered to Greenland to escort his commander's betrothed to their Irish stronghold, Thomas Lachlann is unexpectedly drawn to the beguiling beauty he was sent to find. Bewitched and bewildered, Thomas knows that if he takes Yngveld as his beloved his life will be forfeit—but if he loses the golden-haired enchantress his heart will break.

_3305-4 $4.50 US/$5.50 CAN

APACHE CONQUEST

THERESA SCOTT

Bestselling Author of *Forbidden Passion*

Sent to the New World to wed a stranger, beautiful young Carmen is prepared to love the man her uncle has chosen. But on the trail to Sante Fe, a recklessly virile half-breed Indian sets her blood afire, tempting her to forget her betrothed. And though Puma has suffered greatly at the hands of the Spanish, he vows to do anything, to defy anyone to make the fiery senorita his own.

_3471-9 $4.99 US/$5.99 CAN

TIMESWEPT ROMANCE
A TIME TO LOVE AGAIN
Flora Speer
Bestselling Author of *Viking Passion*

While updating her computer files, India Baldwin accidentally backdates herself to the time of Charlemagne—and into the arms of a rugged warrior. Although there is no way a modern-day career woman can adjust to life in the barbaric eighth century, a passionate night of Theuderic's masterful caresses leaves India wondering if she'll ever want to return to the twentieth century.

__0-505-51900-3 $4.99 US/$5.99 CAN

FUTURISTIC ROMANCE
HEART OF THE WOLF
Saranne Dawson
Bestselling Author of *The Enchanted Land*

Long has Jocelyn heard of Daken's people and their magical power to assume the shape of wolves. If the legends prove true, the Kassid will be all the help the young princess needs to preserve her empire—unless Daken has designs on her kingdom as well as her love.

__0-505-51901-1 $4.99 US/$5.99 CAN

LEISURE BOOKS
ATTN: Order Department
276 5th Avenue, New York, NY 10001

Please add $1.50 for shipping and handling for the first book and $.35 for each book thereafter. PA., N.Y.S. and N.Y.C. residents, please add appropriate sales tax. No cash, stamps, or C.O.D.s. All orders shipped within 6 weeks via postal service book rate. Canadian orders require $2.00 extra postage and must be paid in U.S. dollars through a U.S. banking facility.

Name _____

Address _____

City _____ State _____ Zip _____

I have enclosed $_____ in payment for the checked book(s).
Payment <u>must</u> accompany all orders.☐ Please send a free catalog.

Futuristic Romance

Journey to the distant future where love rules and passion is the lifeblood of every man and woman.

Heart's Lair by Kathleen Morgan. Although Karic is the finest male specimen Liane has ever seen, her job is not to admire his nude body, but to discover the lair where his rebellious followers hide. Never does Liane imagine that when the Cat Man escapes he will take her as his hostage— or that she will fulfill her wildest desires in his arms.

_3549-9 $4.50 US/$5.50 CAN

The Knowing Crystal by Kathleen Morgan. On a seemingly hopeless search for the Knowing Crystal, sheltered Alia has desperate need of help. Teran, with his warrior skills and raw strength, seems to be the answer to her prayers, but his rugged masculinity threatens Alia. Even though Teran is only a slave, Alia will learn in his powerful arms that love can break all bonds.

_3548-0 $4.50 US/$5.50 CAN

LEISURE BOOKS
ATTN: Order Department
276 5th Avenue, New York, NY 10001

Please add $1.50 for shipping and handling for the first book and $.35 for each book thereafter. PA., N.Y.S. and N.Y.C. residents, please add appropriate sales tax. No cash, stamps, or C.O.D.s. All orders shipped within 6 weeks via postal service book rate. Canadian orders require $2.00 extra postage and must be paid in U.S. dollars through a U.S. banking facility.

Name _____

Address _____

City _____ State _____ Zip _____

I have enclosed $_____ in payment for the checked book(s).
Payment <u>must</u> accompany all orders.□ Please send a free catalog.

THE OUTBACK SAGA — AARON FLETCHER

Outback. Innocent in the ways of Europeans, Mayrah is the native girl Partick Garrity has bought to satisfy his passions. Divided by competing cultures, they are nevertheless united by their fierce love of the land—and eventually, each other.
_3113-2 $4.95 US/$5.95 CAN

Outback Station. Wealthy and beautiful, Alexandra Hammond has every reason to disdain David Kerrick, the penniless convict who has killed her cousin. But Alexandra is a woman with the strength to judge the truth for herself. Together, Alexandra and David will take on the vast outback, burying the bitterness of the past and planting the seeds of a shining future.
_3104-3 $4.95 US/$5.95 CAN

Walkabout. The golden legacy of Tibooburra outback station is threatened by the disappearance of the young boy who will one day inherit it all. Drawing from the land an indomitable strength, Jeremy Kerrick grows to manhood and wins the woman of his dreams. Together, they will meet the challenge of the outback or die trying.
_3292-9 $5.99 US/$6.99 CAN